APPOINTMENT AT
THE DEATH STAR

The star ahead continued to brighten, its glow evidently coming from within. It assumed a circular outline.

As they drew nearer, craters and mountains gradually became visible. Yet there was something extremely odd about them. The craters were far too regular in outline, the mountains far too vertical.

"That's no moon," Kenobi said softly, "that's a space station. Let's get out of here!"

Gauges began to whine in protest and by ones and twos every instrument on the control console went berserk. Try as they might they couldn't keep the surface of the gargantuan station from looming steadily larger.

The true size of the battle station became apparent as the freighter was pulled closer and closer. Now only a miniscule speck against the gray bulk of the station, the *Millennium Falcon* was sucked toward one of these steel pseudopods and was instantly swallowed up.

A lake of metal closed off the entryway and the freighter vanished as if it had never existed . . .

STAR WARS

Starring

Mark Hamill   **Harrison Ford**   **Carrie Fisher**

Peter Cushing

and

Alec Guinness

with

**Anthony Daniels   Kenny Baker
Peter Mayhew** and **Dave Prowse**

Written and Directed by
George Lucas

Produced by
Gary Kurtz

Production Designer ——— **John Barry**
Director of Photography ——— **Gil Taylor**
Music by ——————— **John Williams**

Special Visual Effects Supervisors:
Miniatures & Optical Effects ———
John Dykstra
Production & Mechanical Effects ———
John Stears

Film Editors ——— **Marcia Lucas
Richard Chew
Paul Hirsch**

A Lucasfilm Ltd. Production
A Twentieth Century-Fox Release
Panavision*
Technicolor*
Prints by Deluxe*

Making Films Sound Better
□□ | DOLBY SYSTEM | ®
Noise Reduction—High Fidelity

STAR WARS

From the Adventures of Luke Skywalker

A Novel by
George Lucas

A Del Rey Book

BALLANTINE BOOKS • NEW YORK

☐ prologue

ANOTHER galaxy, another time.

The Old Republic was the Republic of legend, greater than distance or time. No need to note where it was or whence it came, only to know that . . . it was *the* Republic.

Once, under the wise rule of the Senate and the protection of the Jedi Knights, the Republic throve and grew. But as often happens when wealth and power pass beyond the admirable and attain the awesome, then appear those evil ones who have greed to match.

So it was with the Republic at its height. Like the greatest of trees, able to withstand any external attack, the Republic rotted from within though the danger was not visible from outside.

Aided and abetted by restless, power-hungry individuals within the government, and the massive organs of commerce, the ambitious Senator Palpatine caused himself to be elected President of the Republic. He promised to reunite the disaffected among the people and to restore the remembered glory of the Republic.

Once secure in office he declared himself Emperor, shutting himself away from the populace. Soon he was controlled by the very assistants and boot-lickers he had appointed to high office, and the cries of the people for justice did not reach his ears.

Having exterminated through treachery and deception the Jedi Knights, guardians of justice in the galaxy, the Imperial governors and bureaucrats prepared to institute a reign of terror among the disheartened worlds of the galaxy. Many used the imperial forces and the name of the increasingly isolated Emperor to further their own personal ambitions.

But a small number of systems rebelled at these new outrages. Declaring themselves opposed to the New Order they began the great battle to restore the Old Republic.

From the beginning they were vastly outnumbered by the systems held in thrall by the Emperor. In those first dark days it seemed certain the bright flame of resistance would be extinguished before it could cast the light of new truth across a galaxy of oppressed and beaten peoples . . .

From the First Saga
Journal of the Whills

"They were in the wrong place at the wrong time. Naturally they became heroes."

Leia Organa of Alderaan, Senator

☐ I

IT was a vast, shining globe and it cast a light of lambent topaz into space—but it was not a sun. Thus, the planet had fooled men for a long time. Not until entering close orbit around it did its discoverers realize that this was a world in a binary system and not a third sun itself.

At first it seemed certain nothing could exist on such a planet, least of all humans. Yet both massive G1 and G2 stars orbited a common center with peculiar regularity, and Tatooine circled them far enough out to permit the development of a rather stable, if exquisitely hot, climate. Mostly this was a dry desert of a world, whose unusual starlike yellow glow was the result of double sunlight striking sodium-rich sands and flats. That same sunlight suddenly shone on the thin skin of a metallic shape falling crazily toward the atmosphere.

The erratic course the galactic cruiser was traveling was intentional, not the product of injury but of a desperate desire to avoid it. Long streaks of intense energy slid close past its hull, a multihued storm of destruction like a school of rainbow remoras fighting to attach themselves to a larger, unwilling host.

One of those probing, questing beams succeeded in touching the fleeing ship, striking its principal solar fin. Gemlike fragments of metal and plastic erupted into space as the end of the fin disintegrated. The vessel seemed to shudder.

The source of those multiple energy beams suddenly hove into view—a lumbering Imperial cruiser, its massive outline bristling cactuslike with dozens of heavy weapons emplacements. Light ceased arching from those spines now as the cruiser moved in close. Intermittent explosions and flashes of light could be seen in those portions of the smaller ship which had taken hits. In the absolute cold of space, the cruiser snuggled up alongside its wounded prey.

Another distant explosion shook the ship—but it certainly didn't feel distant to Artoo Detoo or See Threepio. The concussion bounced them around the narrow corridor like bearings in an old motor.

To look at these two, one would have supposed that the tall, human-like machine, Threepio, was the master and the stubby, tripodal robot, Artoo Detoo, an inferior. But while Threepio might have sniffed disdainfully at the suggestion, they were in fact equal in everything save loquacity. Here Threepio was clearly —and necessarily—the superior.

Still another explosion rattled the corridor, throwing Threepio off balance. His shorter companion had the better of it during such moments with his squat, cylindrical body's low center of gravity well balanced on thick, clawed legs.

Artoo glanced up at Threepio, who was steadying himself against a corridor wall. Lights blinked enigmatically around a single mechanical eye as the smaller robot studied the battered casing of his friend. A patina of metal and fibrous dust coated the usually gleaming bronze finish, and there were some visible dents—all the result of the pounding the rebel ship they were on had been taking.

Accompanying the last attack was a persistent deep hum which even the loudest explosion had not been able to drown out. Then for no apparent reason, the basso thrumming abruptly ceased, and the only sounds in the otherwise deserted corridor came from the eerie dry-twig crackle of shorting relays or the pops of dying circuitry. Explosions began to echo through the ship once more, but they were far away from the corridor.

Threepio turned his smooth, humanlike head to one

side. Metallic ears listened intently. The imitation of a human pose was hardly necessary—Threepio's auditory sensors were fully omnidirectional—but the slim robot had been programmed to blend perfectly among human company. This programming extended even to mimicry of human gestures.

"Did you hear that?" he inquired rhetorically of his patient companion, referring to the throbbing sound. "They've shut down the main reactor and the drive." His voice was as full of disbelief and concern as that of any human. One metallic palm rubbed dolefully at a patch of dull gray on his side, where a broken hull brace had fallen and scored the bronze finish. Threepio was a fastidious machine, and such things troubled him.

"Madness, this is madness." He shook his head slowly. "This time we'll be destroyed for sure."

Artoo did not comment immediately. Barrel torso tilted backward, powerful legs gripping the deck, the meter-high robot was engrossed in studying the roof overhead. Though he did not have a head to cock in a listening posture like his friend, Artoo still somehow managed to convey that impression. A series of short beeps and chirps issued from his speaker. To even a sensitive human ear they would have been just so much static, but to Threepio they formed words as clear and pure as direct current.

"Yes, I suppose they did have to shut the drive down," Threepio admitted, "but what are we going to do now? We can't enter atmosphere with our main stablizer fin destroyed. I can't believe we're simply going to surrender."

A small band of armed humans suddenly appeared, rifles held at the ready. Their expressions were as worry-wrinkled as their uniforms, and they carried about them the aura of men prepared to die.

Threepio watched silently until they had vanished around a far bend in the passageway, then looked back at Artoo. The smaller robot hadn't shifted from his position of listening. Threepio's gaze turned upward also though he knew Artoo's senses were slightly sharper than his own.

"What is it, Artoo?" A short burst of beeping came in response. Another moment, and there was no need for highly attuned sensors. For a minute or two more, the corridor remained deathly silent. Then a faint *scrape, scrape* could be heard, like a cat at a door, from somewhere above. That strange noise was produced by heavy footsteps and the movement of bulky equipment somewhere on the ship's hull.

When several muffled explosions sounded, Threepio murmured, "They've broken in somewhere above us. There's no escape for the Captain this time." Turning, he peered down at Artoo. I think we'd better—"

The shriek of overstressed metal filled the air before he could finish, and the far end of the passageway was lit by a blinding actinic flash. Somewhere down there the little cluster of armed crew who had passed by minutes before had encountered the ship's attackers.

Threepio turned his face and delicate photoreceptors away—just in time to avoid the fragments of metal that flew down the corridor. At the far end a gaping hole appeared in the roof, and reflective forms like big metal beads began dropping to the corridor floor. Both robots knew that no machine could match the fluidity with which those shapes moved and instantly assumed fighting postures. The new arrivals were humans in armor, not mechanicals.

One of them looked straight at Threepio—no, not at him, the panicked robot throught frantically, but past him. The figure shifted its big rifle around in armored hands—too late. A beam of intense light struck the head, sending pieces of armor, bone, and flesh flying in all directions.

Half the invading Imperial troops turned and began returning fire up the corridor—aiming past the two robots.

"Quick—this way!" Threepio ordered, intending to retreat from the Imperials. Artoo turned with him. They had taken only a couple of steps when they saw the rebel crewmen in position ahead, firing *down* the corridor. In seconds the passageway was filled with smoke and crisscrossing beams of energy.

Red, green and blue bolts ricocheted off polished sections of wall and floor or ripped long gashes in metal surfaces. Screams of injured and dying humans —a peculiarly unrobotic sound, Threepio thought— echoed piercingly above the inorganic destruction.

One beam struck near the robot's feet at the same time as a second one burst the wall directly behind him, exposing sparking circuitry and rows of conduits. The force of the twin blast tumbled Threepio into the shredded cables, where a dozen different currents turned him into a jerking, twisting display.

Strange sensations coursed through his metal nerve-ends. They caused no pain, only confusion. Every time he moved and tried to free himself there was another violent crackling as a fresh cluster of componentry broke. The noise and man-made lightning remained constant around him as the battle continued to rage.

Smoke began to fill the corridor. Artoo Detoo bustled about trying to help free his friend. The little robot evidenced a phlegmatic indifference to the ravening energies filling the passageway. He was built so low that most of the beams passed over him anyhow.

"Help!" Threepio yelled, suddenly frightened at a new message from an internal sensor. "I think something is melting. Free my left leg—the trouble's near the pelvic servomotor." Typically, his tone turned abruptly from pleading to berating.

"This is all your fault!" he shouted angrily. "I should have known better than to trust the logic of a half-sized thermocapsulary dehousing assister. I don't know why you insisted we leave our assigned stations to come down this stupid access corridor. Not that it matters now. The whole ship must be—" Artoo Detoo cut him off in midspeech with some angry beepings and hoots of his own, though he continued to cut and pull with precision at the tangled high-voltage cables.

"Is that so?" Threepio sneered in reply. "The same to you, you little . . . !"

An exceptionally violent explosion shook the passage, drowning him out. A lung-searing miasma of carbonized component filled the air, obscuring everything.

Two meters tall. Bipedal. Flowing black robes trailing from the figure and a face forever masked by a functional if bizarre black metal breath screen—a Dark Lord of the Sith was an awesome, threatening shape as it strode through the corridors of the rebel ship.

Fear followed the footsteps of all the Dark Lords. The cloud of evil which clung tight about this particular one was intense enough to cause hardened Imperial troops to back away, menacing enough to set them muttering nervously among themselves. Once-resolute rebel crewmembers ceased resisting, broke and ran in panic at the sight of the black armor—armor which, though black as it was, was not nearly as dark as the thoughts drifting through the mind within.

One purpose, one thought, one obsession dominated that mind now. It burned in the brain of Darth Vader as he turned down another passageway in the broken fighter. There smoke was beginning to clear, though the sounds of faraway fighting still resounded through the hull. The battle here had ended and moved on.

Only a robot was left to stir freely in the wake of the Dark Lord's passing. See Threepio finally stepped clear of the last restraining cable. Somewhere behind him human screams could be heard from where relentless Imperial troops were mopping up the last remnants of rebel resistance.

Threepio glanced down and saw only scarred deck. As he looked around, his voice was full of concern. "Artoo Detoo—where are you?" The smoke seemed to part just a bit more. Threepio found himself staring up the passageway.

Artoo Detoo, it seemed, was there. But he wasn't

looking in Threepio's direction. Instead, the little robot appeared frozen in an attitude of attention. Leaning over him was—it was difficult for even Threepio's electronic photoreceptors to penetrate the clinging, acidic smoke—a human figure. It was young, slim, and by abstruse human standards of aesthetics, Threepio mused, of a calm beauty. One small hand seemed to be moving over the front of Artoo's torso.

Threepio started toward them as the haze thickened once more. But when he reached the end of the corridor, only Artoo stood there, waiting. Threepio peered past him, uncertain. Robots were occasionally subject to electronic hallucinations—but why should he hallucinate a human?

He shrugged . . . Then again, why not, especially when one considered the confusing circumstances of the past hour and the dose of raw current he had recently absorbed. He shouldn't be surprised at anything his concatenated internal circuits conjured up.

"Where have you been?" Threepio finally asked. "Hiding, I suppose." He decided not to mention the maybe-human. If it had been a hallucination, he wasn't going to give Artoo the satisfaction of knowing how badly recent events had unsettled his logic circuits.

"They'll be coming back this way," he went on, nodding down the corridor and not giving the small automaton a chance to reply, "looking for human survivors. What are we going to do now? They won't trust the word of rebel-owned machines that we don't know anything of value. We'll be sent to the spice mines of Kessel or taken apart for spare components for other, less deserving robots. That's if they don't consider us potential program traps and blow us apart on sight. If we don't . . ." But Artoo had already turned and was ambling quickly back down the passageway.

"Wait, where are you going? Haven't you been listening to me?" Uttering curses in several languages, some purely mechanical, Threepio raced fluidly after his friend. The Artoo unit, he thought to himself, could be downright close-circuited when it wanted to.

Outside the galactic cruiser's control center the corridor was crowded with sullen prisoners gathered by Imperial troops. Some lay wounded, some dying. Several officers had been separated from the enlisted ranks and stood in a small group by themselves, bestowing belligerent looks and threats on the silent knot of troops holding them at bay.

As if on command, everyone—Imperial troops as well as rebels—became silent as a massive caped form came into view from behind a turn in the passage. Two of the heretofore resolute, obstinate rebel officers began to shake. Stopping before one of the men, the towering figure reached out wordlessly. A massive hand closed around the man's neck and lifted him off the deck. The rebel officer's eyes bulged, but he kept his silence.

An Imperial officer, his armored helmet shoved back to reveal a recent scar where an energy beam had penetrated his shielding, scrambled down out of the fighter's control room, shaking his head briskly. "Nothing, sir. Information retrieval system's been wiped clean."

Darth Vader acknowledged this news with a barely perceptible nod. The impenetrable mask turned to regard the officer he was torturing. Metal-clad fingers contracted. Reaching up, the prisoner desperately tried to pry them loose, but to no avail.

"Where is the data you intercepted?" Vader rumbled dangerously. "What have you done with the information tapes?"

"We—intercepted—no information," the dangling officer gurgled, barely able to breathe. From somewhere deep within, he dredged up a squeal of outrage. "This is a . . . councilor vessel . . . Did you not see our . . . exterior markings? We're on a . . . diplomatic . . . mission."

"Chaos take your mission!" Vader growled. "Where

are those tapes!" He squeezed harder, the threat in his grip implicit.

When he finally replied, the officer's voice was a bare, choked whisper. "Only . . . the Commander knows."

"This ship carries the system crest of Alderaan," Vader growled, the gargoylelike breath mask leaning close. "Is any of the royal family on board? Who are you carrying?" Thick fingers tightened further, and the officer's struggles became more and more frantic. His last words were muffled and choked past intelligibility.

Vader was not pleased. Even though the figure went limp with an awful, unquestionable finality, that hand continued to tighten, producing a chilling snapping and popping of bone, like a dog padding on plastic. Then with a disgusted wheeze Vader finally threw the doll-form of the dead man against a far wall. Several Imperial troops ducked out of the way just in time to avoid the grisly missile.

The massive form whirled unexpectedly, and Imperial officers shrank under that baleful sculptured stare. "Start tearing this ship apart piece by piece, component by component, until you find those tapes. As for the passengers, if any, I want them alive." He paused a moment, then added, *"Quickly!"*

Officers and men nearly fell over themselves in their haste to leave—not necessarily to carry out Vader's orders, but simply to retreat from that malevolent presence.

Artoo Detoo finally came to a halt in an empty corridor devoid of smoke and the signs of battle. A worried, confused Threepio pulled up behind him.

"You've led us through half the ship, and to what . . . ?" He broke off, staring in disbelief as the squat robot reached up with one clawed limb and snapped the seal on a lifeboat hatch. Immediately a red warning light came on and a low hooting sounded in the corridor.

Threepio looked wildly in all directions, but the passageway remained empty. When he looked back, Artoo was already working his way into the cramped boat pod. It was just large enough to hold several humans, and its design was not laid out to accommodate mechanicals. Artoo had some trouble negotiating the awkward little compartment.

"Hey," a startled Threepio called, admonishing, "you're not permitted in there! It's restricted to humans only. We just might be able to convince the Imperials that we're not rebel programmed and are too valuable to break up, but if someone sees you in there we haven't got a chance. Come on out."

Somehow Artoo had succeeded in wedging his body into position in front of the miniature control board. He cocked his body slightly and threw a stream of loud beeps and whistles at his reluctant companion.

Threepio listened. He couldn't frown, but he managed to give a good impression of doing so. "Mission . . . what mission? What are you talking about? You sound like you haven't got an integrated logic terminal left in your brain. No . . . no more adventures. I'll take my chances with the Imperials—and I'm *not* getting in there."

An angry electronic twang came from the Artoo unit.

"Don't call *me* a mindless philosopher," Threepio snapped back, "you overweight, unstreamlined glob of grease!"

Threepio was concocting an additional rejoinder when an explosion blew out the back wall of the corridor. Dust and metal debris whooshed through the narrow subpassageway, followed instantly by a series of secondary explosions. Flames began jumping hungrily from the exposed interior wall, reflecting off Threepio's isolated patches of polished skin.

Muttering the electronic equivalent of consigning his soul to the unknown, the lanky robot jumped into the life pod. "I'm going to regret this," he muttered more audibly as Artoo activated the safety door behind him. The smaller robot flipped a series of switches, snapped back a cover, and pressed three buttons in a certain sequence. With the thunder of explosive latches the life pod ejected from the crippled fighter.

When word came over the communicators that the last pocket of resistance on the rebel ship had been cleaned out, the Captain of the Imperial cruiser relaxed considerably. He was listening with pleasure to the proceedings on the captured vessel when one of his chief gunnery officers called to him. Moving to the man's position, the Captain stared into the circular viewscreen and saw a tiny dot dropping away toward the fiery world below.

"There goes another pod, sir. Instructions?" The officer's hand hovered over a computerized energy battery.

Casually, confident in the firepower and total control under his command, the Captain studied the nearby readouts monitoring the pod. All of them read blank.

"Hold your fire, Lieutenant Hija. Instruments show no life forms aboard. The pod's release mechanism must have short-circuited or received a false instruction. Don't waste your power." He turned away, to listen with satisfaction to the reports of captured men and material coming from the rebel ship.

Glare from exploding panels and erupting circuitry reflected crazily off the armor of the lead storm trooper as he surveyed the passageway ahead. He was about to turn and call for those behind him to follow him forward when he noticed something moving off to one side. It appeared to be crouching back in a small, dark alcove. Holding his pistol ready, he moved cautiously forward and peered into the recess.

A small, shivering figure clad in flowing white hugged the back of the recess and stared up at the man. Now he could see that he faced a young woman, and her physical description fit that of the one individual the Dark Lord was most interested in. The trooper grinned behind his helmet. A lucky encounter for him. He would be commended.

Within the armor his head turned slightly, directing his voice to the tiny condenser microphone. "Here she is," he called to those behind him. "Set for stun forc—"

He never finished the sentence, just as he would never receive the hoped-for commendation. Once his attention turned from the girl to his communicator her shivering vanished with startling speed. The energy pistol she had held out of sight behind her came up and around as she burst from her hiding place.

The trooper who had been unlucky enough to find her fell first, his head a mass of melted bone and metal. The same fate met the second armored form coming up fast behind him. Then a bright green energy pole touched the woman's side and she slumped instantly to the deck, the pistol still locked in her small palm.

Metal-encased shapes clustered around her. One whose arm bore the insignia of a lower officer knelt and turned her over. He studied the paralyzed form with a practiced eye.

"She'll be all right," he finally declared, looking up at his subordinates. "Report to Lord Vader."

Threepio stared, mesmerized, out the small viewport set in the front of the tiny escape pod as the hot yellow eye of Tatooine began to swallow them up. Somewhere behind them, he knew, the crippled fighter and the Imperial cruiser were receding to imperceptibility.

That was fine with him. If they landed near a civilized city, he would seek elegant employment in a halcyon atmosphere, something more befitting his status and training. These past months had gifted him with entirely too much excitement and unpredictability for a mere machine.

Artoo's seemingly random manipulation of the pod controls promised anything but a smooth landing, however. Threepio regarded his squat companion with concern.

"Are you sure you know how to pilot this thing?"

Artoo replied with a noncommittal whistle that did nothing to alter the taller robot's jangled state of mind.

□ II

It was an old settlers' saying that you could burn your eyes out faster by staring straight and hard at the sun-scorched flatlands of Tatooine than by looking directly at its two huge suns themselves, so powerful was the penetrating glare reflected from those endless wastes. Despite the glare, life could and did exist in the flatlands formed by long-evaporated seabeds. One thing made it possible: the reintroduction of water.

For human purposes, however, the water of Tatooine was only marginally accessible. The atmosphere yielded its moisture with reluctance. It had to be coaxed down out of the hard blue sky—coaxed, forced, yanked down to the parched surface.

Two figures whose concern was obtaining that moisture were standing on a slight rise of one of those inhospitable flats. One of the pair was stiff and metallic—a sand-pitted vaporator sunk securely through sand and into deeper rock. The figure next to it was a good deal more animated, though no less sun-weathered.

Luke Skywalker was twice the age of the ten-year-old vaporator, but much less secure. At the moment he was swearing softly at a recalcitrant valve adjuster on the temperamental device. From time to time he resorted to some unsubtle pounding in place of using

the appropriate tool. Neither method worked very
well. Luke was sure that the lubricants used on the
vaporators went out of their way to attract sand,
beckoning seductively to small abrasive particles with
an oily gleam. He wiped sweat from his forehead and
leaned back for a moment. The most prepossessing
thing about the young man was his name. A light
breeze tugged at his shaggy hair and baggy work tunic
as he regarded the device. No point in staying angry
at it, he counseled himself. It's only an unintelligent
machine.

As Luke considered his predicament, a third figure
appeared, scooting out from behind the vaporator to
fumble awkwardly at the damaged section. Only three
of the Treadwell model robot's six arms were functioning, and these had seen more wear than the boots
on Luke's feet. The machine moved with unsteady,
stop-and-start motions.

Luke gazed at it sadly, then inclined his head to
study the sky. Still no sign of a cloud, and he knew
there never would be unless he got that vaporator
working. He was about to try once again when a
small, intense gleam of light caught his eye. Quickly
he slipped the carefully cleaned set of macrobinoculars
from his utility belt and focused the lenses skyward.

For long moments he stared, wishing all the while
that he had a real telescope instead of the binocs. As
he stared, vaporators, the heat, and the day's remaining chores were forgotten. Clipping the binoculars
back onto his belt, Luke turned and dashed for the
landspeeder. Halfway to the vehicle he thought to
call behind him.

"Hurry up," he shouted impatiently. "What are you
waiting for? Get it in gear."

The Treadwell started toward him, hesitated, and
then commenced spinning in a tight circle, smoke
belching from every joint. Luke shouted further instructions, then finally gave up in disgust when he realized that it would take more than words to motivate
the Treadwell again.

For a moment Luke hesitated at leaving the machine behind—but, he argued to himself, its vital components were obviously shot. So he jumped into the landspeeder, causing the recently repaired repulsion floater to list alarmingly to one side until he was able to equalize weight distribution by sliding behind the controls. Maintaining its altitude slightly above the sandy ground, the light-duty transport vehicle steadied itself like a boat in a heavy sea. Luke gunned the engine, which whined in protest, and sand erupted behind the floater as he aimed the craft toward the distant town of Anchorhead.

Behind him, a pitiful beacon of black smoke from the burning robot continued to rise into the clear desert air. It wouldn't be there when Luke returned. There were scavengers of metal as well as flesh in the wide wastes of Tatooine.

Metal and stone structures bleached white by the glaze of twin Tatoo I and II huddled together tightly, for company as much as for protection. They formed the nexus of the widespread farming community of Anchorhead.

Presently the dusty, unpaved streets were quiet, deserted. Sandflies buzzed lazily in the cracked eaves of pourstone buildings. A dog barked in the distance, the sole sign of habitation until a lone old woman appeared and started across the street. Her metallic sun shawl was pulled tight around her.

Something made her look up, tired eyes squinting into the distance. The sound suddenly leaped in volume as a shining rectangular shape came roaring around a far corner. Her eyes popped as the vehicle bore down on her, showing no sign of altering its path. She had to scramble to get out of its way.

Panting and waving an angry fist after the landspeeder, she raised her voice over the sound of its passage. "Won't you kids ever learn to slow down!"

Luke might have seen her, but he certainly didn't hear her. In both cases his attention was focused elsewhere as he pulled up behind a low, long concrete station. Various coils and rods jutted from its top and sides. Tatooine's relentless sand waves broke in frozen yellow spume against the station's walls. No one had bothered to clear them away. There was no point. They would only return again the following day.

Luke slammed the front door aside and shouted, "Hey!"

A rugged young man in mechanic's dress sat sprawled in a chair behind the station's unkempt control desk. Sunscreen oil had kept his skin from burning. The skin of the girl on his lap had been equally protected, and there was a great deal more of the protected area in view. Somehow even dried sweat looked good on her.

"Hey, everybody!" Luke yelled again, having elicited something less than an overwhelming response with his first cry. He ran toward the instrument room at the rear of the station while the mechanic, half asleep, ran a hand across his face and mumbled, "Did I hear a young noise blast through here?"

The girl on his lap stretched sensuously, her well-worn clothing tugging in various intriguing directions. Her voice was casually throaty. "Oh," she yawned, "that was just Wormie on one of his rampages."

Deak and Windy looked up from the computer-assisted pool game as Luke burst into the room. They were dressed much like Luke, although their clothing was of better fit and somewhat less exercised.

All three youths contrasted strikingly with the burly, handsome player at the far side of the table. From neatly clipped hair to his precision-cut uniform he stood out in the room like an Oriental poppy in a sea of oats. Behind the three humans a soft hum came from where a repair robot was working patiently on a broken piece of station equipment.

"Shape it up, you guys," Luke yelled excitedly. Then he noticed the older man in the uniform. The subject of his suddenly startled gaze recognized him simultaneously.

"Biggs!"

The man's face twisted in a half grin. "Hello, Luke." Then they were embracing each other warmly.

Luke finally stood away, openly admiring the other's uniform. "I didn't know you were back. When did you get in?"

The confidence in the other's voice bordered the realm of smugness without quite entering it. "Just a little while ago. I wanted to surprise you, hotshot." He indicated the room. "I thought you'd be here with these other two nightcrawlers." Deak and Windy both smiled. "I certainly didn't expect you to be out working." He laughed easily, a laugh few people found resistible.

"The academy didn't change you much," Luke commented. "But you're back so soon." His expression grew concerned. "Hey, what happened—didn't you get your commission?"

There was something evasive about Biggs as he replied, looking slightly away, "Of course I got it. Signed to serve aboard the freighter *Rand Ecliptic* just last week. First Mate Biggs Darklighter, at your service." He performed a twisting salute, half serious and half humorous, then grinned that overbearing yet ingratiating grin again.

"I just came back to say good-bye to all you unfortunate landlocked simpletons." They all laughed, until Luke suddenly remembered what had brought him here in such a hurry.

"I almost forgot," he told them, his initial excitement returning, "there's a battle going on right here in our system. Come and look."

Deak looked disappointed. "Not another one of your epic battles, Luke. Haven't you dreamed up enough of them? Forget it."

"Forget it, hell—I'm serious. It's a battle, all right."

With words and shoves he managed to cajole the occupants of the station out into the strong sunlight. Camie in particular looked disgusted.

"This had better be worth it, Luke," she warned him, shading her eyes against the glare.

Luke already had his macrobinoculars out and was searching the heavens. It took only a moment for him to fix on a particular spot. "I told you," he insisted. "There they are."

Biggs moved alongside him and reached for the binoculars as the others strained unaided eyes. A slight readjustment provided just enough magnification for Biggs to make out two silvery specks against the dark blue.

"That's no battle, hotshot," he decided, lowering the binocs and regarding his friend gently. "They're just sitting there. Two ships, all right—probably a barge loading a freighter, since Tatooine hasn't got an orbital station."

"There was a lot of firing—earlier," Luke added. His initial enthusiasm was beginning to falter under the withering assurance of his older friend.

Camie grabbed the binoculars away from Biggs, banging them slightly against a support pillar in the process. Luke took them away from her quickly, inspecting the casing for damage. "Take it easy with those."

"Don't worry so much, Wormie," she sneered. Luke took a step toward her, then halted as the huskier mechanic easily interposed himself between them and favored Luke with a warning smile. Luke considered, shrugged the incident away.

"I keep telling you, Luke," the mechanic said, with the air of a man tired of repeating the same story to no avail, "the rebellion is a long way from here. I doubt if the Empire would fight to keep this system. Believe me, Tatooine is a big hunk of nothing."

His audience began to fade back into the station before Luke could mutter a reply. Fixer had his arm around Camie, and the two of them were chuckling over Luke's ineptitude. Even Deak and Windy were murmuring among themselves—about him, Luke was certain.

He followed them, but not without a last glance back and up to the distant specks. One thing he was sure of were the flashes of light he had seen between the two ships. They hadn't been caused by the suns of Tatooine reflecting off metal.

The binding that locked the girl's hands behind her back was primitive and effective. The constant attention the squad of heavily armed troopers favored her with might have been out of place for one small female, except for the fact that their lives depended on her being delivered safely.

When she deliberately slowed her pace, however, it became apparent that her captors did not mind mistreating her a little. One of the armored figures shoved her brutally in the small of the back, and she nearly fell. Turning, she gave the offending soldier a vicious look. But she could not tell if it had any effect, since the man's face was completely hidden by his armored helmet.

The hallway they eventually emerged into was still smoking around the edges of the smoldering cavity blasted through the hull of the fighter. A portable accessway had been sealed to it and a circlet of light showed at the far end of the tunnel, bridging space between the rebel craft and the cruiser. A shadow moved over her as she turned from inspecting the accessway, startling her despite her usually unshakable self-control.

Above her towered the threatening bulk of Darth Vader, red eyes glaring behind the hideous breath mask. A muscle twitched in one smooth cheek, but other than that the girl didn't react. Nor was there the slightest shake in her voice.

"Darth Vader . . . I should have known. Only you would be so bold—and so stupid. Well, the Imperial Senate will not sit still for this. When they hear that you have attacked a diplomatic miss—"

"Senator Leia Organa," Vader rumbled softly, though strongly enough to override her protests. His pleasure at finding her was evident in the way he savored every syllable.

"Don't play games with me, Your Highness," he continued ominously. "You aren't on any mercy mission this time. You passed directly through a restricted system, ignoring numerous warnings and completely disregarding orders to turn about—until it no longer mattered."

The huge metal skull dipped close. "I know that several transmissions were beamed to this vessel by spies within that system. When we traced those transmissions back to the individuals with whom they originated, they had the poor grace to kill themselves before they could be questioned. I want to know what happened to the data they sent you."

Neither Vader's words nor his inimical presence appeared to have any effect on the girl. "I don't know what you're blathering about," she snapped, looking away from him. "I'm a member of the Senate on a diplomatic mission to—"

"To your part of the rebel alliance," Vader declared, cutting her off accusingly. "You're also a traitor." His gaze went to a nearby officer. "Take her away."

She succeeded in reaching him with her spit, which hissed against still-hot battle armor. He wiped the offensive matter away silently, watching her with interest as she was marched through the accessway into the cruiser.

A tall, slim soldier wearing the sign of an Imperial Commander attracted Vader's attention as he came up next to him. "Holding her is dangerous," he ventured, likewise looking after her as she was escorted toward the cruiser. "If word of this does get out, there will be much unrest in the Senate. It will generate sympathy for the rebels." The Commander looked up at the unreadable metal face, then added in an off-handed manner, "She should be destroyed immediately."

"No. My first duty is to locate that hidden fortress of theirs," Vader replied easily. "All the rebel spies have been eliminated—by our hand or by their own. Therefore she is now my only key to discovering its location. I intend to make full use of her. If necessary, I will use her up—but I *will* learn the location of the rebel base."

The Commander pursed his lips, shook his head slightly, perhaps a bit sympathetically, as he considered the woman. "She'll die before she gives you any information." Vader's reply was chilling in its indifference. "Leave that to me." He considered a moment, then went on. "Send out a wide-band distress signal. Indicate that the Senator's ship encountered an unexpected meteorite cluster it could not avoid. Readings indicate that the shift shields were overriden and the ship was hulled to the point of vacating ninety-five percent of its atmosphere. Inform her father and the Senate that all aboard were killed."

A cluster of tired-looking troops marched purposefully up to their Commander and the Dark Lord. Vader eyed them expectantly.

"The data tapes in question are not aboard the ship. There is no valuable information in the ship's storage banks and no evidence of bank erasure," the officer in charge recited mechanically. "Nor were any transmissions directed outward from the ship from the time we made contact. A malfunctioning lifeboat pod was ejected during the fighting, but it was confirmed at the time that no life forms were on board."

Vader appeared thoughtful. "It *could* have been a malfunctioning pod," he mused, "that might also have contained the tapes. Tapes are not life forms. In all probability any native finding them would be ignorant of their importance and would likely clear them for his own use. Still . . .

"Send down a detachment to retrieve them, or to make certain they are not in the pod," he finally ordered the Commander and attentive officer. "Be as subtle as possible; there is no need to attract attention, even on this miserable outpost world."

As the officer and troops departed, Vader turned his gaze back to the Commander. "Vaporize this fighter—we don't want to leave anything. As for the pod, I cannot take the chance it was a simple malfunction. The data it might contain could prove too damaging. See to this personally, Commander. If those data tapes exist, they must be retrieved or destroyed at all costs." Then he added with satisfaction, "With that accomplished and the Senator in our hands, we will see the end of this absurd rebellion."

"It shall be as you direct, Lord Vader," the Commander acknowledged. Both men entered the accessway to the cruiser.

"What a forsaken place this is!"

Threepio turned cautiously to look back at where the pod lay half buried in sand. His internal gyros were still unsteady from the rough landing. Landing! Mere application of the term unduly flattered his dull associate.

On the other hand, he supposed he ought to be grateful they had come down in one piece. Although, he mused as he studied the barren landscape, he still wasn't sure they were better off here than they would have been had they remained on the captured cruiser. High sandstone mesas dominated the skyline to one side. Every other direction showed only endless series of marching dunes like long yellow teeth stretching for kilometer on kilometer into the distance. Sand ocean blended into sky-glare until it was impossible to distinguish where one ended and the other began.

A faint cloud of minute dust particles rose in their wake as the two robots marched away from the pod. That vehicle, its intended function fully discharged, was now quite useless. Neither robot had been designed for pedal locomotion on this kind of terrain, so they had to fight their way across the unstable surface.

"We seem to have been made to suffer," Threepio moaned in self-pity. "It's a rotten existence." Something squeaked in his right leg and he winced. "I've got to rest before I fall apart. My internals still haven't recovered from that headlong crash you called a landing."

He paused, but Artoo Detoo did not. The little automaton had performed a sharp turn and was now ambling slowly but steadily in the direction of the nearest outjut of mesa.

"Hey," Threepio yelled. Artoo ignored the call and continued striding. "Where do you think you're going?"

Now Artoo paused, emitting a stream of electronic explanation as Threepio exhaustedly walked over to join him.

"Well, I'm not going that way," Threepio declared when Artoo had concluded his explanation. "It's too rocky." He gestured in the direction they had been walking, at an angle away from the cliffs. "This way is much easier." A metal hand waved disparagingly at the high mesas. "What makes you think there are any settlements that way, anyhow?"

A long whistle issued from the depths of Artoo.

"Don't get technical with me," Threepio warned. "I've had just about enough of your decisions."

Artoo beeped once.

"All right, go your way," Threepio announced grandly. "You'll be sandlogged within a day, you nearsighted scrap pile." He gave the Artoo unit a contemptuous shove, sending the smaller robot tumbling down a slight dune. As it struggled at the bottom to regain its feet, Threepio started off toward the blurred, glaring horizon, glancing back over his shoulder. "Don't let me catch you following me, begging for help," he warned, "because you won't get it."

Below the crest of the dune, the Artoo unit righted itself. It paused briefly to clean its single electronic eye with an auxiliary arm. Then it produced an electronic squeal which was almost, though not quite, a human expression of rage. Humming quietly to itself then, it turned and trudged off toward the sandstone ridges as if nothing had happened.

Several hours later a straining Threepio, his internal thermostat overloaded and edging dangerously toward overheat shutdown, struggled up the top of what he hoped was the last towering dune. Nearby, pillars and buttresses of bleached calcium, the bones of some enormous beast, formed an unpromising landmark. Reaching the crest of the dune, Threepio peered anxiously ahead. Instead of the hoped-for greenery of human civilization he saw only several dozen more dunes, identical in form and promise to the one he now stood upon. The farthest rose even higher than the one he presently surmounted.

Threepio turned and looked back toward the now far-off rocky plateau, which was beginning to grow indistinct with distance and heat distortion. "You malfunctioning little twerp," he muttered, unable even now to admit to himself that perhaps, just possibly, the Artoo unit might have been right. "This is all your fault. You tricked me into going this way, but you'll do no better."

Nor would he if he didn't continue on. So he took a step forward and heard something grind dully within a leg joint. Sitting down in an electronic funk, he began picking sand from his encrusted joints.

He could continue on his present course, he told himself. Or he could confess to an error in judgment and try to catch up again with Artoo Detoo. Neither prospect held much appeal for him.

But there was a third choice. He could sit here, shining in the sunlight, until his joints locked, his internals overheated, and the ultraviolet burned out his photoreceptors. He would become another monument to the destructive power of the binary, like the colossal organism whose picked corpse he had just encountered.

Already his receptors were beginning to go, he reflected. It seemed he saw something moving in the distance. Heat -distortion, probably. No—no—it was definitely light on metal, and it was moving toward him. His hopes soared. Ignoring the warnings from his damaged leg, he rose and began waving frantically.

It was, he saw now, definitely a vehicle, though of a type unfamiliar to him. But a vehicle it was, and that implied intelligence and technology.

He neglected in his excitement to consider the possibility that it might not be of human origin.

"So I cut off my power, shut down the afterburners, and dropped in low on Deak's tail," Luke finished, waving his arms wildly. He and Biggs were walking in the shade outside the power station. Sounds of metal being worked came from somewhere within, where Fixer had finally joined his robot assistant in performing repairs.

"I was so close to him," Luke continued excitedly, "I thought I was going to fry my instrumentation. As it was, I busted up the skyhopper pretty bad." That recollection inspired a frown.

"Uncle Owen was pretty upset. He grounded me for the rest of the season." Luke's depression was brief. Memory of his feat overrode its immorality.

"You should have been there, Biggs!"

"You ought to take it a little easier," his friend cautioned. "You may be the hottest bush pilot this side of Mos Eisley, Luke, but those little skyhoppers can be dangerous. They move awfully fast for tropospheric craft—faster than they need to. Keep playing engine jockey with one and someday, whammo!" He slammed one fist violently into his open palm. "You're going to be nothing more than a dark spot on the damp side of a canyon wall."

"Look who's talking," Luke retorted. "Now that you've been on a few big, automatic starships you're beginning to sound like my uncle. You've gotten soft in the cities." He swung spiritedly at Biggs, who blocked the movement easily, making a halfhearted gesture of counterattack.

Biggs's easygoing smugness dissolved into something warmer. "I've missed you, kid."

Luke looked away, embarrassed. "Things haven't exactly been the same since you left, either, Biggs. It's been so—" Luke hunted for the right word and finally finished helplessly, "—so *quiet.*" His gaze traveled across the sandy, deserted streets of Anchorhead. "Its always been quiet, really."

Biggs grew silent, thinking. He glanced around. They were alone out here. Everyone else was back inside the comparative coolness of the power station. As he leaned close Luke sensed an unaccustomed solemnness in his friend's tone.

"Luke, I didn't come back just to say good-bye, or to crow over everyone because I got through the Academy." Again he seemed to hesitate, unsure of himself. Then he blurted out rapidly, not giving himself a chance to back down, "But I want somebody to know. I can't tell my parents."

Gaping at Biggs, Luke could only gulp, "Know what? What are you talking about?"

"I'm talking about the talking that's been going on at the Academy—and other places, Luke. Strong talking. I made some new friends, outsystem friends. We agreed about the way certain things are developing, and—" his voice dropped conspiratorially—"When we reach one of the peripheral systems, we're going to jump ship and join the Alliance."

Luke stared back at his friend, tried to picture Biggs —fun-loving, happy-go-lucky, live-for-today Biggs— as a patriot afire with rebellious fervor.

"You're going to join the rebellion?" he started. "You've got to be kidding. How?"

"Damp down, will you?" the bigger man cautioned. glancing furtively back toward the power station. "You've got a mouth like a crater."

"I'm sorry," Luke whispered rapidly. "I'm quiet— listen how quiet I am. You can barely hear me—"

Biggs cut him off and continued. "A friend of mine from the Academy has a friend on Bestine who might enable us to make contact with an armed rebel unit."

"A friend of a— You're crazy," Luke announced with conviction, certain his friend had gone mad. "You could wander around forever trying to find a real rebel outpost. Most of them are only myths. This twice removed friend could be an imperial agent. You'd end up on Kessel, or worse. If rebel outposts were so easy to find, the Empire would have wiped them out years ago."

"I know it's a long shot," Biggs admitted reluctantly. "If I don't contact them, then"—a peculiar light came into Biggs's eyes, a conglomeration of newfound maturity and . . . something else—"I'll do what I can, on my own."

He stared intensely at his friend. "Luke, I'm not going to wait for the Empire to conscript me into its service. In spite of what you hear over the official information channels, the rebellion is growing, spreading. And I want to be on the right side—the side I believe in." His voice altered unpleasantly, and Luke wondered what he saw in his mind's eye.

"You should have heard some of the stories I've heard, Luke, learned of some of the outrages I've learned about. The Empire may have been great and beautiful once, but the people in charge now—" He shook his head sharply. "It's rotten, Luke, rotten."

"And I can't do a damn thing," Luke muttered morosely. "I'm stuck here." He kicked futilely at the ever-present sand of Anchorhead.

"I thought you were going to enter the Academy soon," Biggs observed. "If that's so, then you'll have your chance to get off this sandpile."

Luke snorted derisively. "Not likely. I had to withdraw my application." He looked away, unable to meet his friend's disbelieving stare. "I had to. There's been a lot of unrest among the sandpeople since you left, Biggs. They've even raided the outskirts of Anchorhead."

Biggs shook his head, disregarding the excuse. "Your uncle could hold off a whole colony of raiders with one blaster."

"From the house, sure," Luke agreed, "but Uncle Owen's finally got enough vaporators installed and running to make the farm pay off big. But he can't guard all that land by himself, and he says he needs me for one more season. I can't run out on him now."

Biggs sighed sadly. "I feel for you, Luke. Someday you're going to have to learn to separate what seems to be important from what really is important." He gestured around them.

"What good is all your uncle's work if it's taken over by the Empire? I've heard that they're starting to imperialize commerce in all the outlying systems. It won't be long before your uncle and everyone else on Tatooine are just tenants slaving for the greater glory of the Empire."

"That couldn't happen here," Luke objected with a confidence he didn't quite feel. "You've said it yourself—the Empire won't bother with this rock."

"Things change, Luke. Only the threat of rebellion keeps many in power from doing certain unmentionable things. If that threat is completely removed—well, there are two things men have never been able to satisfy: their curiosity and their greed. There isn't much the high Imperial bureaucrats are curious about."

Both men stood silent. A sandwhirl traversed the street in silent majesty, collapsing against a wall to send newborn baby zephyrs in all directions.

"I wish I was going with you," Luke finally murmured. He glanced up. "Will you be around long?"

"No. As a matter of fact, I'm leaving in the morning to rendezvous with the *Ecliptic*."

"Then I guess . . . I won't be seeing you again."

"Maybe someday," Biggs declared. He brightened, grinning that disarming grin. "I'll keep a look out for you, hotshot. Try not to run into any canyon walls in the meantime."

"I'll be at the Academy the season after," Luke insisted, more to encourage himself than Biggs. "After that, who knows where I'll end up?" He sounded determined. "I won't be drafted into the starfleet, that's for sure. Take care of yourself. You'll . . . always be the best friend I've got." There was no need for a handshake. These two had long since passed beyond that.

"So long, then, Luke," Biggs said simply. He turned and reentered the power station.

Luke watched him disappear through the door, his own thoughts as chaotic and frenetic as one of Tatooine's spontaneous dust storms.

There were any number of extraordinary features unique to Tatooine's surface. Outstanding among them were the mysterious mists which rose regularly from the ground at the points where desert sands washed up against unyielding cliffs and mesas.

Fog in a steaming desert seemed as out of place as cactus on a glacier, but it existed nonetheless. Meteorologists and geologists argued its origin among themselves, muttering hard-to-believe theories about water suspended in sandstone veins beneath the sand and incomprehensible chemical reactions which made water rise when the ground cooled, then fall underground again with the double sunrise. It was all very backward and very real.

Neither the mist nor the alien moans of nocturnal desert dwellers troubled Artoo Detoo, however, as he made his careful way up the rocky arroyo, hunting for the easiest pathway to the mesa top. His squarish, broad footpads made clicking sounds loud in the evening light as sand underfoot gave way gradually to gravel.

For a moment, he paused. He seemed to detect a noise—like metal on rock—ahead of him, instead of rock on rock. The sound wasn't repeated, though, and he quickly resumed his ambling ascent.

Up the arroyo, too far up to be seen from below, a pebble trickled loose from the stone wall. The tiny figure which had accidentally dislodged the pebble retreated mouselike into shadow. Two glowing points of light showed under overlapping folds of brown cape a meter from the narrowing canyon wall.

Only the reaction of the unsuspecting robot indicated the presence of the whining beam as it struck him. For a moment Artoo Detoo fluoresced eerily in the dimming light. There was a single short electronic squeak. Then the tripodal support unbalanced and the tiny automaton toppled over onto its back, the lights on its front blinking on and off erratically from the effects of the paralyzing beam.

Three travesties of men scurried out from behind concealing boulders. Their motions were more indicative of rodent than humankind, and they stood little taller than the Artoo unit. When they saw that the single burst of enervating energy had immobilized the robot, they holstered their peculiar weapons. Nevertheless, they approached the listless machine cautiously, with the trepidation of hereditary cowards.

Their cloaks were thickly coated with dust and sand. Unhealthy red-yellow pupils glowed catlike from the depths of their hoods as they studied their captive. The jawas conversed in low guttural croaks and scrambled analogs of human speech. If, as anthropologists hypothesized, they had ever been human, they had long since degenerated past anything resembling the human race.

Several more jawas appeared. Together, they succeeded in alternately hoisting and dragging the robot back down the arroyo.

At the bottom of the canyon—like some monstrous prehistoric beast—was a sandcrawler as enormous as its owners and operators were tiny. Several dozen meters high, the vehicle towered above the ground on multiple treads that were taller than a tall man.

Its metal epidermis was battered and pitted from with-standing untold sandstorms.

On reaching the crawler, the jawas resumed jab-bering among themselves. Artoo Detoo could hear them but failed to comprehend anything. He need not have been embarrassed at his failure. If they so wished, only jawas could understand other jawas, for they employed a randomly variable language that drove linguists mad.

One of them removed a small disk from a belt pouch and sealed it to the Artoo unit's flank. A large tube protruded from one side of the gargantuan vehicle. They rolled him over to it and then moved clear. There was a brief moan, the *whoosh* of power-ful vacuum, and the small robot was sucked into the bowels of the sandcrawler as neatly as a pea up a straw. This part of the job completed, the jawas en-gaged in another bout of jabbering, following which they scurried into the crawler via tubes and ladders, for all the world like a nest of mice returning to their holes.

None too gently, the suction tube deposited Artoo in a small cubical. In addition to varied piles of bro-ken instruments and outright scrap, a dozen or so ro-bots of differing shapes and sizes populated the prison. A few were locked in electronic conversation. Others muddled aimlessly about. But when Artoo tumbled into the chamber, one voice burst out in surprise.

"Artoo Detoo—it's you, it's you!" called an excited Threepio from the near darkness. He made his way over to the still immobilized repair unit and embraced it most unmechanically. Spotting the small disk sealed onto Artoo's side, Threepio turned his gaze thought-fully down to his own chest, where a similar device had likewise been attached.

Massive gears, poorly lubricated, started to move. With a groaning and grinding, the monster sand-crawler turned and lumbered with relentless patience into the desert night.

☐ III

THE burnished conference table was as soulless and unyielding as the mood of the eight Imperial Senators and officers ranged around it. Imperial troopers stood guard at the entrance to the chamber, which was sparse and coldly lit from lights in the table and walls. One of the youngest of the eight was declaiming. He exhibited the attitude of one who had climbed far and fast by methods best not examined too closely. General Tagge did possess a certain twisted genius, but it was only partly that ability which had lifted him to his present exalted position. Other noisome talents had proven equally efficacious.

Though his uniform was as neatly molded and his body as clean as that of anyone else in the room, none of the remaining seven cared to touch him. A certain sliminess clung cloyingly to him, a sensation inferred rather than tactile. Despite this, many respected him. Or feared him.

"I tell you, he's gone too far this time," the General was insisting vehemently. "This Sith Lord inflicted on us at the urging of the Emperor will be our undoing. Until the battle station is fully operational, we remain vulnerable.

"Some of you still don't seem to realize how well equipped and organized the rebel Alliance is. Their vessels are excellent, their pilots better. And they are propelled by something more powerful than mere engines: this perverse, reactionary fanaticism of theirs. They're more dangerous than most of you realize."

An older officer, with facial scars so deeply engraved that even the best cosmetic surgery could not fully repair them, shifted nervously in his chair.

34

"Dangerous to your starfleet, General Tagge, but not to this battle station." Wizened eyes hopped from man to man, traveling around the table. "I happen to think Lord Vader knows what he's doing. The rebellion will continue only as long as those cowards have a sanctuary, a place where their pilots can relax and their machines can be repaired."

Tagge objected. "I beg to differ with you, Romodi. I think the construction of this station has more to do with Governor Tarkin's bid for personal power and recognition than with any justifiable military strategy. Within the Senate the rebels will continue to increase their support as long—"

The sound of the single doorway sliding aside and the guards snapping to attention cut him off. His head turned as did everyone else's.

Two individuals as different in appearance as they were united in objectives had entered the chamber. The nearest to Tagge was a thin, hatchet-faced man with hair and form borrowed from an old broom and the expression of a quiescent piranha. The Grand Moff Tarkin, Governor of numerous outlying Imperial territories, was dwarfed by the broad, armored bulk of Lord Darth Vader.

Tagge, unintimidated but subdued, slowly resumed his seat as Tarkin assumed his place at the end of the conference table. Vader stood next to him, a dominating presence behind the Governor's chair. For a minute Tarkin stared directly at Tagge, then glanced away as if he had seen nothing. Tagge fumed but remained silent.

As Tarkin's gaze roved around the table a razor-thin smile of satisfaction remained frozen in his features. "The Imperial Senate will no longer be of any concern to us, gentlemen. I have just received word that the Emperor has permanently dissolved that misguided body."

A ripple of astonishment ran through the assembly. "The last remnants," Tarkin continued, "of the Old Republic have finally been swept away."

"This is impossible," Tagge interjected. "How will the Emperor maintain control of the Imperial bureaucracy?"

"Senatorial representation has not been formally abolished, you must understand," Tarkin explained. "It has merely been superseded for the—" he smiled a bit more—"duration of the emergency. Regional Governors will now have direct control and a free hand in administering their territories. This means that the Imperial presence can at last be brought to bear properly on the vacillating worlds of the Empire. From now on, fear will keep potentially traitorous local governments in line. Fear of the Imperial fleet—and fear of this battle station."

"And what of the existing rebellion?" Tagge wanted to know.

"If the rebels somehow managed to gain access to a complete technical schema of this battle station, it is remotely possible that they might be able to locate a weakness susceptible to minor exploitation." Tarkin's smile shifted to a smirk. "Of course, we all know how well guarded, how carefully protected, such vital data is. It could not possibly fall into rebel hands."

"The technical data to which you are obliquely referring," rumbled Darth Vader angrily, "will soon be back in our hands. If—"

Tarkin shook the Dark Lord off, something no one else at the table would have dared to do. "It is immaterial. Any attack made against this station by the rebels would be a suicidal gesture, suicidal and useless—regardless of any information they managed to obtain. After many long years of secretive construction," he declared with evident pleasure, "this station has become the decisive force in this part of the universe. Events in this region of the galaxy will no longer be determined by fate, by decree, or by any other agency. They will be decided by this station!"

A huge metal-clad hand gestured slightly, and one of the filled cups on the table drifted responsively into it. With a slightly admonishing tone the Dark

Lord continued. "Don't become too proud of this technological terror you've spawned, Tarkin. The ability to destroy a city, a world, a whole system is still insignificant when set against the force."

" 'The Force,' " Tagge sneered. "Don't try to frighten *us* with your sorcerer's ways, Lord Vader. Your sad devotion to that ancient mythology has not helped you to conjure up those stolen tapes, or gifted you with clairvoyance sufficient to locate the rebels' hidden fortress. Why, it's enough to make one laugh fit to—"

Tagge's eyes abruptly bulged and his hands went to his throat as he began to turn a disconcerting shade of blue.

"I find," Vader ventured mildly, "this lack of faith disturbing."

"Enough of this," Tarkin snapped, distressed. "Vader, release him. This bickering among ourselves is pointless."

Vader shrugged as if it were of no consequence. Tagge slumped in his seat, rubbing his throat, his wary gaze never leaving the dark giant.

"Lord Vader will provide us with the location of the rebel fortress by the time this station is certified operational," Tarkin declared. "That known, we will proceed to it and destroy it utterly, crushing this pathetic rebellion in one swift stroke."

"As the Emperor wills it," Vader added, not without sarcasm, "so shall it be."

If any of the powerful men seated around the table found this disrespectful tone objectionable, a glance at Tagge was sufficient to dissuade them from mentioning it.

The dim prison reeked of rancid oil and stale lubricants, a veritable metallic charnel house. Threepio endured the discomfiting atmosphere as best he could. It was a constant battle to avoid being thrown by every unexpected bounce into the walls or into a fellow machine.

To conserve power—and also to avoid the steady stream of complaints from his taller companion— Artoo Detoo had shut down all exterior functions. He lay inert among a pile of secondary parts, sublimely unconcerned at the moment as to their fate.

"Will this never end?" Threepio was moaning as another violent jolt roughly jostled the inhabitants of the prison. He had already formulated and discarded half a hundred horrible ends. He was certain only that their eventual disposition was sure to be worse than anything he could imagine.

Then, quite without warning, something more unsettling than even the most battering bump took place. The sandcrawler's whine died, and the vehicle came to a halt—almost as if in response to Threepio's query. A nervous buzz rose from those mechanicals who still retained a semblance of sentience as they speculated on their present location and probable fate.

At least Threepio was no longer ignorant of his captors or of their likely motives. Local captives had explained the nature of the quasi-human mechanic migrants, the jawas. Traveling in their enormous mobile fortress-homes, they scoured the most inhospitable regions of Tatooine in search of valuable minerals—and salvageable machinery. They had never been seen outside of their protective cloaks and sandmasks, so no one knew exactly what they looked like. But they were reputed to be extraordinarily ugly. Threepio did not have to be convinced.

Leaning over his still-motionless companion, he began a steady shaking of the barrellike torso. Epidermal sensors were activated on the Artoo unit, and the lights on the front side of the little robot began a sequential awakening.

"Wake up, wake up," Threepio urged. "We've stopped someplace." Like several of the other, more imaginative robots, his eyes were warily scanning metal walls, expecting a hidden panel to slide aside at any moment and a giant mechanical arm to come probing and fumbling for him.

"No doubt about it, we're doomed," he recited mournfully as Artoo righted himself, returning to full activation. "Do you think they'll melt us down?" He became silent for several minutes, then added, "It's this waiting that gets to me."

Abruptly the far wall of the chamber slid aside and the blinding white glare of a Tatooine morning rushed in on them. Threepio's sensitive photoreceptors were hard pressed to adjust in time to prevent serious damage.

Several of the repulsive-looking jawas scrambled agilely into the chamber, still dressed in the same swathings and filth Threepio had observed on them before. Using hand weapons of an unknown design, they prodded at the machines. Certain of them, Threepio noted with a mental swallow, did not stir.

Ignoring the immobile ones, the jawas herded those still capable of movement outside, Artoo and Threepio among them. Both robots found themselves part of an uneven mechanical line.

Shielding his eyes against the glare, Threepio saw that five of them were arranged alongside the huge sandcrawler. Thoughts of escape did not enter his mind. Such a concept was utterly alien to a mechanical. The more intelligent a robot was, the more abhorrent and unthinkable the concept. Besides, had he tried to escape, built-in sensors would have detected the critical logic malfunction and melted every circuit in his brain.

Instead, he studied the small domes and vaporators that indicated the presence of a larger underground human homestead. Though he was unfamiliar with this type of construction, all signs pointed to a modest, if isolated, habitation. Thoughts of being dismembered for parts or slaving in some high-temperature mine slowly faded. His spirits rose correspondingly.

"Maybe this won't be so bad after all," he murmured hopefully. "If we can convince these bipedal vermin to unload us here, we may enter into sensible human service again instead of being melted into slag."

Artoo's sole reply was a noncommittal chirp. Both machines became silent as the jawas commenced scurrying around them, striving to straighten one poor machine with a badly bent spine, to disguise a dent or scrape with liquid and dust.

As two of them bustled about, working on his sand-coated skin, Threepio fought to stifle an expression of disgust. One of his many human-analog functions was the ability to react naturally to offensive odors. Apparently hygiene was unknown among the jawas. But he was certain no good would come of pointing this out to them.

Small insects drifted in clouds about the faces of the jawas, who ignored them. Apparently the tiny individualized plagues were regarded as just a different sort of appendage, like an extra arm or leg.

So intent was Threepio on his observation that he failed to notice the two figures moving toward them from the region of the largest dome. Artoo had to nudge him slightly before he looked up.

The first man wore an air of grim, semiperpetual exhaustion, sandblasted into his face by too many years of arguing with a hostile environment. His graying hair was frozen in tangled twists like gypsum helicites. Dust frosted his face, clothes, hands, and thoughts. But the body, if not the spirit, was still powerful.

Proportionately dwarfed by his uncle's wrestlerlike body, Luke strode slump-shouldered in his shadow, his present attitude one of dejection rather than exhaustion. He had a great deal on his mind, and it had very little to do with farming. Mostly it involved the rest of his life, and the commitment made by his best friend who had recently departed beyond the blue sky above to enter a harsher, yet more rewarding career.

The bigger man stopped before the assembly and

entered into a peculiar squeaky dialogue with the jawa in charge. When they wished it, the jawas could be understood.

Luke stood nearby, listening indifferently. Then he shuffled along behind his uncle as the latter began inspecting the five machines, pausing only to mutter an occasional word or two to his nephew. It was hard to pay attention, even though he knew he ought to be learning.

"Luke—oh, Luke!" a voice called.

Turning away from the conversation, which consisted of the lead jawa extolling the unmatched virtues of all five machines and his uncle countering with derision, Luke walked over to the near edge of the subterranean courtyard and peered down.

A stout woman with the expression of a misplaced sparrow was busy working among decorative plants. She looked up at him. "Be sure and tell Owen that if he buys a translator to make sure it speaks Bocce, Luke."

Turning, Luke looked back over his shoulder and studied the motley collection of tired machines. "It looks like we don't have much of a choice," he called back down to her, "but I'll remind him anyway."

She nodded up at him and he turned to rejoin his uncle.

Apparently Owen Lars had already come to a decision, having settled on a small semi-agricultural robot. This one was similar in shape to Artoo Detoo, save that its multiple subsidiary arms were tipped with different functions. At an order it had stepped out of the line and was wobbling along behind Owen and the temporarily subdued jawa.

Proceeding to the end of the line, the farmer's eyes narrowed as he concentrated on the sand-scoured but still flashy bronze finish of the tall, humanoid Threepio.

"I presume you function," he grumbled at the robot. "Do you know customs and protocol?"

"Do I know protocol?" Threepio echoed as the

farmer looked him up and down. Threepio was determined to embarrass the jawa when it came to selling his abilities. "Do I know protocol! Why, it's my primary function. I am also well—"

"Don't need a protocol 'droid," the farmer snapped dryly.

"I don't blame you, sir," Threepio rapidly agreed. "I couldn't be more in agreement. What could be more of a wasteful luxury in a climate like this? For someone of your interests, sir, a protocol 'droid would be a useless waste of money. No, sir—versatility is my middle name. See Vee Threepio—Vee for versatility—at your service. I've been programmed for over thirty secondary functions that require only . . ."

"I need," the farmer broke in, demonstrating imperious disregard for Threepio's as yet unenumerated secondary functions, "a 'droid that knows something about the binary language of independently programmable moisture vaporators."

"Vaporators! We are both in luck," Threepio countered. "My first post-primary assignment was in programming binary load lifters. Very similar in construction and memory-function to your vaporators. You could almost say . . ."

Luke tapped his uncle on the shoulder and whispered something in his ear. His uncle nodded, then looked back at the attentive Threepio again.

"Do you speak Bocce?"

"Of course, sir," Threepio replied, confident for a change with a wholly honest answer. "It's like a second language to me. I'm as fluent in Bocce as—"

The farmer appeared determined never to allow him to conclude a sentence. "Shut up." Owen Lars looked down at the jawa. "I'll take this one, too."

"Shutting up, sir," responded Threepio quickly, hard put to conceal his glee at being selected.

"Take them down to the garage, Luke," his uncle instructed him. "I want you to have both of them cleaned up by suppertime."

Luke looked askance at his uncle. "But I was going into Tosche station to pick up some new power converters and . . ."

"Don't lie to me, Luke," his uncle warned him sternly. "I don't mind you wasting time with your idle friends, but only after you've finished your chores. Now hop to it—and before supper, mind."

Downcast, Luke directed his words irritably to Threepio and the small agricultural robot. He knew better than to argue with his uncle.

"Follow me, you two." They started for the garage as Owen entered into price negotiations with the jawa.

Other jawas were leading the three remaining machines back into the sandcrawler when something let out an almost pathetic beep. Luke turned to see a Artoo unit breaking formation and starting toward him. It was immediately restrained by a jawa wielding a control device that activated the disk sealed on the machine's front plate.

Luke studied the rebellious 'droid curiously. Threepio started to say something, considered the circumstances and thought better of it. Instead, he remained silent, staring straight ahead.

A minute later, something pinged sharply nearby. Glancing down, Luke saw that a head plate had popped off the top of the agricultural 'droid. A grinding noise was coming from within. A second later the machine was throwing internal components all over the sandy ground.

Leaning close, Luke peered inside the expectorating mechanical. He called out, "Uncle Owen! The servomotor-central on this cultivator unit is shot. Look . . ." He reached in, tried to adjust the device, and pulled away hurriedly when it began a wild sparking. The odor of crisped insulation and corroded circuitry filled the clear desert air with a pungency redolent of mechanized death.

Owen Lars glared down at the nervous jawa. "What kind of junk are you trying to push on us?"

The jawa responded loudly, indignantly, while simultaneously taking a couple of precautionary steps away from the big human. He was distressed that the man was between him and the soothing safety of the sandcrawler.

Meanwhile, Artoo Detoo had scuttled out of the group of machines being led back toward the mobile fortress. Doing so turned out to be simple enough, since all the jawas had their attention focused on the argument between their leader and Luke's uncle.

Lacking sufficient armature for wild gesticulation, the Artoo unit suddenly let out a high whistle, then broke it off when it was apparent he had gained Threepio's attention.

Tapping Luke gently on the shoulder, the tall 'droid whispered conspiratorially into his ear. "If I might say so, young sir, that Artoo unit is a real bargain. In top condition. I don't believe these creatures have any idea what good shape he's really in. Don't let all the sand and dust deceive you."

Luke was in the habit of making instant decisions —for good or bad—anyway. "Uncle Owen!" he called.

Breaking off the argument without taking his attention from the jawa, his uncle glanced quickly at him. Luke gestured toward Artoo Detoo. "We don't want any trouble. What about swapping this—" he indicated the burned-out agricultural 'droid—"for that one?"

The older man studied the Artoo unit professionally, then considered the jawas. Though inherently cowards, the tiny desert scavengers *could* be pushed too far. The sandcrawler could flatten the homestead —at the risk of inciting the human community to lethal vengeance.

Faced with a no-win situation for either side if he pressed too hard, Owen resumed the argument for show's sake before gruffly assenting. The head jawa consented reluctantly to the trade, and both sides breathed a mental sigh of relief that hostilities had been avoided. While the jawa bowed and whined with impatient greed, Owen paid him off.

Meanwhile, Luke had led the two robots toward an opening in the dry ground. A few seconds later they were striding down a ramp kept clear of drifting sand by electrostatic repellers.

"Don't you ever forget this," Threepio muttered to Artoo, leaning over the smaller machine. "Why I stick my neck out for you, when all you ever bring me is trouble, is beyond my capacity to comprehend."

The passage widened into the garage proper, which was cluttered with tools and sections of farming machinery. Many looked heavily used, some to the point of collapse. But the lights were comforting to both 'droids, and there was a homeliness to the chamber which hinted at a tranquillity not experienced by either machine for a long time. Near the center of the garage was a large tub, and the aroma drifting from it made Threepio's principal olfactory sensors twitch.

Luke grinned, noting the robot's reaction. "Yes, it's a lubrication bath." He eyed the tall bronze robot appraisingly. "And from the looks of it, you could use about a week's submergence. But we can't afford that so you'll have to settle for an afternoon." Then Luke turned his attention to Artoo Detoo, walking up to him and flipping open a panel that shielded numerous gauges.

"As for you," he continued, with a whistle of surprise, "I don't know how you've kept running. Not surprising, knowing the jawas' reluctance to part with any erg-fraction they don't have to. It's recharge time for you." He gestured toward a large power unit.

Artoo Detoo followed Luke's gesture, then beeped once and waddled over to the boxy construction. Finding the proper cord, he automatically flipped open a panel and plugged the triple prongs into his face.

Threepio had walked over to the large cistern, which was filled almost full with aromatic cleansing oil. With a remarkably humanlike sigh he lowered himself slowly into the tank.

"You two behave yourselves," Luke cautioned them as he moved to a small two-man skyhopper. A powerful little suborbital spacecraft, it rested in the hangar section of the garage-workshop. "I've got work of my own to do."

Unfortunately, Luke's energies were still focused on his farewell encounter with Biggs, so that hours later he had finished few of his chores. Thinking about his friend's departure, Luke was running a caressing hand over the damaged port fin of the 'hopper—the fin he had damaged while running down an imaginary Tie fighter in the wrenching twists and turns of a narrow canyon. That was when the projecting ledge had clipped him as effectively as an energy beam.

Abruptly something came to a boil within him. With atypical violence he threw a power wrench across a worktable nearby. "It just isn't fair!" he declared to no one in particular. His voice dropped disconsolately. "Biggs is right. I'll never get out of here. He's planning rebellion against the Empire, and I'm trapped on a blight of a farm."

"I beg your pardon, sir."

Luke spun, startled, but it was only the tall 'droid, Threepio. The contrast in the robot was striking compared with Luke's initial sight of him. Bronze-colored alloy gleamed in the overhead lights of the garage, cleaned of pits and dust by the powerful oils.

"Is there anything I might do to help?" the robot asked solicitously.

Luke studied the machine, and as he did so some of his anger drained away. There was no point in yelling cryptically at a robot.

"I doubt it," he replied, "unless you can alter time and speed up the harvest. Or else teleport me off this sandpile under uncle Owen's nose."

Sarcasm was difficult for even an extremely sophisticated robot to detect, so Threepio considered the question objectively before finally replying, "I don't think so, sir. I'm only a third-degree 'droid and not very knowledgeable about such things as transatomic physics." Suddenly, the events of the past couple of days seemed to catch up with him all at once. "As a matter of fact, young sir," Threepio went on while looking around him with fresh vision, "I'm not even sure which planet I'm on."

Luke chuckled sardonically and assumed a mocking pose. "If there's a bright center to this universe, you're on the world farthest from it."

"Yes, Luke sir."

The youth shook his head irritably. "Never mind the 'sir'—it's just Luke. And this world is called Tatooine."

Threepio nodded slightly. "Thank you, Luke s— Luke. I am See Threepio, human-droid relations specialist." He jerked a casual metal thumb back toward the recharge unit. "That is my companion, Artoo Detoo."

"Pleased to meet you, Threepio," Luke said easily. "You too, Artoo." Walking across the garage, he checked a gauge on the smaller machine's front panel, then gave a grunt of satisfaction. As he began unplugging the charge cord he saw something which made him frown and lean close.

"Something wrong, Luke?" Threepio inquired.

Luke went to a nearby tool wall and selected a small many-armed device. "I don't know yet, Threepio."

Returning to the recharger, Luke bent over Artoo and began scraping at several bumps in the small 'droid's top with a chromed pick. Occasionally he jerked back sharply as bits of corrosion were flicked into the air by the tiny tool.

Threepio watched, interested, as Luke worked. "There's a lot of strange carbon scoring here of a type I'm not familiar with. Looks like you've both seen a lot of action out of the ordinary."

"Indeed, sir," Threepio admitted, forgetting to drop the honorific. This time Luke was too absorbed elsewhere to correct him. "Sometimes I'm amazed we're in as good shape as we are." He added as an afterthought, while still shying away from the thrust of Luke's question, "What with the rebellion and all."

Despite his caution, it seemed to Threepio that he must have given something away, for an almost jawa-like blaze appeared in Luke's eyes. "You know about the rebellion against the Empire?" he demanded.

"In a way," Threepio confessed reluctantly. "The rebellion was responsible for our coming into your service. We are refugees, you see." He did not add from where.

Not that Luke appeared to care. *"Refugees!"* Then I *did* see a space battle!" He rambled on rapidly, excited. "Tell me where you've been——in how many encounters. How is the rebellion going? Does the Empire take it seriously? Have you seen many ships destroyed?"

"A bit slower, please, sir," Threepio pleaded. "You misinterpret our status. We were innocent bystanders. Our involvement with the rebellion was of the most marginal nature.

"As to battles, we were in several, I think. It is difficult to tell when one is not directly in contact with the actual battle machinery." He shrugged neatly. "Beyond that, there is not much to say. Remember, sir, I am little more than a cosmeticized interpreter and not very good at telling stories or relating histories, and even less proficient at embellishing them. I am a very literal machine."

Luke turned away, disappointed, and returned to his cleaning of Artoo Detoo. Additional scraping turned up something puzzling enough to demand his full attention. A small metal fragment was tightly lodged between two bar conduits that would normally form a linkage. Setting down the delicate pick, Luke switched to a larger instrument.

"Well, my little friend," he murmured, "you've got something jammed in here real good." As he pushed and pried Luke directed half his attention to Three-pio. "Were you on a star freighter or was it—"

Metal gave way with a powerful *crack,* and the re-coil sent Luke tumbling head over heels. Getting to his feet, he started to curse—then froze, motionless.

The front of the Artoo unit had begun to glow, exuding a three-dimensional image less than one-third of a meter square but precisely defined. The portrait formed within the box was so exquisite that in a couple of minutes Luke discovered he was out of breath —because he had forgotten to breathe.

Despite a superficial sharpness, the image flickered and jiggled unsteadily, as if the recording had been made and installed with haste. Luke stared at the foreign colors being projected into the prosaic at-mosphere of the garage and started to form a question. But it was never finished. The lips on the figure moved, and the girl spoke—or rather, seemed to speak. Luke knew the aural accompaniment was gen-erated somewhere within Artoo Detoo's squat torso.

"Obi-wan Kenobi," the voice implored huskily, "help me! You're my only remaining hope." A burst of static dissolved the face momentarily. Then it coa-lesced again, and once more the voice repeated, "Obi-wan Kenobi, you're my only remaining hope."

With a raspy hum the hologram continued. Luke sat perfectly still for a long moment, considering what he was seeing, then he blinked and directed his words to the Artoo unit.

"What's this all about, Artoo Detoo?"

The stubby 'droid shifted slightly, the cubish por-trait shifting with him, and beeped what sounded vaguely like a sheepish reply.

Threepio appeared as mystified as Luke. "What is that?" he inquired sharply, gesturing at the speaking portrait and then at Luke. "You were asked a ques-tion. What and who is that, and how are you origi-nating it—and why?"

The Artoo unit generated a beep of surprise, for all the world as if just noticing the hologram. This was followed by a whistling stream of information.

Threepio digested the data, tried to frown, couldn't, and strove to convey his own confusion via the tone of his voice. "He insists it's nothing, sir. Merely a malfunction—old data. A tape that should have been erased but was missed. He insists we pay it no mind."

That was like telling Luke to ignore a cache of Durindfires he might stumble over in the desert. "Who is she?" he demanded, staring enraptured at the hologram. "She's beautiful."

"I really don't know who she is," Threepio confessed honestly. "I think she might have been a passenger on our last voyage. From what I recall, she was a personage of some importance. This might have something to do with the fact that our Captain was attaché to—"

Luke cut him off, savoring the way sensuous lips formed and reformed the sentence fragment. "Is there any more to this recording? It sounds like it's incomplete." Getting to his feet, Luke reached out for the Artoo unit.

The robot moved backward and produced whistles of such frantic concern that Luke hesitated and held off reaching for the internal controls.

Threepio was shocked. "Behave yourself, Artoo," he finally chastised his companion. "You're going to get us into trouble." He had visions of the both of them being packed up as uncooperative and shipped back to the jawas, which was enough to make him imitate a shudder.

"It's all right—he's our master now." Threepio indicated Luke. "You can trust him. I feel that he has our best interests in mind."

Detoo appeared to hesitate, uncertain. Then he whistled and beeped a long complexity at his friend.

"Well?" Luke prompted impatiently.

Threepio paused before replying. "He says that he is the property of one Obi-wan Kenobi, a resident of this world. Of this very region, in fact. The sentence fragment we are hearing is part of a private message intended for this person."

Threepio shook his head slowly. "Quite frankly, sir, I don't know what he's talking about. Our last master was Captain Colton. I never heard Artoo mention a prior master. I've certainly never heard of an Obi-wan Kenobi. But with all we've been through," he concluded apologetically, "I'm afraid his logic circuits have gotten a bit scrambled. He's become decidedly eccentric at times." And while Luke considered this turn of events, Threepio took the opportunity to throw Artoo a furious look of warning.

"Obi-wan Kenbi," Luke recited thoughtfully. His expression suddenly brightened. "Say . . . I wonder if he could be referring to old Ben Kenobi."

"Begging your pardon," Threepio gulped, astonished beyond measure, "but you actually know of such a person?"

"Not exactly," he admitted in a more subdued voice. "I don't know anyone named Obi-wan—but old Ben lives somewhere out on the fringe of the Western Dune Sea. He's kind of a local character— a hermit. Uncle Owen and a few of the other farmers say he's a sorcerer.

"He comes around once in a while to trade things. I hardly ever talk to him, though. My uncle usually runs him off." He paused and glanced across at the small robot again. "But I never heard that old Ben owned a 'droid of any kind. At least, none that I ever heard tell of."

Luke's gaze was drawn irresistibly back to the hologram. "I wonder who she is. She must be important—especially if what you told me just now is true, Threepio. She sounds and looks as if she's in some kind of trouble. Maybe the message *is* important. We ought to hear the rest of it."

He reached again for the Artoo's internal controls, and the robot scurried backward again, squeaking a blue streak.

"He says there's a restraining separator bolt that's

circuiting out his self-motivation components." Three-pio translated. "He suggests that if you move the bolt he might be able to repeat the entire message," Threepio finished uncertainly. When Luke continued to stare at the portrait, Threepio added, more loudly "*Sir!*"

Luke shook himself. "What . . . ? Oh, yes." He considered the request. Then he moved and peered into the open panel. This time Artoo didn't retreat.

"I see it, I think. Well, I guess you're too small to run away from me if I take this off. I wonder what someone would be sending a message to old Ben for."

Selecting the proper tool, Luke reached down into the exposed circuitry and popped the restraining bolt free. The first noticeable result of this action was that the portrait disappeared.

Luke stood back. "There, now." There was an uncomfortable pause during which the hologram showed no sign of returning. "Where did she go?" Luke finally prompted. "Make her come back. Play the entire message, Artoo Detoo."

An innocent-sounding beep came from the robot. Threepio appeared embarrassed and nervous as he translated. "He said, 'What message?' "

Threepio's attention turned half angrily to his companion. "What message? You know what message! The one you just played a fragment of for us. The one you're hauling around inside your recalcitrant, rust-ridden innards, you stubborn hunk of junk!"

Artoo sat and hummed softly to himself.

"I'm sorry, sir," Threepio said slowly, "but he shows signs of having developed an alarming flutter in his obedience-rational module. Perhaps if we—"

A voice from down a corridor interrupted him. "Luke . . . oh, Luke—come to dinner!"

Luke hesitated, then rose and turned away from the puzzling little 'droid. "Okay," he called, "I'm coming, Aunt Beru!" He lowered his voice as he spoke to Threepio. "See what you can do with him. I'll be

back soon." Tossing the just-removed restraining bolt
on the workbench, he hurried from the chamber.

As soon as the human was gone, Threepio whirled
on his shorter companion. "You'd better consider
playing that whole recording for him," he growled,
with a suggestive nod toward a workbench laden with
dismembered machine parts. "Otherwise he's liable to
take up that cleaning pick again and go digging for it.
He might not be too careful what he cuts through
if he believes you're deliberately withholding something
from him."

A plaintive beep came from Artoo.

"No," Threepio responded, "I don't think he likes
you at all."

A second beep failed to alter the stern tone in the
taller robot's voice. "No, I don't like you, either."

☐ IV

LUKE'S Aunt Beru was filling a pitcher with blue
liquid from a refrigerated container. Behind her, in
the dining area, a steady buzz of conversation reached
to the kitchen.

She sighed sadly. The mealtime discussions between
her husband and Luke had grown steadily more ac-
rimonious as the boy's restlessness pulled him in
directions other than farming. Directions for which
Owen, a stolid man of the soil if there ever was one,
had absolutely no sympathy.

Returning the bulk container to the refrigerator
unit, she placed the pitcher on a tray and hurried back
to the dining room. Beru was not a brilliant woman,
but she possessed an instinctive understanding of her
important position in this household. She functioned
like the damping rods in a nuclear reactor. As long
as she was present, Owen and Luke would continue

to generate a lot of heat, but if she was out of their presence for too long—*boom!*

Condenser units built into the bottom of each plate kept the food on the dining-room table hot as she hurried in. Immediately, both men lowered their voices to something civilized and shifted the subject. Beru pretended not to notice the change.

"I think that Artoo unit might have been stolen, Uncle Owen," Luke was saying, as if that had been the topic of conversation all along.

His uncle helped himself to the milk pitcher, mumbling his reply around a mouthful of food. "The jawas have a tendency to pick up anything that's not tied down, Luke, but remember, they're basically afraid of their own shadows. To resort to outright theft, they'd have to have considered the consequences of being pursued and punished. Theoretically, their minds shouldn't be capable of that. What makes you think the 'droid is stolen?"

"For one thing, it's in awfully good shape for a discard. It generated a hologram recording while I was cleaning—" Luke tried to conceal his horror at the slip. He added hastily, "But that's not important. The reason I think it might be stolen is because it claims to be the property of someone it calls Obi-wan Kenobi."

Maybe something in the food, or perhaps the milk, caused Luke's uncle to gag. Then again, it might have been an expression of disgust, which was Owen's way of indicating his opinion of that peculiar personage. In any case, he continued eating without looking up at his nephew.

Luke pretended the display of graphic dislike had never happened. "I thought," he continued determinedly, "it might have meant old Ben. The first name is different, but the last is identical."

When his uncle steadfastly maintained his silence, Luke prompted him directly. "Do *you* know who he's talking about, Uncle Owen?"

Surprisingly, his uncle looked uncomfortable instead

of angry. "It's nothing," he mumbled, still not meeting Luke's gaze. "A name from another time." He squirmed nervously in his seat. "A name that can only mean trouble."

Luke refused to heed the implied warning and pressed on. "Is it someone related to old Ben, then? I didn't know he had any relatives."

"You stay away from that old wizard, you hear me!" his uncle exploded, awkwardly substituting threat for reason.

"Owen . . ." Aunt Beru started to interject gently, but the big farmer cut her off sternly.

"Now, this is important, Beru." He turned his attention back to his nephew. "I've told you about Kenobi before. He's a crazy old man; he's dangerous and full of mischief, and he's best left well alone."

Beru's pleading gaze caused him to quiet somewhat. "That 'droid has nothing to do with him. Couldn't have," he grumbled half to himself. "Recording—huh! Well, tomorrow I want you to take the unit into Anchorhead and have its memory flushed."

Snorting, Owen bent to his half-eaten meal with determination. "That will be the end of this foolishness. I don't care where that machine thinks it came from. I paid hard credit for it, and it belongs to us now."

"But suppose it *does* belong to someone else" Luke wondered. "What if this Obi-wan person comes looking for his 'droid?"

As expression between sorrow and a sneer crossed his uncle's seamed face at a remembrance. "He won't. I don't think that man exists anymore. He died about the same time as your father." A huge mouthful of hot food was shoveled inward. "Now forget about it."

"Then it *was* a real person," Luke murmured, staring down at his plate. He added slowly, "Did he know my father?"

"I said forget about it," Owen snapped. "Your only worry as far as those two 'droids are concerned is having them ready for work tomorrow. Remember, the last of our savings is tied up in those two. Wouldn't even have bought them if it wasn't so near harvest." He shook a spoon at his nephew. "In the morning I want you to have them working with the irrigation units up on the south ridge.

"You know," Luke replied distantly, "I think these 'droids are going to work out fine. In fact, I—" He hesitated, shooting his uncle a surreptitious glare. "I was thinking about our agreement about me staying on for another season."

His uncle failed to react, so Luke rushed on before his nerve failed. "If these new 'droids do work out, I want to transmit my application to enter the Academy for next year."

Owen scowled, trying to hide his displeasure with food. "You mean, you want to transmit the *application* next year—after the harvest."

"You have more than enough 'droids now, and they're in good condition. They'll last."

" 'Droids, yes," his uncle agreed, "but 'droids can't replace a man, Luke. You know that. The harvest is when I need you the most. It's just for one more season after this one." He looked away, bluster and anger gone now.

Luke toyed with his food, not eating, saying nothing.

"Listen," his uncle told him, "for the first time we've got a chance for a real fortune. We'll make enough to hire some extra hands for next time. Not 'droids—people. Then you can go to the Academy." He fumbled over words, unaccustomed to pleading. "I need you here, Luke. You understand that, don't you?"

"It's another year," his nephew objected sullenly. "Another *year*."

How many times had he heard that before? How many times had they repeated this identical charade with the same result?

Convinced once more that Luke had come round

to his way of thinking, Owen shrugged the objection off. "Time will pass before you know it."

Abruptly Luke rose, shoving his barely touched plate of food aside. "That's what you said last year when Biggs left." He spun and half ran from the room.

"Where are you going, Luke?" his aunt yelled worriedly after him.

Luke's reply was bleak, bitter. "Looks like I'm going nowhere." Then he added, out of consideration for his aunt's sensibilities, "I have to finish cleaning those 'droids if they're going to be ready to work tomorrow."

Silence hung in the air of the dining room after Luke departed. Husband and wife ate mechanically. Eventually Aunt Beru stopped shoving her food around her plate, looked up, and pointed out earnestly, "Owen, you can't keep him here forever. Most of his friends are gone, the people he grew up with. The Academy means so much to him."

Listlessly her husband replied, "I'll make it up to him next year. I promise. We'll have money—or maybe, the year after that."

"Luke's just not a farmer, Owen," she continued firmly. "He never will be, no matter how hard you try to make him one." She shook her head slowly. "He's got too much of his father in him."

For the first time all evening Owen Lars looked thoughtful as well as concerned as he gazed down the passage Luke had taken. "That's what I'm afraid of," he whispered.

Luke had gone topside. He stood on the sand watching the double sunset as first one and then the other of Tatooine's twin suns sank slowly behind the distant range of dunes. In the fading light the sands turned gold, russet, and flaming red-orange before advancing night put the bright colors to sleep for another day. Soon, for the first time, those sands would blossom with food plants. This former wasteland would see an eruption of green.

The thought ought to have sent a thrill of anticipation through Luke. He should have been as flushed with excitement as his uncle was whenever he described the coming harvest. Instead, Luke felt nothing but a vast indifferent emptiness. Not even the prospect of having a lot of money for the first time in his life excited him. What was there to do with money in Anchorhead—anywhere on Tatooine, for that matter?

Part of him, an increasingly large part, was growing more and more restless at remaining unfulfilled. This was not an uncommon feeling in youths his age, but for reasons Luke did not understand it was much stronger in him than in any of his friends.

As the night cold came creeping over the sand and up his legs, he brushed the grit from his trousers and descended into the garage. Maybe working on the 'droids would bury some of the remorse a little deeper in his mind. A quick survey of the chamber showed no movement. Neither of the new machines was in sight. Frowning slightly, Luke took a small control box from his belt and activated a couple of switches set into the plastic.

A low hum came from the box. The caller produced the taller of the two robots, Threepio. In fact, he gave a yell of surprise as he jumped up behind the skyhopper.

Luke started toward him, openly puzzled. "What are you hiding back there for?"

The robot came stumbling around the prow of the craft, his attitude one of desperation. It occurred to Luke then that despite his activating the caller, the Artoo unit was still nowhere to be seen.

The reason for his absence—or something related to it—came pouring unbidden from Threepio. "It wasn't my fault," the robot begged frantically. "Please don't deactivate me! I told him not to go, but he's faulty. He must be malfunctioning. Something has totally boiled his logic circuits. He kept babbling on about some sort of mission, sir. I never heard a robot with delusions of grandeur before. Such things shouldn't even be within the cogitative theory units of one that's as basic as an Artoo unit, and . . ."

"You mean . . . ?" Luke started to gape.

"Yes, sir . . . he's gone."

"And I removed his restraining coupling myself," Luke muttered slowly. Already he could visualize his uncle's face. The last of their savings tied up in these 'droids, he had said.

Racing out of the garage, Luke hunted for nonexistent reasons why the Artoo unit should go berserk. Threepio followed on his heels.

From a small ridge which formed the highest point close by the homestead, Luke had a panoramic view of the surrounding desert. Bringing out the precious macrobinoculars, he scanned the rapidly darkening horizons for something small, metallic, three-legged, and out of its mechanical mind.

Threepio fought his way up through the sand to stand beside Luke. "That Artoo unit has always caused nothing but trouble," he groaned. "Astromech 'droids are becoming too iconoclastic even for me to understand, sometimes."

The binoculars finally came down, and Luke commented matter-of-factly, "Well, he's nowhere in sight." He kicked furiously at the ground. "Damn it—how could I have been so stupid, letting it trick me into removing that restrainer! Uncle Owen's going to kill me."

"Begging your pardon, sir," ventured a hopeful Threepio, visions of jawas dancing in his head, "but can't we go after him?"

Luke turned. Studiously he examined the wall of black advancing toward them. "Not at night. It's too dangerous with all the raiders around. I'm not too concerned about the jawas, but sandpeople . . . no, not in the dark. We'll have to wait until morning to try to track him."

A shout rose from the homestead below. "Luke—Luke, are you finished with those 'droids yet? I'm turning down the power for the night."

"All right!" Luke responded, sidestepping the question. "I'll be down in a few minutes, Uncle Owen!" Turning, he took one last look at the vanished horizon. "Boy, am I in for it!" he muttered. "That little 'droid's going to get me in a lot of trouble."

"Oh, he excells at that, sir." Threepio confirmed with mock cheerfulness. Luke threw him a sour look, and together they turned and descended into the garage.

"Luke . . . Luke!" Still rubbing the morning sleep from his eyes, Owen glanced from side to side, loosening his neck muscles. "Where could that boy be loafing now?" he wondered aloud at the lack of response. There was no sign of movement in the homestead, and he had already checked above.

"Luke!" he yelled again. *Luke, luke, luke . . .* the name echoed teasingly back at him from the homestead walls. Turning angrily, he stalked back into the kitchen, where Beru was preparing breakfast.

"Have you seen Luke this morning?" he asked as softly as he could manage.

She glanced briefly at him, then returned to her cooking. "Yes. He said he had some things to do before he started out to the south ridge this morning, so he left early."

"Before breakfast?" Owen frowned worriedly. "That's not like him. Did he take the new 'droids with him?"

"I think so. I'm sure I saw at least one of them with him."

"Well," Owen mused, uncomfortable but with nothing to really hang imprecations on, "he'd better have those ridge units repaired by midday or there'll be hell to pay."

An unseen face shielded by smooth white metal emerged from the half-buried life pod that now formed the backbone of a dune slightly higher than its neighbors. The voice sounded efficient, but tired.

"Nothing," the inspecting trooper muttered to his several companions. "No tapes, and no sign of habitation."

Powerful handguns lowered at the information that the pod was deserted. One of the armored men turned, calling out to an officer standing some distance away. "This is definitely the pod that cleared the rebel ship, sir, but there's nothing on board."

"Yet it set down intact," the officer was murmuring to himself. "It *could* have done so on automatics, but if it was a true malfunction, then they shouldn't have been engaged." Something didn't make sense.

"Here's why there's nothing on board and no hint of life, sir," a voice declared.

The officer turned and strode several paces to where another trooper was kneeling in the sand. He held up an object for the officer's inspection. It shone in the sun.

" 'Droid plating," the officer observed after a quick glance at the metal fragment. Superior and underling exchanged a significant glance. Then their eyes turned simultaneously to the high mesas off to the north.

Gravel and fine sand formed a gritty fog beneath the landspeeder as it slid across the rippling wasteland of Tatooine on humming repulsors. Occasionally the craft would jog slightly as it encountered a dip or slight rise, to return to its smooth passage as its pilot compensated for the change in terrain.

Luke leaned back in the seat, luxuriating in unaccustomed relaxation as Threepio skillfully directed the powerful landcraft around dunes and rocky outcrops. "You handle a landspeeder pretty well, for a machine," he noted admiringly.

"Thank you, sir," a gratified Threepio responded,

his eyes never moving from the landscape ahead. "I was not lying to your uncle when I claimed versatility as my middle name. In fact, on occasion I have been called upon to perform unexpected functions in circumstances which would have appalled my designers."

Something pinged behind them, then pinged again.

Luke frowned and popped the speeder canopy. A few moments of digging in the motor casing eliminated the metallic bark.

"How's that?" he yelled forward.

Threepio signaled that the adjustment was satisfactory. Luke turned back into the cockpit and closed the canopy over them again. Silently he brushed his wind-whipped hair back out of his eyes as his attention returned to the dry desert ahead of them.

"Old Ben Kenobi is supposed to live out in this general direction. Even though nobody knows exactly where, I don't see how that Artoo unit could have come this far so quickly." His expression was downcast. "We must have missed him back in the dunes somewhere. He could be anywhere out here. And Uncle Owen must be wondering why I haven't called in from the south ridge by now."

Threepio considered a moment, then ventured, "Would it help, sir, if you told him that it was my fault?"

Luke appeared to brighten at the suggestion. "Sure . . . he needs you twice as much now. Probably he'll only deactivate you for a day or so, or give you a partial memory flush."

Deactivate? Memory flush? Threepio added hastily, "On second thought, sir, Artoo would still be around if you hadn't removed his restraining module."

But something more important than fixing responsibility for the little robot's disappearance was on Luke's mind at the moment. "Wait a minute," he advised Threepio as he stared fixedly at the instrument panel. "There's something dead ahead on the metal scanner. Can't distinguish outlines at this distance, but

judging by size alone, it *could* be our wandering
'droid. Hit it."

The landspeeder jumped forward as Threepio engaged the accelerator, but its occupants were totally
unaware that other eyes were watching as the craft
increased its speed.

Those eyes were not organic, but then, they weren't
wholly mechanical, either. No one could say for certain, because no one had ever made that intimate a
study of the Tusken Raiders—known less formally to
the margin farmers of Tatooine simply as the sandpeople.

The Tuskens didn't permit close study of themselves, discouraging potential observers by methods
as effective as they were uncivilized. A few xenologists
thought they must be related to the jawas. Even fewer
hypothesized that the jawas were actually the mature
form of the sandpeople, but this theory was dis-
counted by the majority of serious scientists.

Both races affected tight clothing to shield them
from Tatooine's twin dose of solar radiation, but
there most comparisons ended. Instead of heavy
woven cloaks like the jawas wore, the sandpeople
wrapped themselves mummylike in endless swathings
and bandages and loose bits of cloth.

Where the jawas feared everything, a Tusken
Raider feared little. The sandpeople were larger,
stronger, and far more aggressive. Fortunately for the
human colonists of Tatooine, they were not very numerous and elected to pursue their nomadic existence
in some of Tatooine's most desolate regions. Contact between human and Tusken, therefore, was in-
frequent and uneasy, and they murdered no more than
a handful of humans per year. Since the human population had claimed its share of Tuskens, not always
with reason, a peace of a sort existed between the
two—as long as neither side gained an advantage.

One of the pair felt that that unstable condition
had temporarily shifted in his favor, and he was about

to take full advantage of it as he raised his rifle toward the landspeeder. But his companion grabbed the weapon and shoved down on it before it could be fired. This set off a violent argument between the two. And, as they traded vociferous opinions in a language consisting mostly of consonants, the landspeeder sped on its way.

Either because the speeder had passed out of range or because the second Tusken had convinced the other, the two broke off the discussion and scrambled down the back side of the high ridge. Snuffling and a shifting of weight took place at the ridge bottom as the two Banthas stirred at the approach of their masters. Each was as large as a small dinosaur, with bright eyes and long, thick fur. They hissed anxiously as the two sandpeople approached, then mounted them from knee to saddle.

With a kick Banthas rose. Moving slowly but with enormous strides, the two massive horned creatures swept down the back of the rugged bluff, urged on by their anxious, equally outrageous mahouts.

"It's him, all right," Luke declared with mixed anger and satisfaction as the tiny tripodal form came into view. The speeder banked and swung down onto the floor of a huge sandstone canyon. Luke slipped his rifle out from behind the seat and swung it over his shoulder. "Come round in front of him, Threepio," he instructed.

"With pleasure, sir."

The Artoo unit obviously noted their approach, but made no move to escape; it could hardly have outrun the landspeeder anyway. Artoo simply halted as soon as it detected them and waited until the craft swung around in a smooth arc. Threepio came to a sharp halt, sending up a low cloud of sand on the smaller robot's right. Then the whine from the landspeeder's engine dropped to a low idling hum as Threepio put it in parking mode. A last sigh and the craft stopped completely.

After finishing a cautious survey of the canyon, Luke led his companion out onto the gravelly surface and up to Artoo Detoo. "Just where," he inquired sharply, "did you think you were going?"

A feeble whistle issued from the apologetic robot, but it was Threepio and not the recalcitrant rover who was abruptly doing most of the talking.

"Master Luke here is now your rightful owner, Artoo. How could you just amble away from him like this? Now that he's found you, let's have no more of this 'Obi-wan Kenobi' gibberish. I don't know where you picked that up—or that melodramatic hologram, either."

Artoo started to beep in protest, but Threepio's indignation was too great to permit excuses. "And don't talk to me about your mission. What rot! You're fortunate Master Luke doesn't blast you into a million pieces right here and now."

"Not much chance of that," admitted Luke, a bit overwhelmed by Threepio's casual vindictiveness. "Come on—it's getting late." He eyed the rapidly rising suns. "I just hope we can get back before Uncle Owen really lets go."

"If you don't mind my saying so," Threepio suggested, apparently unwilling that the Artoo unit should get off so easily, "I think you ought to deactivate the little fugitive until you've gotten him safely back in the garage."

"No. He's not going to try anything." Luke studied the softly beeping 'droid sternly. "I hope he's learned his lesson. There's no need to—"

Without warning the Artoo unit suddenly leaped off the ground—no mean feat considering the weakness of the spring mechanisms in his three thick legs. His cylindrical body was twisting and spinning as he let out a frantic symphony of whistles, hoots, and electronic exclamations.

Luke was tired, not alarmed. "What is it? What's wrong with him now?" He was beginning to see how

Threepio's patience could be worn thin. He had had about enough of this addled instrument himself.

Undoubtedly the Artoo unit had acquired the holo of the girl by accident, then used it to entice Luke into removing his restraining module. Threepio probably had the right attitude. Still, once Luke got its circuits realigned and its logic couplings cleaned, it would make a perfectly serviceable farm unit. Only . . . if that was the case, then why was Threepio looking around so anxiously?

'Oh my, sir. Artoo claims there are several creatures of unknown type approaching from the southeast.'

That *could* be another attempt by Artoo to distract them, but Luke couldn't take the chance. Instantly he had his rifle off his shoulder and had activated the energy cell. He examined the horizon in the indicated direction and saw nothing. But then, sandpeople were experts at making themselves unseeable.

Luke suddenly realized exactly how far out they were, how much ground the landspeeder had covered that morning. "I've never been out in this direction this far from the farm before," he informed Threepio. "There are some awfully strange things living out here. Not all of them have been classified. It's better to treat anything as dangerous until determined otherwise. Of course, if it's something utterly new . . ." His curiosity prodded him. In any case, this was probably just another ruse of Artoo Detoo's. "Let's take a look," he decided.

Moving cautiously forward and keeping his rifle ready, he led Threepio toward the crest of a nearby high dune. At the same time he took care not to let Artoo out of his sight.

Once at the top he lay flat and traded his rifle for the macrobinoculars. Below, another canyon spread out before them, rising to a wind-weathered wall of rust and ocher. Advancing the binocs slowly across the canyon floor, he settled unexpectedly on two tethered shapes. Banthas—and riderless!

"Did you say something, sir?" wheezed Threepio, struggling up behind Luke. His locomotors were not designed for such outer climbing and scrambling.

"Banthas, all right," Luke whispered over his shoulder, not considering in the excitement of the moment that Threepio might not know a Bantha from a panda.

He looked back into the eyepieces, refocusing slightly. "Wait . . . it's sandpeople, sure. I see one of them."

Something dark suddenly blocked his sight. For a moment he thought that a rock might have moved in front of him. Irritably he dropped the binoculars and reached out to move the blinding object aside. His hand touched something like soft metal.

It was a bandaged leg about as big around as both of Luke's together. Shocked, he looked up . . . and up. The towering figure glaring down at him was no jawa. It had seemingly erupted straight from the sand.

Threepio took a startled step backward and found no footing. As gyros whined in protest the tall robot tumbled backward down the side of the dune. Frozen in place, Luke heard steadily fading bangs and rattles as Threepio bounced down the steep slope behind him.

As the moment of confrontation passed, the Tusken let out a terrifying grunt of fury and pleasure and brought down his heavy gaderffii. The double-edged ax would have cleaved Luke's skull neatly in two, except that he threw the rifle up in a gesture more instinctive than calculated. His weapon deflected the blow, but would never do so again. Made from cannibalized freighter plating the huge ax shattered the barrel and made metallic confetti of the gun's delicate insides.

Luke scrambled backward and found himself against a steep drop. The Raider stalked him slowly, weapon held high over its rag-enclosed head. It uttered a gruesome, chuckling laugh, the sound made all the more inhuman by the distortion effect of its gridlike sandfilter.

Luke tried to view his situation objectively, as he had been instructed to do in survival school. Trouble was, his mouth was dry, his hands were shaking, and he was paralyzed with fear. With the Raider in front of him and a probably fatal drop behind, something else in his mind took over and opted for the least painful response. He fainted.

None of the Raiders noticed Artoo Detoo as the tiny robot forced himself into a small alcove in the rocks near the landspeeder. One of them was carrying the inert form of Luke. He dumped the unconscious youth in a heap next to the speeder, then joined his fellows as they began swarming over the open craft.

Supplies and spare parts were thrown in all directions. From time to time the plundering would be interrupted as several of them quibbled or fought over a particularly choice bit of booty.

Unexpectedly, distribution of the landspeeder's contents ceased, and with frightening speed the Raiders became part of the desertscape, looking in all directions.

A lost breeze idled absently down the canyon. Far off to the west, something howled. A rolling, booming drone ricocheted off canyon walls and crawled nervously up and down a gorgon scale.

The sandpeople remained poised a moment longer. Then they were uttering loud grunts and moans of fright as they rushed to get away from the highly visible landspeeder.

The shivering howl sounded again, nearer this time. By now the sandpeople were halfway to their waiting Banthas, that were likewise lowing tensely and tugging at their tethers.

Although the sound held no meaning for Artoo Detoo, the little 'droid tried to squeeze himself even deeper into the almost-cave. The booming howl came closer. Judging by the way the sandpeople had reacted, something monstrous beyond imagining had to be behind that rolling cry. Something monstrous and murder-bent which might not have the sense to distinguish between edible organics and inedible machines.

Not even the dust of their passing remained to mark where the Tusken Raiders had only minutes before been dismembering the interior of the landspeeder. Artoo Detoo shut down all but vital functions, trying to minimize noise and light as a swishing sound grew gradually audible. Moving toward the landspeeder, the creature appeared above the top of a nearby dune. . . .

☐ V

IT was tall, but hardly monstrous. Artoo frowned inwardly as he checked ocular circuitry and reactivated his innards.

The monster looked very much like an old man. He was clad in a shabby cloak and loose robes hung with a few small straps, packs, and unrecognizable instruments. Artoo searched the human's wake but detected no evidence of a pursuing nightmare. Nor did the man appear threatened. Actually, Artoo thought, he looked kind of pleased.

It was impossible to tell where the odd arrival's overlapping attire ended and his skin began. That aged visage blended into the sand-stroked cloth, and his beard appeared but an extension of the loose threads covering his upper chest.

Hints of extreme climates other than desert, of ultimate cold and humidity, were etched into that seamed face. A questing beak of nose, like a high rock, protruded outward from a flashflood of wrinkles and scars. The eyes bordering it were a liquid crystal-azure. The man smiled through sand and dust and beard, squinting at the sight of the crumpled form lying quietly alongside the landspeeder.

Convinced that the sandpeople had been the victims of an auditory delusion of some kind—conveniently ignoring the fact that he had experienced it also—and likewise assured that this stranger meant Luke no harm, Artoo shifted his position slightly, trying to obtain a better view. The sound produced by a tiny pebble he dislodged was barely perceptible to his electronic sensors, but the man whirled as if shot. He stared straight at Artoo's alcove, still smiling gently.

"Hello there," he called in a deep, surpringly cheerful voice. "Come here, my little friend. No need to be afraid."

Something forthright and reassuring was in that voice. In any case, the association of an unknown human was preferable to remaining isolated in this wasteland. Waddling out into the sunlight, Artoo made his way over to where Luke lay sprawled. The robot's barrellike body inclined forward as he examined the limp form. Whistles and beeps of concern came from within.

Walking over, the old man bent beside Luke and reached out to touch his forehead, then his temple. Shortly. the unconscious youth was stirring and mumbling like a dreaming sleeper.

"Don't worry," the human told Artoo, "he'll be all right."

As if to confirm this opinion, Luke blinked, stared upward uncomprehendingly, and muttered, "What happened?'

"Rest easy, son," the man instructed him as he sat back on his heels. "You've had a busy day." Again the boyish grin. "You're mighty lucky your head's still attached to the rest of you."

Luke looked around, his gaze coming to rest on the elderly face hovering above him. Recognition did wonders for his condition.

"Ben . . . it's got to be!" A sudden remembrance

made him look around fearfully. But there was no sign of sandpeople. Slowly he raised his body to a sitting position. "Ben Kenobi . . . am I glad to see you!"

Rising, the old man surveyed the canyon floor and rolling rimwall above. One foot played with the sand. "The Jundland wastes are not to be traveled lightly. It's the misguided traveler who tempts the Tuskens' hospitality." His gaze went back to his patient. "Tell me, young man, what brings you out this far into nowhere?"

Luke indicated Artoo Detoo. "This little 'droid. For a while I thought he'd gone crazy, claiming he was searching for a former master. Now I don't think so. I've never seen such devotion in a 'droid—misguided or otherwise. There seems to be no stopping him; he even resorted to tricking me."

Luke's gaze shifted upward. "He claims to be the property of someone called Obi-wan Kenobi." Luke watched closely, but the man showed no reaction. "Is that a relative of yours? My uncle thinks he was a real person. Or is it just some unimportant bit of scrambled information that got shifted into his primary performance bank?"

An introspective frown did remarkable things to that sandlbasted face. Kenobi appeared to ponder the question, scratching absently at his scruffy beard. "Obi-wan Kenobi!," he recited. "Obi-wan . . . now, that's a name I haven't heard in a long time. A long time. Most curious."

"My uncle said he was dead," Luke supplied helpfully.

"Oh, he's not dead," Kenobi corrected him easily. "Not yet, not yet."

Luke climbed excitedly to his feet, all thoughts of Tusken Raiders forgotten now. "You know him, then?"

A smile of perverse youthfulness split that collage of wrinkled skin and beard. "Of course I know him: he's me. Just as you probably suspected, Luke. I haven't gone by the name *Obi-wan*, though, since before you were born."

"Then," Luke essayed, gesturing at Artoo Detoo, "this 'droid does belong to you, as he claims."

"Now, that's the peculiar part," an openly puzzled Kenobi confessed, regarding the silent robot. "I can't seem to remember owning a 'droid, least of all a modern Artoo unit. Most interesting, most interesting."

Something drew the old man's gaze suddenly to the brow of nearby cliffs. "I think it's best we make use of your landspeeder some. The sandpeople are easily startled, but they'll soon return in greater numbers. A landspeeder's not a prize readily conceded, and after all, jawas they're not."

Placing both hands over his mouth in a peculiar fashion, Kenobi inhaled deeply and let out an unearthly howl that made Luke jump. "That ought to keep any laggards running for a while yet," the old man concluded with satisfaction.

"That's a krayt dragon call!" Luke gaped in astonishment "How did you do that?"

"I'll show you sometime, son. It's not too hard. Just takes the right attitude, a set of well-used vocal cords, and a lot of wind. Now, if you were an imperial bureaucrat, I could teach you right off, but you're not." He scanned the cliff-spine again. "And I don't think this is the time or place for it."

"I won't argue that." Luke was rubbing at the back of his head. "Let's get started."

That was when Artoo let out a pathetic beep and whirled. Luke couldn't interpret the electronic squeal, but he suddenly comprehended the reason behind it. "Threepio." Luke exclaimed, worriedly. Artoo was already moving as fast as possible away from the landspeeder. "Come on, Ben."

The little robot led them to the edge of a large sandpit. It stopped there, pointing downward and squeaking mournfully. Luke saw where Artoo was pointing, then started cautiously down the smooth, shifting slope while Kenobi followed effortlessly.

Threepio lay in the sand at the base of the slope down which he had rolled and tumbled. His casing was dented and badly mangled. One arm lay broken and bent a short distance away.

"Threepio!" Luke called. There was no response. Shaking the 'droid failed to activate anything. Opening a plate on the robot's back, Luke flipped a hidden switch on and off several times in succession. A low hum started, stopped, started again, and then dropped to a normal purr.

Using his remaining arm, Threepio rolled over and sat up. "Where am I," he murmured, as his photo-receptors continued to clear. Then he recognized Luke. "Oh, I'm sorry, sir. I must have taken a bad step."

"You're lucky any of your main circuits are still operational," Luke informed him. He looked significantly toward the top of the hill. "Can you stand? We've got to get out of here before the sandpeople return."

Servomotors whined in protest until Threepio ceased struggling. "I don't think I can make it. You go on, Master Luke. It doesn't make sense to risk yourself on my account. I'm finished."

"No, you're not," Luke shot back, unaccountably affected by this recently encountered machine. But then, Threepio was not the usual uncommunicative, agrifunctional device Luke was accustomed to dealing with. "What kind of talk is that?"

"Logical," Threepio informed him.

Luke shook his head angrily. "Defeatist."

With Luke and Ben Kenobi's aid, the battered 'droid somehow managed to struggle erect. Little Artoo watched from the pit's rim.

Hesitating part way up the slope, Kenobi sniffed the air suspiciously. "Quickly, son. They're on the move again."

Trying to watch the surrounding rocks and his footsteps simultaneously, Luke fought to drag Threepio clear of the pit.

The decor of Ben Kenobi's well-concealed cave was Spartan without appearing uncomfortable. It would not have suited most people, reflecting as it did it's owner's peculiarly eclectic tastes. The living area radiated an aura of lean comfort with more importance attached to mental comforts than those of the awkward human body.

They had succeeded in vacating the canyon before the Tusken Raiders could return in force. Under Kenobi's direction, Luke left a trail behind them so confusing that not even a hypernasal jawa could have followed it.

Luke spent several hours ignoring the temptations of Kenobi's cave. Instead he remained in the corner which was equipped as a compact yet complete repair shop, working to fix Threepio's severed arm.

Fortunately, the automatic overload disconnects had given way under the severe strain, sealing electronic nerves and ganglia without real damage. Repair was merely a matter of reattaching the limb to the shoulder, then activating the self-reseals. Had the arm been broken in mid-"bone" instead of at a joint, such repairs would have been impossible save at a factory shop.

While Luke was thus occupied, Kenobi's attention was concentrated on Artoo Detoo. The squat 'droid sat passively on the cool cavern floor while the old man fiddled with its metal insides. Finally the man sat back with a "Humph!" of satisfaction and closed the open panels in the robot's rounded head. "Now let's see if we can figure out what you are, my little friend, and where you came from."

Luke was almost finished anyway, and Kenobi's words were sufficient to pull him away from the repair area. "I saw part of the message," he began, "and I..."

Once more the striking portrait was being projected into empty space from the front of the little robot. Luke broke off, enraptured by its enigmatic beauty once again.

"Yes, I think that's got it," Kenobi murmured contemplatively.

The image continued to flicker, indicating a tape hastily prepared. But it was much sharper, better defined now, Luke noted with admiration. One thing was apparent: Kenobi was skilled in subjects more specific than desert scavenging.

"General Obi-wan Kenobi," the mellifluous voice was saying, "I present myself in the name of the world family of Alderaan and of the Alliance to Restore the Republic. I break your solitude at the bidding of my father, Bail Organa, Viceroy and First Chairman of the Alderaan system."

Kenobi absorbed this extraordinary declamation while Luke's eyes bugged big enough to fall from his face.

"Years ago, General," the voice continued, "you served the Old Republic in the Clone Wars. Now my father begs you to aid us again in our most desperate hour. He would have you join him on Alderaan. You *must* go to him.

"I regret that I am unable to present my father's request to you in person. My mission to meet personally with you has failed. Hence I have been forced to resort to this secondary method of communication.

"Information vital to the survival of the Alliance has been secured in the mind of this Detoo 'droid. My father will know how to retrieve it. I plead with you to see this unit safely delivered to Alderaan."

She paused, and when she continued, her words were hurried and less laced with formality. "You *must* help me, Obi-wan Kenobi. You are my last hope. I will be captured by agents of the Empire. They will learn nothing from me. Everything to be learned lies locked in the memory cells of this 'droid. Do not fail us, Obi-wan Kenobi. Do not fail *me*."

A small cloud of tridimensional static replaced the delicate portrait, then it vanished entirely. Artoo Detoo gazed up expectantly at Kenobi.

Luke's mind was as muddy as a pond laced with petroleum. Unanchored, his thoughts and eyes turned for stability to the quiet figure seated nearby.

The old man. The crazy wizard. The desert bum and all-around character whom his uncle and everyone else had known of for as long as Luke could recall.

If the breathless, anxiety-ridden message the unknown woman had just spoken into the cool air of the cave had affected Kenobi in any way he gave no hint of it. Instead, he leaned back against the rock wall and tugged thoughtfully at his beard, puffing slowly on a water pipe of free-form tarnished chrome.

Luke visualized that simple yet lovely portrait. "She's so—so—" His farming background didn't provide him with the requisite words. Suddenly something in the message caused him to stare disbelievingly at the oldster. "General Kenobi, you fought in the Clone Wars? But . . . that was so long ago."

"Um, yes," Kenobi acknowledged, as casually as he might have discussed the recipe for shang stew. "I guess it was a while back. I was a Jedi knight once. Like," he added, watching the youth appraisingly, "your father."

"A Jedi knight," Luke echoed. Then he looked confused. "But my father didn't fight in the Clone Wars. He was no knight—just a navigator on a space freighter."

Kenobi's smile enfolded the pipe's mouthpiece. "Or so your uncle has told you." His attention was suddenly focused elsewhere. "Owen Lars didn't agree with your father's ideas, opinions, or with his philosophy of life. He believed that your father should have stayed here on Tatooine and not gotten involved in . . ." Again the seemingly indifferent shrug. "Well, he thought he should have remained here and minded his farming."

Luke said nothing, his body tense as the old man related bits and pieces of a personal history Luke had viewed only through his uncle's distortions.

"Owen was always afraid that your father's adventurous life might influence you, might pull you away from Anchorhead." He shook his head slowly, regretfully at the remembrance. "I'm afraid there wasn't much of the farmer in your father."

Luke turned away. He returned to cleaning the last particles of sand from Threepio's healing armature. "I wish I'd known him," he finally whispered.

"He was the best pilot I ever knew," Kenobi went on, "and a smart fighter. The force . . . the instinct was strong in him." For a brief second Kenobi actually appeared old. "He was also a good friend."

Suddenly the boyish twinkle returned to those piercing eyes along with the old man's natural humor. "I understand you're quite a pilot yourself. Piloting and navigation aren't hereditary, but a number of the things that can combine to make a good small-ship pilot are. Those you may have inherited. Still, even a duck has to be taught to swim."

"What's a duck?" Luke asked curiously.

"Never mind. In many ways, you know, you are much like your father." Kenobi's unabashed look of evaluation made Luke nervous. "You've grown up quite a bit since the last time I saw you."

Having no reply for that, Luke waited silently as Kenobi sank back into deep contemplation. After a while the old man stirred, evidently having reached an important decision.

"All this reminds me," he declared with deceptive casualness, "I have something here for you." He rose and walked over to a bulky, old-fashioned chest and started rummaging through it. All sorts of intriguing items were removed and shoved around, only to be placed back in the bin. A few of them Luke recognized. As Kenobi was obviously intent on something important, he forbore inquiring about any of the other tantalizing flotsam.

"When you were old enough," Kenobi was saying, "your father wanted you to have this . . . if I can ever find the blasted device. I tried to give it to you once before, but your uncle wouldn't allow it. He believed you might get some crazy ideas from it and end up following old Obi-wan on some idealistic crusade.

"You see, Luke, that's where your father and your uncle Owen disagreed. Lars is not a man to let idealism interfere with business, whereas your father didn't think the question even worth discussing. His decision on such matters came like his piloting—instinctively."

Luke nodded. He finished picking out the last of the grit and looked around for one remaining component to snap back into Threepio's open chest plate. Locating the restraining module, he opened the receiving latches in the machine and set about locking it back in place. Threepio watched the process and appeared to wince ever so perceptibly.

Luke stared into those metal and plastic photo-receptors for a long moment. Then he set the module pointedly on the workbench and closed the 'droid up. Threepio said nothing.

A grunt came from behind them, and Luke turned to see a pleased Kenobi walking over. He handed Luke a small, innocuous-looking device, which the youth studied with interest.

It consisted primarily of a short, thick handgrip with a couple of small switches set into the grip. Above this small post was a circular metal disk barely larger in diameter than his spread palm. A number of unfamiliar, jewellike components were built into both handle and disk, including what looked like the smallest power cell Luke had ever seen. The reverse side of the disk was polished to a mirror brightness. But it was the power cell that puzzled Luke the most. Whatever the thing was, it required a great deal of energy, according to the rating form of the cell.

Despite the claim that it had belonged to his father, the gizmo looked newly manufactured. Kenobi had obviously kept it carefully. Only a number of minute scratches on the handgrip hinted at previous usage.

"Sir?" came a familiar voice Luke hadn't heard in a while.

"What?" Luke was startled out of his examination.

"If you'll not be needing me," Threepio declared, "I think I'll shut down for a bit. It will help the armature nerves to knit, and I'm due for some internal self-cleansing anyhow."

"Sure, go ahead," Luke said absently, returning to his fascinated study of the whatever-it-was. Behind him, Threepio became silent, the glow fading temporarily from his eyes. Luke noticed that Kenobi was watching him with interest. "What is it?" he finally asked, unable despite his best efforts to identify the device.

"Your father's lightsaber," Kenobi told him. "At one time they were widely used. Still are, in certain galactic quarters."

Luke examined the controls on the handle, then tentatively touched a brightly colored button up near the mirrored pommel. Instantly the disk put forth a blue-white beam as thick around as his thumb. It was dense to the point of opacity and a little over a meter in length. It did not fade, but remained as brilliant and intense at its far end as it did next to the disk. Strangely, Luke felt no heat from it, though he was very careful not to touch it. He knew what a lightsaber could do, though he had never seen one before. It could drill a hole right through the rock wall of Kenobi's cave—or through a human being.

"This was the formal weapon of a Jedi knight," explained Kenobi. "Not as clumsy or random as a blaster. More skill than simple sight was required for its use. An elegant weapon. It was a symbol as well. Anyone can use a blaster or fusioncutter—but to use a lightsaber *well* was a mark of someone a cut above the ordinary." He was pacing the floor of the cave as he spoke.

"For over a thousand generations, Luke, the Jedi knights were the most powerful, most respected force in the galaxy. They served as the guardians and guarantors of peace and justice in the Old Republic."

When Luke failed to ask what had happened to them since, Kenobi looked up to see that the youth was staring vacantly into space, having absorbed little if any of the oldster's instruction. Some men would have chided Luke for not paying attention. Not Kenobi. More sensitive than most, he waited patiently until the silence weighed strong enough on Luke for him to resume speaking.

"How," he asked slowly, "did my father die?"

Kenobi hesitated, and Luke sensed that the old man had no wish to talk about this particular matter. Unlike Owen Lars, however, Kenobi was unable to take refuge in a comfortable lie.

"He was betrayed and murdered," Kenobi declared solmenly, "by a very young Jedi named Darth Vader." He was not looking at Luke. "A boy I was training. One of my brightest disciples . . . one of my greatest failures."

Kenobi resumed his pacing. "Vader used the training I gave him and the force within him for evil, to help the later corrupt Emperors. With the Jedi knights disbanded, disorganized, or dead, there were few to oppose Vader. Today they are all but extinct."

An indecipherable expression crossed Kenobi's face. "In many ways they were too good, too trusting for their own health. They put too much trust in the stability of the Republic, failing to realize that while the body might be sound, the head was growing diseased and feeble, leaving it open to manipulation by such as the Emperor.

"I wish I knew what Vader was after. Sometimes I have the feeling he is marking time in preparation for some incomprehensible abomination. Such is the destiny of one who masters the force and is consumed by its dark side."

Luke's face twisted in confusion. "A force? That's the second time you've mentioned a 'force.' "

Kenobi nodded. "I forget sometimes in whose presence I babble. Let us say simply that the force is something a Jedi must deal with. While it has never been properly explained, scientists have theorized it is an energy field generated by living things. Early man suspected its existence, yet remained in ignorance of its potential for millennia.

"Only certain individuals could recognize the force for what it was. They were mercilessly labeled: charlatans, fakers, mystics—and worse. Even fewer could make use of it. As it was usually beyond their primitive controls, it frequently was too powerful for them. They were misunderstood by their fellows—and worse."

Kenobi made a wide, all-encompassing gesture with both arms. "The force surrounds each and every one of us. Some men believe it directs our actions, and not the other way around. Knowledge of the force and how to manipulate it was what gave the Jedi his special power."

The arms came down and Kenobi stared at Luke until the youth began to fidget uncomfortably. When he spoke again it was in a tone so crisp and unaged that Luke jumped in spite of himself. "You must learn the ways of the force also, Luke—if you are to come with me to Alderaan."

"Alderaan!" Luke hopped off the repair seat, looking dazed. "I'm not going to Alderaan. I don't even know where Alderaan is." Vaporators, 'droids, harvest—abruptly the surroundings seemed to close in on him, the formerly intriguing furnishings and alien artifacts now just a mite frightening. He looked around wildly, trying to avoid the piercing gaze of Ben Kenobi . . . old Ben . . . crazy Ben . . . General Obi-wan . . .

"I've got to get back home," he found himself muttering thickly. "It's late. I'm in for it as it is." Remembering something, he gestured toward the motionless bulk of Artoo Detoo. "You can keep the 'droid. He seems to want you to. I'll think of something to tell my uncle—I hope," he added forlornly.

"I need your help, Luke," Kenobi explained, his manner a combination of sadness and steel. "I'm getting too old for this kind of thing. Can't trust myself to finish it properly on my own. This mission is far too important." He nodded toward Artoo Detoo. "You heard and saw the message."

"But . . . I can't get involved with anything like that," protested Luke. "I've got work to do; we've got crops to bring in—even though Uncle Owen could always break down and hire a little extra help. I mean, one, I guess. But there's nothing I can do about it. Not now. Besides, that's all such a long way from here. The whole thing is really none of my business."

"That sounds like your uncle talking," Kenobi observed without rancor.

"Oh! My uncle Owen . . . How am I going to explain all this to him?"

The old man suppressed a smile, aware that Luke's destiny had already been determined for him. It had been ordained five minutes before he had learned about the manner of his father's death. It had been ordered before that when he had heard the complete message. It had been fixed in the nature of things when he had first viewed the pleading portrait of the beautiful Senator Organa awkwardly projected by the little 'droid. Kenobi shrugged inwardly. Likely it had been finalized even before the boy was born. Not that Ben believed in predestination, but he did believe in heredity—and in the force.

"Remember, Luke, the suffering of one man is the suffering of all. Distances are irrelevant to injustice. If not stopped soon enough, evil eventually reaches out to engulf all men, whether they have opposed it or ignored it."

"I suppose," Luke confessed nervously, "I *could* take you as far as Anchorhead. You can get transport from there to Mos Eisley, or wherever it is you want to go."

"Very well," agreed Kenobi. "That will do for a beginning. Then you must do what you feel is *right*."

Luke turned away, now thoroughly confused. "Okay. Right now I don't feel too good . . ."

The holding hole was deathly dim, with only the bare minimum of illumination provided. There was barely enough to see the black metal walls and the high ceiling overhead. The cell was designed to maximize a prisioner's feelings of helplessness, and this it achieved well. So much so that the single occupant started tensely as a hum came from one end of the chamber. The metal door which began moving aside was as thick as her body—as if, she mused bitterly, they were afraid she might break through anything less massive with her bare hands.

Straining to see outside, the girl saw several imperial guards assume positions just outside the doorway. Eyeing them defiantly, Leia Organa backed up against the far wall.

Her determined expression collapsed as soon as a monstrous black form entered the room, gliding smoothly as if on treads. Vader's presence crushed her spirit as thoroughly as an elephant would crush an eggshell. That villain was followed by an antiqued whip of a man who was only slightly less terrifying, despite his miniscule appearance alongside the Dark Lord.

Darth Vader made a gesture to someone outside. Something that hummed like a huge bee moved close and slipped inside the doorway. Leia choked on her own breath at the sight of the dark metal globe. It hung suspended on independent repulsors, a farrago of metal arms protruding from its sides. The arms were tipped with a multitude of delicate instruments.

Leia studied the contraption fearfully. She had heard rumors of such machines, but had never really believed that Imperial technicians would construct such a monstrosity. Incorporated into its soulless memory was every barbarity, every substantiated outrage known to mankind—and to several alien races as well.

Vader and Tarkin stood there quietly, giving her plenty of time to study the hovering nightmare. The Governor in particular did not delude himself into thinking that the mere presence of the device would shock her into giving up the information he needed. Not, he reflected, that the ensuing session would be especially unpleasant. There was always enlightenment and knowledge to be gained from such encounters, and the Senator promised to be a most interesting subject.

After a suitable interval had passed, he motioned to the machine. "Now, Senator Organa, Princess Organa, we will discuss the location of the principal rebel base."

The machine moved slowly toward her, traveling on a rising hum. Its indifferent spherical form blocked out Vader, the Governor, the rest of the cell . . . the light . . .

Muffled sounds penetrated the cell walls and thick door, drifting out into the hallway beyond. They barely intruded on the peace and quiet of the walkway running past the sealed chamber. Even so, the guards stationed immediately outside managed to find excuses to edge a sufficient distance away to where those oddly modulated sounds could no longer be heard at all.

☐ VI

"LOOK over there, Luke," Kenobi ordered, pointing to the southwest. The landspeeder continued to race over the gravelly desert floor beneath them. "Smoke, I should think."

Luke spared a glance at the indicated direction. "I don't see anything, sir."

"Let's angle over that way anyhow. Someone may be in trouble."

Luke turned the speeder. Before long the rising wisps of smoke that Kenobi had somehow detected earlier became visible to him also.

Topping a slight rise, the speeder dropped down a gentle slope into a broad, shallow canyon that was filled with twisted, burned shapes, some of them inorganic, some not. Dead in the center of this carnage and looking like a beached metal whale lay the shattered hulk of a jawa sandcrawler.

Luke brought the speeder to a halt. Kenobi followed him onto the sand, and together they began to examine the detritus of destruction.

Several slight depressions in the sand caught Luke's attention. Walking a little faster, he came up next to them and studied them for a moment before calling back to Kenobi.

"Looks like the sandpeople did it, all right. Here's Bantha tracks . . ." Luke noticed a gleam of metal half buried in the sand. "And there's a piece of one of those big double axes of theirs." He shook his head in confusion. "But I never heard of the Raiders hitting something this big." He leaned back, staring up at the towering, burned-out bulk of the sandcrawler.

Kenobi had passed him. He was examining the broad, huge footprints in the sand. "They didn't," he declared casually, "but they intended that we—and anyone else who might happen onto this—should think so." Luke moved up alongside him.

"I don't understand, sir."

"Look at these tracks carefully," the older man directed him, pointing down at the nearest and then up at the others. "Notice anything funny about them?" Luke shook his head. "Whoever left here was riding Banthas side by side. Sandpeople always ride one Bantha behind another, single file, to hide their strength from any distant observers."

Leaving Luke to gape at the parallel sets of tracks, Kenobi turned his attention to the sandcrawler. He pointed out where single weapons' bursts had blasted away portals, treads, and support beams. "Look at the precision with which this firepower was applied. Sandpeople aren't this accurate. In fact, no one on Tatooine fires and destroys with this kind of efficiency." Turning, he examined the horizon. One of those nearby bluffs concealed a secret—and a threat. "Only Imperial troops would mount an attack on a sandcrawler with this kind of cold accuracy."

Luke had walked over to one of the small, crumpled bodies and kicked it over onto its back. His face screwed up in distaste as he saw what remained of the pitiful creature.

"These are the same jawas who sold Uncle Owen and me Artoo and Threepio. I recognize this one's cloak design. Why would Imperial troops be slaughtering jawas and sandpeople? They must have killed some Raiders to get those Banthas." His mind worked furiously, and he found himself growing unnaturally tense as he stared back at the landspeeder, past the rapidly deteriorating corpses of the jawas.

"But . . . if they tracked the 'droids to the jawas, then they had to learn first who they sold them to. That would lead them back to . . ." Luke was sprinting insanely for the landspeeder.

"Luke, wait . . . wait, Luke!" Kenobi called. "It's too dangerous! You'd never . . . !"

Luke heard nothing except the roaring in his ears, felt nothing save the burning in his heart. He jumped into the speeder and was throwing the accelerator full over almost simultaneously. In an explosion of sand and gravel he left Kenobi and the two robots standing alone in the midst of smoldering bodies, framed by the still smoking wreck of the sandcrawler.

The smoke that Luke saw as he drew near the homestead was of a different consistency from that which had boiled out of the jawa machine. He barely remembered to shut down the landspeeder's engine as he popped the cockpit canopy and threw himself out.

Dark smoke was drifting steadily from holes in the ground.

Those holes had been his home, the only one he had ever known. They might as well have been throats of small volcanoes now. Again and again he tried to penetrate the surface entrances to the below-ground complex. Again and again the still-intense heat drove him back, coughing and choking.

Weakly he found himself stumbling clear, his eyes watering not entirely from the smoke. Half blinded, he staggered over to the exterior entrance to the garage. It too was burning. But perhaps they managed to escape in the other landspeeder.

"Aunt Beru . . . Uncle Owen!" It was difficult to make out much of anything through the eye-stinging haze. Two smoking shapes showed down the tunnel, barely visible through tears and haze. They almost looked like— He squinted harder, wiping angrily at his uncooperative eyes.

No.

Then he was spinning away, falling to his stomach and burying his face in the sand so he wouldn't have to look anymore.

The tridimensional solid screen filled one wall of the vast chamber from floor to ceiling. It showed a million star systems. A tiny portion of the galaxy, but an impressive display nonetheless when exhibited in such a fashion.

Below, far below, the huge shape of Darth Vader stood flanked on one side by Governor Tarkin and on the other by Admiral Motti and General Tagge, their private antagonisms forgotten in the awesomeness of this moment.

"The final checkout is complete," Motti informed them. "All systems are operational." He turned to the others. "What shall be the first course we set?"

Vader appeared not to have heard as he mumbled softly, half to himself, "She has a surprising amount of control. Her resistance to the interrogator is considerable." He glanced down at Tarkin. "It will be some time before we can extract any useful information from her."

"I've always found the methods you recommend rather quaint, Vader."

"They are efficient," the Dark Lord argued softly. "In the interests of accelerating the procedure, however, I am open to your suggestions."

Tarkin looked thoughtful. "Such stubbornness can often be detoured by applying threats to something other than the one involved."

"What do you mean?"

"Only that I think it is time we demonstrated the full power of this station. We may do so in a fashion doubly useful." He instructed the attentive Motti, "Tell your programmers to set course for the Alderaan system."

Kenobi's pride did not prevent him from wrapping an old scarf over nose and mouth to filter out a portion of the bonfire's drifting putrid odor. Though possessed of olfactory sensory apparatus, Artoo Detoo and Threepio had no need of such a screen. Even Threepio, who was equipped to discriminate among aromatic aesthetics, could be artificially selective when he so desired.

Working together, the two 'droids helped Kenobi throw the last of the bodies onto the blazing pyre, then stood back and watched the dead continue to burn. Not that the desert scavengers wouldn't have been equally efficient in picking the burned-out sandcrawler clean of flesh, but Kenobi retained values most modern men would have deemed archaic. He would consign no one to the bone-gnawers and gravel-maggots, not even a filthy jawa.

At a rising thrumming Kenobi turned from the residue of the noisome business to see the landspeeder approaching, now traveling at a sensible pace, far different from when it had left. It slowed and hovered nearby, but showed no signs of life.

Gesturing for the two robots to follow, Ben started toward the waiting craft. The canopy flipped open and up to reveal Luke sitting motionless in the pilot's seat. He didn't look up at Kenobi's inquiring glance. That in itself was enough to tell the old man what had happened.

"I share your sorrow, Luke," he finally ventured softly. "There was nothing you could have done. Had you been there, you'd be dead now, too, and the 'droids would be in the hands of the Imperials. Not even the force——"

"Damn your force!" Luke snarled with sudden violence. Now he turned and glared at Kenobi. There was a set to his jaw that belonged on a much older face.

"I'll take you to the spaceport at Mos Eisley, Ben. I want to go with you——to Alderaan. There's nothing left for me here now." His eyes turned to look out across the desert, to focus on something beyond sand and rock and canyon walls. "I want to learn to be like a Jedi, like my father. I want . . ." He paused, the words backing up like a logjam in his throat.

Kenobi slid into the cockpit, put a hand gently on the youth's shoulder, then went forward to make room for the two robots. "I'll do my best to see that you get what you want, Luke. For now, let's go to Mos Eisley."

Luke nodded and closed the canopy. The landspeeder moved away to the southeast, leaving behind the still-smoldering sandcrawler, the jawa funeral pyre, and the only life Luke had ever known.

Leaving the speeder parked near the edge of the sandstone bluff, Luke and Ben walked over and peered down at the tiny regularized bumps erupting from the sun-baked plain below. The haphazard collage of low-grade concrete, stone, and plastoid structures spread outward from a central power-and-water-distribution plant like the spokes of a wheel.

Actually the town was considerably larger than it

appeared, since a good portion of it lay underground. Looking like bomb craters from this distance, the smooth circular depressions of launch stations pockmarked the cityscape.

A brisk gale was scouring the tired ground. It whipped the sand about Luke's feet and legs as he adjusted his protective goggles.

"There it is," Kenobi murmured, indicating the unimpressive collection of buildings, "Mos Eisley Spaceport—the ideal place for us to lose ourselves while we seek passage offplanet. Not a more wretched collection of villainy and disreputable types exists anywhere on Tatooine. The Empire has been alerted to us, so we must be very cautious, Luke. The population of Mos Eisley should disguise us well."

Luke wore a determined look. "I'm ready for anything, Obi-wan."

I wonder if you comprehend what that might entail, Luke, Kenobi thought. But he only nodded as he led the way back to the landspeeder.

Unlike Anchorhead, there were enough people in Mos Eisley to require movement in the heat of day. Built from the beginning with commerce in mind, even the oldest of the town's buildings had been designed to provide protection from the twin suns. They looked primitive from the outside, and many were. But oftentimes walls and arches of old stone masked durasteel double walls with circulating coolant flowing freely between.

Luke was maneuvering the landspeeder through the town's outskirts when several tall, gleaming forms appeared from nowhere and began to close a circle around him. For one panicked moment he considered gunning the engine and racing through the pedestrians and other vehicles. A startlingly firm grip on his arm both restrained and relaxed him. He glanced over to see Kenobi smiling, warning him.

So they continued at a normal town cruising speed, Luke hoping that the imperial troops were bent on business elsewhere. No such luck. One of the troopers raised an armored hand. Luke had no choice but to respond. As he pulled the speeder over, he grew aware of the attention they were receiving from curious passersby. Worse yet, it seemed that the trooper's attention was in fact reserved not for Kenobi or himself, but for the two unmoving robots seated in the speeder behind them.

"How long have you had these 'droids?" the trooper who had raised his hand barked. Polite formalities were to be dispensed with, it appeared.

Looking blank for a second, Luke finally came up with "Three or four seasons, I guess."

"They're up for sale, if you want them—and the price is right," Kenobi put in, giving a wonderful impression of a desert finagler out to cajole a few quick credits from ignorant Imperials.

The trooper in charge did not deign to reply. He was absorbed in a thorough examination of the landspeeder's underside.

"Did you come in from the south?" he asked.

"No . . . no," Luke answered quickly, "we live in the west, near Bestine township."

"Bestine?" the trooper murmured, walking around to study the speeder's front. Luke forced himself to stare straight ahead. Finally the armored figure concluded his examination. He moved to stand ominously close to Luke and snapped, "Let me see your identification."

Surely the man sensed his terror and nervousness by now, Luke thought wildly. His resolution of not long before to be ready to take on anything had already disintegrated under the unwinking stare of this professional soldier. He knew what would happen if they got a look at his formal ID, with the location of his homestead and the names of his nearest relatives on it. Something seemed to be buzzing inside his head; he felt faint.

Kenobi had leaned over and was talking easily to the trooper. "You don't need to see his identification," the old man informed the Imperial in an extremely peculiar voice.

Staring blankly back at him, the officer replied, as if it were self-evident, "I don't need to see your identification." His reaction was the opposite of Kenobi's: his voice was normal, but his expression peculiar.

"These aren't the 'droids you're looking for," Kenobi told him pleasantly.

"These aren't the 'droids we're looking for."

"He can go about his business.

"You can go about your business," the metal-masked officer informed Luke.

The expression of relief that spread across Luke's face ought to have been as revealing as his previous nervousness, but the Imperial ignored it.

"Move along," Kenobi whispered.

"Move along," the officer instructed Luke.

Unable to decide whether he should salute, nod, or give thanks to the man, Luke settled for nudging the accelerator. The landspeeder moved forward, drawing away from the circle of troops. As they prepared to round a corner, Luke risked a glance backward. The officer who had inspected them appeared to be arguing with several comrades, though at this distance Luke couldn't be sure.

He peered up at his tall companion and started to say something. Kenobi only shook his head slowly and smiled. Swallowing his curiosity, Luke concentrated on guiding the speeder through steadily narrowing streets.

Kenobi seemed to have some idea where they were headed. Luke studied the run-down structures and equally unwholesome-looking individuals they were passing. They had entered the oldest section of Mos Eisley and consequently the one where the old vices flourished most strongly.

Kenobi pointed and Luke pulled the landspeeder up in front of what appeared to be one of the original spaceport's first blockhouses. It had been converted into a cantina whose clientele was suggested by the diverse nature of transport parked outside. Some of them Luke recognized, others he had only heard rumors of. The cantina itself, he knew from the design of the building, must lie partially underground.

As the dusty but still sleek craft pulled into an open spot, a jawa materialized from nowhere and began running covetous hands over the metal sides. Luke leaned out and barked something harsh at the sub-human which caused it to scurry away.

"I can't abide those jawas," murmured Threepio with lofty disdain. "Disgusting creatures."

Luke's mind was too full of their narrow escape for him to comment on Threepio's sentiments. "I still can't understand how we got by those troops. I thought we were as good as dead."

"The force is in the mind, Luke, and can sometimes be used to influence others. It's a powerful ally. But as you come to know the force, you will discover that it can also be a danger."

Nodding without really understanding, Luke indicated the run-down though obviously popular cantina. "Do you really think we can find a pilot here capable of taking us all the way to Alderaan?"

Kenobi was exiting from the speeder. "Most of the good, independent freighter pilots frequent this place, though many can afford better. They can talk freely here. You should have learned by now, Luke, not to equate ability with appearance." Luke saw the old man's shabby clothing anew and felt ashamed. "Watch yourself, though. This place can be rough."

Luke found himself squinting as they entered the cantina. It was darker inside than he would have liked. Perhaps the regular habitués of this place were unaccustomed to the light of day, or didn't wish to be seen clearly. It didn't occur to Luke that the dim interior in combination with the brilliantly lit entrance permitted everyone inside to see each newcomer before he could see them.

Moving inward, Luke was astonished at the variety

of beings making use of the bar. There were one-eyed creatures and thousand-eyed, creatures with scales, creatures with fur, and some with skin that seemed to ripple and change consistency according to their feelings of the moment.

Hovering near the bar itself was a towering insectoid that Luke glimpsed only as a threatening shadow. It contrasted with two of the tallest women Luke had ever seen. They were among the most normal-looking of the outrageous assemblage of humans that mixed freely among alien counterparts. Tentacles, claws, and hands were wrapped around drinking utensils of various sizes and shapes. Conversation was a steady babble of human and alien tongues.

Leaning close, Kenobi gestured toward the far end of the bar. A small knot of rough-looking humans lounged there, drinking, laughing, and trading stories of dubious origin.

"Corellians—pirates, most likely."

"I thought we were looking for an independent freighter captain with his own ship for hire," Luke whispered back.

"So we are, young Luke, so we are," agreed Kenobi. "And there's bound to be one or two adequate for our needs among that group. It's just that in Corellian terminology the distinction between who owns what cargo tends to get a little muddled from time to time. Wait here."

Luke nodded and watched as Kenobi worked his way through the crowd. The Corellians' suspicion at his approach vanished as soon as he engaged them in conversation.

Something grabbed Luke's shoulder and spun him around.

"Hey" Looking around and struggling to regain his composure, he found himself staring up at an enormous, scruffy-looking human. Luke saw by the man's clothing that he must be the bartender, if not the owner of this cantina.

"We don't serve their kind in here," the glaring form growled.

"What?" Luke replied dumbly. He still hadn't recovered from his sudden submergence into the cultures of several dozen races. It was rather different from the poolroom behind the Anchorhead power station. "Your 'droids," the bartender explained impatiently, gesturing with a thick thumb. Luke peered in the indicated direction, to see Artoo and Threepio standing quietly nearby. "They'll have to wait outside. We don't serve them in here. I only carry stuff for organics, not," he concluded with an expression of distaste, "mechanicals."

Luke didn't like the idea of kicking Threepio and Artoo out, but he didn't know how else to deal with the problem. The bartender didn't appear to be the sort who would readily respond to reason, and when he looked around for old Ben, Luke saw that he was locked in deep conversation with one of the Corellians.

Meanwhile, the discussion had attracted the attention of several especially gruesome-looking types who happened to be clustered within hearing range. All were regarding Luke and the two 'droids in a decidely unfriendly fashion.

"Yes, of course," Luke said, realizing this wasn't the time or place to force the issue of 'droid rights. "I'm sorry." He looked over at Threepio. "You'd better stay outside with the speeder. We don't want any trouble in here."

"I heartily agree with you, sir," Threepio said, his gaze traveling past Luke and the bartender to take in the unfriendly stares at the bar. "I don't feel the need for lubrication at the moment anyway." With Artoo waddling in his wake, the tall robot hastily headed for the exit.

That finished things as far as the bartender was concerned, but Luke now found himself the subject of some unwanted attention. He abruptly became aware of his isolation and felt as if at one time or another every eye in the place rested a moment on him, that things human and otherwise were smirking and making comments about him behind his back.

Trying to maintain an air of quiet confidence, he returned his gaze to old Ben, and started when he saw what the oldster was talking to now. The Corellian was gone. In its place Kenobi was chatting with a towering anthropoid that showed a mouthful of teeth when it smiled.

Luke had heard about Wookies, but he had never expected to see one, much less meet one. Despite an almost comical quasi-monkey face, the Wookie was anything but gentle-looking. Only the large, glowing yellow eyes softened its otherwise awesome appearance. The massive torso was covered entirely with soft, thick russet fur. Less appealing cover consisted of a pair of chromed bandoliers which held lethal projectiles of a type unknown to Luke. Other than these, the Wookies wore little.

Not, Luke knew, that anyone would laugh at the creature's mode of dress. He saw that other denizens of the bar eddied and swirled around the huge form without ever coming too close. All but old Ben—Ben who was talking to the Wookie in its own language, quarreling and hooting softly like a native.

In the course of the conversation the old man had occasion to gesture in Luke's direction. Once the huge anthropoid stared directly at Luke and let out a horrifying howling laugh.

Disgruntled by the role he was evidently playing in the discussion, Luke turned away and pretended to ignore the whole conversation. He might be acting unfairly toward the creature, but he doubted that spine-quaking laugh was meant in gentle good-fellowship.

For the life of him he couldn't understand what Ben wanted with the monster, or why he was spending his time in guttural conversation with it instead of with the now-vanished Corellians. So he sat and sipped his drink in splendid silence, his eyes roving

over the crowd in hopes of meeting a responsive gaze
that held no belligerence.

Suddenly, something shoved him roughly from behind, so hard he almost fell. He turned angrily, but his
fury spent itself in astonishment. He found himself
confronted by a large squarish monstrosity of multiple
eyes and indeterminate origin.

"Negola dewaghi wooldugger?" the apparition bub-
bled challengingly.

Luke had never seen its like before; he knew neither its species nor its language. The gabbling might
have been an invitation to a fight, a request to share a
drink, or a marriage proposal. Despite his ignorance,
however, Luke could tell by the way the creature bobbed and wove unsteadily on its podal supports that it
had imbibed too much of whatever it considered a
pleasing intoxicant.

Not knowing what else to do, Luke tried turning
back to his own drink while studiously ignoring the
creature. As he did so, a thing—a cross between a
capybara and a small baboon—bounced over to stand
(or squat) next to the quivering many-eye. A short,
grubby-looking human also approached and put a
companionable arm around the snuffling mass.

"He doesn't like you," the stubby human informed Luke in a surprisingly deep voice.

"I'm sorry about that," Luke admitted, wishing
heartily he were somewhere else.

"I don't like you, either," the smiling little man
went on with brotherly negativity.

"I said I was sorry about it."

Whether from the conversation it was having with
the rodentlike creature or the overdose of booze, the
apartment house for wayward eyeballs was obviously
growing agitated. It leaned forward, almost toppling
into Luke, and spewed a stream of unintelligible gibberish at him. Luke felt the eyes of a crowd on him
as he grew increasingly more nervous.

" 'Sorry,' " the human mimicked derisively, clearly
deep into his own cups. "Are you insulting us? You

just better watch yourself. We're all wanted." He indicated his drunken companions. "I have the death sentence on me in twelve different systems."

"I'll be careful, then," Luke muttered.

The little man was smiling broadly. "You'll be dead."

At this the rodent let out a loud grunt. It was either a signal or a warning, because everything human or otherwise which had been leaning up at the bar immediately backed away, leaving a clear space around Luke and his antagonists.

Trying to salvage the situation, Luke essayed a wan smile. That faded rapidly when he saw that the three were readying hand weapons. Not only couldn't he have countered all three of them, he had no idea what a couple of the lethal-looking devices did.

"This little one isn't worth the trouble," a calm voice said. Luke looked up, startled. He hadn't heard Kenobi come up alongside him. "Come, let me buy you all something . . ."

By way of reply the bulky monster chittered hideously and swung out a massive limb. It caught an unprepared Luke across the temple and sent him spinning across the room, crashing through tables and shattering a large jug filled with a foul-smelling liquid.

The crowd edged back farther, a few grunts and warning snorts coming from some of them as the drunken monstrosity pulled a wicked-looking pistol from its service pouch. He started to wave it in Kenobi's direction.

That spurred the heretofore neutral bartender to life. He came charging clumsily around the end of the bar, waving his hands frantically but still taking care to stay out of range.

"No blasters, no blasters! Not in my place!"

The rodent thing chattered threateningly at him, while the weapon-wielding many-eye spared him a warning grunt.

In the split second when the gun and its owner's

attention was off him, the old man's hand had moved to the disk slung at his side. The short human started to yell as a fiery blue-white light appeared in the dimness of the cantina.

He never finished the yell. It turned into a blink. When the blink was finished, the man found himself lying prone against the bar, moaning and whimpering as he stared at the stump of an arm.

In between the start of his yell and the conclusion of the blink, the rodent-thing had been cleft cleanly in half down the middle, its two halves falling in opposite directions. The giant multiocular creature still stood staring, dazed, at the old human who was poised motionless before it, the shining lightsaber held over his head in a peculiar fashion. The creature's chrome pistol fired once, blowing a hole in the door. Then the torso peeled away as neatly as had the body of the rodent, its two cauterized sections falling in opposite directions to lie motionless on the cool stone.

Only then did the suggestion of a sigh escape from Kenobi; only then did his body appear to relax. Bringing the lightsaber down, he flipped it carefully upward in a reflex saluting motion which ended with the de-activated weapon resting innocuously on his hip.

That final movement broke the total quiet which had enshrouded the room. Conversation resumed, as did the movement of bodies in chairs, the scraping of mugs and pitchers and other drinking devices on tabletops. The bartender and several assistants appeared to drag the unsightly corpses out of the room, while the mutilated human vanished wordlessly into the crowd, cradling the stump of his gun arm and counting himself fortunate.

To all appearances the cantina had returned to its former state, with one small exception. Ben Kenobi was given a respectful amount of space at the bar.

Luke barely heard the renewed conversation. He was still shaken by the speed of the fight and by the old man's unimagined abilities. As his mind cleared and he moved to rejoin Kenobi, he could overhear bits and snatches of the talk around him. Much of it centered on admiration for the cleanness and finality of the fight.

"You're hurt, Luke," Kenobi observed solicitously.

Luke felt of the bruise where the big creature had struck him. "I . . ." he started to say, but old Ben cut him off. As if nothing had happened, he indicated the great hairy mass which was shouldering its way through the crowd toward them.

"This is Chewbacca," he explained when the anthropoid had joined them at the bar. "He's first mate on a ship that might suit our needs. He'll take us to her captain-owner now."

"This way," the Wookie grunted—at least, it sounded something like that to Luke. In any case, the huge creature's follow-me gesture was unmistakable. They started to wend their way deeper into the bar, the Wookie parting the crowd like a gravel storm cutting canyonettes.

Out in front of the cantina, Threepio paced nervously next to the landspeeder. Apparently unconcerned, Artoo Detoo was engaged in animated electronic conversation with a bright red R-2 unit be longing to another of the cantina's patrons.

"What could be taking them so long? They went to hire one ship—not a fleet."

Abruptly Threepio paused, beckoning silently for Artoo to be quiet. Two Imperial troopers had appeared on the scene. They were met by an unkempt human who had emerged almost simultaneously from the depths of the cantina.

"I do not like the looks of this," the tall 'droid murmured.

Luke had appropriated someone else's drink from a waiter's tray as they made their way to the rear of the cantina. He gulped at it with the giddy air of one who feels himself under divine protection. That safe he was not, but in the company of Kenobi and the giant Wookie he began to feel confident that no one in the bar would assault him with so much as a dirty look.

In a rear booth they encountered a sharp-featured young man perhaps five years older than Luke, perhaps a dozen—it was difficult to tell. He displayed the openness of the utterly confident—or the insanely reckless. At their approach the man sent the humanoid wench who had been wriggling on his lap on her way with a whispered something which left a wide, if inhuman, grin on her face.

The Wookie Chewbacca rumbled something at the man, and he nodded in response, glancing up at the newcomers pleasantly.

"You're pretty handy with that saber, old man. Not often does one see that kind of swordplay in this part of the Empire anymore." He downed a prodigious portion of whatever filled his mug. "I'm Han Solo, captain of the *Millennium Falcon.*" Suddenly he became all business. "Chewie tells me you're looking for passage to the Alderaan system?"

"That's right, son. If it's on a fast ship," Kenobi told him. Solo didn't bridle at the "son."

"Fast ship? You mean you've never *heard* of the *Millennium Falcon?*"

Kenobi appeared amused. "Should I?"

"It's the ship that made the Kessel run in less than twelve standard timeparts!" Solo told him indignantly. "I've outrun Imperial starships and Corellian cruisers. I think she's fast enough for you, old man." His outrage subsided rapidly. "What's your cargo?"

"Only passengers. Myself, the boy, and two 'droids —no questions asked."

"No questions." Solo regarded his mug, finally looked up. "Is it local trouble?"

"Let's just say we'd like to avoid any Imperial entanglements," Kenobi replied easily.

"These days that can be a real trick. It'll cost you a little extra." He did some mental figuring. "All in all, about ten thousand. In advance." He added with a smile, "And no questions asked."

Luke gaped at the pilot. "Ten thousand! We could almost buy our own ship for that."

Solo shrugged. "Maybe you could and maybe you couldn't. In any case, could you fly it?"

"You bet I could," Luke shot back, rising. "I'm not such a bad pilot myself. I don't—"

Again the firm hand on his arm. "We haven't that much with us," Kenobi explained. "But we could pay you two thousand now, plus another fifteen when we reach Alderaan."

Solo leaned forward uncertainly. "fifteen . . .You can really get your hands on that kind of money?"

"I promise it—from the government on Alderaan itself. At the worst, you'll have earned an honest fee: two thousand."

But Solo seemed not to hear the last. "Seventeen thousand . . . All right, I'll chance it. You've got yourselves a ship. As for avoiding Imperial entanglements, you'd better twist out of here or even the *Millennium Falcon* won't be any help to you." He nodded toward the cantina entrance, and added quickly, "Docking bay ninety-four, first thing in the morning."

Four Imperial troopers, their eyes darting rapidly from table to booth to bar, had entered the cantina. There was muttering from among the crowd, but whenever the eyes of one of the heavily armed troopers went hunting for the mutterers, the words died with sullen speed.

Moving to the bar, the officer in charge asked the bartender a couple of brief questions. The big man hesitated a moment, then pointed toward a place near the back of the room. As he did so, his eyes widened slightly. Those of the officer were unreadable.

The booth he was pointing to was empty.

☐ VII

LUKE and Ben were securing Artoo Detoo in the back of the speeder while Threepio kept a lookout for any additional troops.

"If Solo's ship is as fast as his boasting, we should be all right," the old man observed with satisfaction.

"But two thousand—and fifteen more when we reach Alderaan!"

"It's not the fifteen that worries me; it's the first two," Kenobi explained. "I'm afraid you'll have to sell your speeder."

Luke let his gaze rove over the landspeeder, but the thrill it had once given him was gone—gone along with other things best not dwelt on.

"It's all right," he assured Kenobi listlessly. "I don't think I'll need it again."

From their vantage point in another booth, Solo and Chewbacca watched as the Imperials strode through the bar. Two of them gave the Corellian a lingering glance. Chewbacca growled once and the two soldiers hurried their pace somewhat.

Solo grinned sardonically, turning to his partner. "Chewie, this charter could save our necks. Seventeen thousand!" He shook his head in amazement. "Those two must really be desperate. I wonder what they're wanted for. But I agreed, no questions. They're paying enough for it. Let's get going—the *Falcon* won't check itself out."

"Going somewhere, Solo?"

The Corellian couldn't identify the voice, coming as it did through an electronic translator. But there was no problem recognizing the speaker or the gun it held stuck in Solo's side.

The creature was roughly man-sized and bipedal, but its head was something out of delirium by way of an upset stomach. It had huge, dull-faceted eyes, bulbous on a pea-green face. A ridge of short spines crested the high skull, while nostrils and mouth were contained in a tapirlike snout.

"As a matter of fact," Solo replied slowly," "I was just on my way to see your boss. You can tell Jabba I've got the money I owe him."

"That's what you said yesterday—and last week— and the week prior to that. It's too late, Solo. I'm not going back to Jabba with another one of your stories."

"But I've really got the money this time!" Solo protested.

"Fine. I'll take it now, please."

Solo sat down slowly. Jabba's minions were apt to be cursed with nervous trigger fingers. The alien took the seat across from him, the muzzle of the ugly little pistol never straying from Solo's chest.

"I haven't got it here with me. Tell Jabba—"

"It's too late, I think. Jabba would rather have your ship."

"Over my dead body," Solo said unamiably.

The alien was not impressed. "If you insist. Will you come outside with me, or must I finish it here?"

"I don't think they'd like another killing in here," Solo pointed out.

Something which might have been a laugh came from the creature's translator. "They'd hardly notice. Get up, Solo. I've been looking forward to this for a long time. You've embarrassed me in front of Jabba with your pious excuses for the last time."

"I think you're right."

Light and noise filled the little corner of the cantina, and when it had faded, all that remained of the unctuous alien was a smoking, slimy spot on the stone floor.

Solo brought his hand and the smoking weapon it held out from beneath the table, drawing bemused stares from several of the cantina's patrons and clucking sounds from its more knowledgeable ones. They had known the creature had committed its fatal mistake in allowing Solo the chance to get his hands under cover.

"It'll take a lot more than the likes of you to finish me off. Jabba the Hut always did skimp when it came to hiring his hands."

Leaving the booth, Solo flipped the bartender a handful of coins as he and Chewbacca moved off. "Sorry for the mess. I always was a rotten host."

Heavily armed troopers hurried down the narrow alleyway, glowering from time to time at the darkly clad beings who hawked exotic goods from dingy little stalls. Here in Mos Eisley's inner regions the walls were high and narrow, turning the passageway into a tunnel.

No one stared angrily back at them; no one shouted imprecations or mouthed obscenities. These armored figures moved with the authority of the Empire, their sidearms boldly displayed and activated. All around, men, not-men, and mechanicals were crouched in waste-littered doorways. Among accumulations of garbage and filth they exchanged information and concluded transactions of dubious legality.

A hot wind moaned down the alleyway and the troopers closed their formation. Their precision and order masked a fear of such claustrophobic quarters.

One paused to check a door, only to discover it tightly locked and bolted. A sand-encrusted human shambling nearby visited a half-mad harangue on the trooper. Shrugging inwardly, the soldier gave the crazy human a sour eye before moving on down the alley to join up again with his fellows.

As soon as they were well past, the door slid open a crack and a metallic face peered out. Below Threepio's leg, a squat barrel shape struggled for a view.

"I would rather have gone with Master Luke than stay here with you. Still, orders are orders. I don't quite know what all the trouble is about, but I'm sure it must be your fault."

Artoo responded with a near impossibility: a sniggering beep.

"You watch your language," the taller machine warned.

The number of old landspeeders and other powered transports in the dusty lot which were still capable of motion could be counted on the fingers of one hand. But that was not the concern of Luke and Ben as they stood bargaining with the tall, slightly insectoid owner. They were here not to buy, but to sell.

None of the passersby favored the hagglers with so much as a curious glance. Similar transactions which were the business of no one but the transactors took place half a thousand times daily in Mos Eisley.

Eventually there were no more pleas or threats to be exchanged. As though doling out vials of his own blood, the owner finalized the sale by passing a number of small metal shapes to Luke. Luke and the insectoid traded formal good-byes and then they parted, each convinced he had gotten the better of the deal.

"He says it's the best he can do. Since the XP-38 came out, they just aren't in demand anymore," Luke sighed.

"Don't look so discouraged," Kenobi chided him. "What you've obtained will be sufficient. I've enough to cover the rest."

Leaving the main street, they turned down an alleyway and walked past a small robot herding along a clutch of creatures resembling attenuated anteaters. As they rounded the corner Luke strained for a forlorn glimpse of the old landspeeder—his last link with his former life. Then there was no more time for looking back.

Something short and dark that might have been human underneath all its wrappings stepped out of the shadows as they moved away from the corner. It continued staring after them as they disappeared down a bend in the walkway.

The docking-bay entrance to the small saucer-shaped spacecraft was completely ringed by half a dozen men and aliens, of which the former were by half the most grotesque. A great mobile tub of muscle and suet topped by a shaggy scarred skull surveyed the semicircle of armed assassins with satisfaction. Moving forward from the center of the crescent, he shouted toward the ship.

"Come on out, Solo! We've got you surrounded."

"If so, you're facing the wrong way," came a calm voice.

Jabba the Hut jumped—in itself a remarkable sight. His lackeys likewise whirled—to see Han Solo and Chewbacca standing behind them.

"You see, I've been waiting for you, Jabba."

"I expected you would be," the Hut admitted, at once pleased and alarmed by the fact that neither Solo nor the big Wookie appeared to be armed.

"I'm not the type to run," Solo said.

"Run? Run from what?" Jabba countered. The absence of visible weapons bothered Jabba more than he cared to admit to himself. There was something peculiar here, and it would be better to make no hasty moves until he discovered what was amiss.

"Han, my boy, there are times when you disappoint me. I merely wish to know why you haven't paid me . . . as you should have long ago. And why did you have to fry poor Greedo like that? After all you and I have been through together."

Solo grinned tightly. "Shove it, Jabba. There isn't enough sentiment in your body to warm an orphaned bacterium. As for Greedo, you sent him to kill me."

"Why, Han," Jabba protested in surprise, "why would I do that? You're the best smuggler in the business. You're too valuable to fry. Greedo was only relaying my natural concern at your delays. He wasn't going to kill you."

"I think he thought he was. Next time don't send one of those hired twerps. If you've got something to say, come see me yourself."

Jabba shook his head and his jowls shook—lazy, fleshy echoes of his mock sorrow. "Han, Han—if only you hadn't had to dump that shipment of spice! You understand . . . I just can't make an exception. Where would I be if every pilot who smuggled for me dumped his shipment at the first sign of an Imperial warship? And then simply showed empty pockets when I demanded recompense? It's not good business. I can be generous and forgiving—but not to the point of bankruptcy."

"You know, even I get boarded sometimes, Jabba. Did you think I dumped that spice because I got tired of its smell? I wanted to deliver it as much as you wanted to receive it. I had no choice." Again the sardonic smile. "As you say, I'm too valuable to fry. But I've got a charter now and I can pay you back, plus a little extra. I just need some more time. I can give you a thousand on account, the rest in three weeks."

The gross form seemed to consider, then directed his next words not to Solo but to his hirelings. "Put your blasters away." His gaze and a predatory smile turned to the wary Corellian.

"Han, my boy, I'm only doing this because you're the best and I'll need you again sometime. So, out of the greatness of my soul and a forgiving heart—and for an extra, say, twenty percent—I'll give you a little more time." The voice nearly cracked with restraint. "But this is the last time. If you disappoint me again, if you trample my generosity in your mocking laughter, I'll put a price on your head so large you won't be able to go near a civilized system for the rest of your life, because on every one your name and face will be known to men who'll gladly cut your guts out for one-tenth of what I'll promise them."

"I'm glad we both have my best interests at heart," replied Solo pleasantly as he and Chewbacca started

Six years ago, George Lucas, the man who brought you AMERICAN GRAFFITI, began his first draft of a film that very well may become a milestone in the space fantasy genre.

The high-energy adventure unites the hardware of contemporary science fiction with the romantic fantasies of sword and sorcery.

STAR WARS is an imaginative entertainment experience which takes the audience to an unknown galaxy thousands of light years from earth.

Written and designed for the large screen, the live-action fantasy adventure film follows a young man, Luke Skywalker, through exotic worlds uniquely different from our own.

Beginning on the small arid planet of Tatooine, Luke plunges into an extraordinary intergalactic search for a kidnapped rebel Princess. His odyssey finally culminates in a wild, terrifying space battle over a large satellite battle station, Death Star.

Luke is joined by several friends—space pilots, outlaws, mechanical robots, and a large furry Wookie—and together they battle numerous villains and creatures in a massive Galactic Civil War.

Producer Gary Kurtz and writer-director George Lucas, the team responsible for the highly successful AMERICAN GRAFFITI, began production three years ago to create this impressive space adventure.

A whole new special effects shop was constructed to take advantage of computer technology to implement some of the most elaborate miniature and optical effects ever produced on film.

The same care has gone into casting the unusual roles. Lucas, casting with the same approach he used for AMERICAN GRAFFITI, chose new, fresh talent for three of the five major roles. In the other two roles, he cast British veterans, Alec Guinness and Peter Cushing.

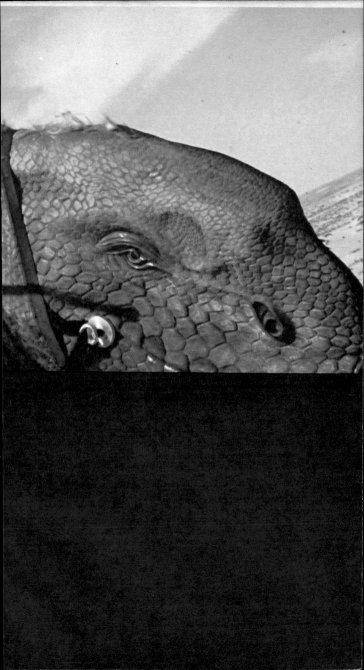

"I think that anyone who goes to the movies loves to have an emotional experience. It's basic — whether you're seven, seventeen or seventy. The more intense the experience, the more successful the film.

"I've always loved adventure films. After I finished AMERICAN GRAFFITI, I came to realize that since the demise of the western, there hasn't been much in the mythological fantasy genre available to the film audience. So, instead of making "isn't-it-terrible-what's-happening-to-mankind" movies, which is how I began, I decided that I'd try to fill that gap. I'd make a film so rooted in imagination that the grimness of everyday life would not follow the audience into the theater. In other words, for two hours, they could forget.

"I'm trying to reconstruct a genre that's been lost and bring it to a new dimension so that the elements of space, fantasy, adventure, suspense and fun all work and feed off each other. So, in a way, STAR WARS is a movie for the kid in all of us."

— George Lucas

Luke Skywalker
●Mark Hamill

Ben (Obi-Wan) Kenobi
●Alec Guinness

Princess Leia Organa
●Carrie Fisher

Luke Skywalker, a twenty-year-old farmboy on the remote planet of Tatooine, is compelled to break from his dull chores on his Uncle's moisture farm. The cryptic message of a kidnapped Princess catapults the brave, impetuous hero into a series of adventures on various worlds of a distant galaxy. Accompanied by his two servant robots, Luke challenges the Galactic Empire's ultimate weapon, the Death Star.

Ben Kenobi, a once respected name in the galaxy, is now an outlaw in the Tatooine mountains. The shabby old desert-rat of a man was, before the rise of the sinister Galactic Empire, one of the greatest warriors in the Old Republic. Even now, in his old age he can still be a threat to the sovereignty of the Empire because of his very special powers.

Princess Leia the very young Senator from Alderaan, has been using her political position to secretly gather information against the Empire. The strong-willed, intelligent Princess has been a unifying force in bringing about the rebellion against the oppression of the powerful Galactic Empire.

Darth Vader

Han Solo • Harrison Ford

Grand Moff Tarkin
• Peter Cushing

Han Solo is the overly confident captain of the Millennium Falcon, a Corellian pirate starship. Accompanied by his Wookie companion, Chewbacca, he plies his mercenary trade outside the restrictive laws of the Empire. At times his insanely reckless manner pushes him into situations from which only his foolhardy courage can save him.

Darth Vader personifies the evil of the Galactic Empire. The awesome, malevolent figure dressed in flowing black robes keeps his face forever masked by a grotesque breath screen. He employs his extrasensory powers to keep the Emperor enthroned and to aid Governor Tarkin in the destruction of the rebellion.

Grand Moff Tarkin is the Governor of the Imperial Outland regions. His insatiable political ambitions to become Emperor have driven him to use ruthless means to quell the rapidly growing rebellion. To this end he has constructed a large and frighteningly powerful new battle station, the Death Star, which is capable of destroying an entire planet.

See-Threepio • C-3PO   **Artoo-Detoo •** R2-D2   **Chewbacca**

See-Threepio is a tall robot with a gleaming metallic surface. As a human-robot relations specialist he translates thousands of the Galactic languages, including the electronic tongues spoken by many robots. His human-like appearance is often matched with his human-like behavior as well.

Artoo-Detoo is a meter-high, cylindrical robot whose face is a mass of computer lights surrounding a single radar eye. Artoo, a sophisticated computer repair and information retrieval robot, can only speak to another robot in a series of electronic sounds. His thick clawed legs carry the feisty, rebellious automaton into a series of dangerous encounters.

Chewbacca, the hundred-year-old giant Wookie, co-pilots the Millennium Falcon. The huge anthropoid has a quasi-monkey face with large blue eyes that soften his awesome appearance. His language includes little more than a series of grunts which can reach a deafening crescendo when his temper is aroused.

Stormtroopers are the drones of the Galactic Empire who carry out a reign of terror among the disheartened worlds of the galaxy. Hidden underneath white armored spacesuits, these fearsome troops enforce the restrictive laws with callous disregard for human rights. Quite often they are tools used to further the personal ambitions of the Imperial governors and bureaucrats.

An alliance of underground freedom fighters are challenging the tyranny and oppression of the awesome Galactic Empire. Idealists and adventurers from a small number of systems joined together to stop the growing outrages. Striking from a fortress hidden among the billion stars of the galaxy, rebel spaceships have been winning a growing number of victories.

Jawas

Tusken Raiders

Jawas are the meter-high creatures who travel the wastes of Tatooine collecting and selling scrap. They scurry about in a rodent-like manner in rough-hewn cloaks thickly coated with dust and sand. These overly cautious creatures jabber in low guttural croaks and hisses. The shrouded creatures smell horribly, attracting small insects to the dark recesses where their mouths and nostrils should be.

Tusken Raiders, or Sandpeople as they are sometimes called, wear abundant clothing to protect themselves from Tatooine's twin suns. These large, strong creatures pursue a nomadic existence in some of Tatooine's most desolate regions. Vicious desert bandits, they fear little and make sudden raids on local settlers. They are marginally human creatures who are not to be trifled with.

past the staring eyes of the Hut's hired guns. "Don't worry, Jabba, I'll pay you. But not because you threaten me. I'll pay you because . . . it's my pleasure."

"They're starting to search the spaceport central," the Commander declared, having to alternately run a couple of steps and then walk to keep pace with the long strides of Darth Vader. The Dark Lord was deep in thought as he strode down one of the battle station's main corridors, trailed by several aides.

"The reports are just starting to come in," the Commander went on. "It's only a matter of time before we have those 'droids."

"Send in more men if you have to. Never mind the protests of the planetary Governor—I must have those 'droids. It's her hope of that data being used against us that is the pillar of her resistance to the mind probes."

"I understand, Lord Vader. Until then we must waste our time with Governor Tarkin's foolish plan to break her."

"There's docking bay ninety-four," Luke told Kenobi and the robots who had rejoined them, "and there's Chewbacca. He seems excited about something."

Indeed, the big Wookie was waving over the heads of the crowd and jabbering loudly in their direction. Speeding their pace, none of the foursome noticed the small, dark-clad thing that had followed them from the transporter lot.

The creature moved into the doorway and pulled a tiny transmitter from a pouch concealed by its multifold robes. The transmitter looked far too new and modern to be in the grasp of so decrepit a specimen, yet its manipulator was speaking into it with steady assurance.

Docking bay ninety-four, Luke noted, was no different in appearance from a host of other grandiosely named docking bays scattered throughout Mos Eisley. It consisted mostly of an entrance rampway and an enormous pit gouged from the rocky soil. This served as clearance radii for the effects of the simple antigrav drive which boosted all spacecraft clear of the gravitational field of the planet.

The mathematics of spacedrive were simple enough even to Luke. Antigrav could operate only when there was a sufficient gravity well to push against—like that of a planet—whereas supralight travel could only take place when a ship was clear of that same gravity. Hence the necessity for the dual-drive system on any extrasystem craft.

The pit which formed docking bay ninety-four was as shabbily cut and run-down as the majority of Mos Eisley. Its sloping sides were crumbling in places instead of being smoothly fashioned as they were on more populous worlds. Luke felt it formed the perfect setting for the spacecraft Chewbacca was leading them toward.

That battered ellipsoid which could only loosely be labeled a ship appeared to have been pieced together out of old hull fragments and components discarded as unusable by other craft. The wonder of it, Luke mused, was that the thing actually held its shape. Trying to picture this vehicle as spaceworthy would have caused him to collapse in hysteria—were the situation not so serious. But to think of traveling to Alderaan in this pathetic . . .

"What a piece of junk," he finally murmured, unable to hide his feelings any longer. They were walking up the rampway toward the open port. "This thing couldn't possibly make it into hyperspace."

Kenobi didn't comment, but merely gestured toward the port, where a figure was coming to meet them.

Either Solo had supernaturally acute hearing, or else he was used to the reaction the sight of the *Millennium Falcon* produced in prospective passengers. "She may not look like much," he confessed as he approached them, "but she's all go. I've added a few unique modifications to her myself. In addition to piloting, I like to tinker. She'll make point five factors beyond lightspeed."

Luke scratched his head as he tried to reassess the craft in view of its owner's claims. Either the Corellian was the biggest liar this side of the galactic center, or there was more to this vessel than met the eye. Luke thought back once more to old Ben's admonition never to trust surface impressions, and decided to reserve judgment on the ship and its pilot until after he had watched them in operation.

Chewbacca had lingered behind at the docking-bay entrance. Now he rushed up the ramp, a hairy whirlwind, and blabbered excitedly at Solo. The pilot regarded him coolly, nodding from time to time, then barked a brief reply. The Wookie charged into the ship, pausing only to urge everyone to follow.

"We seem to be a bit rushed," Solo explained cryptically, "so if you'll hurry aboard, we'll be off."

Luke was about to venture some questions, but Kenobi was already prodding him up the ramp. The 'droids followed.

Inside, Luke was slightly startled to see the bulky Chewbacca squirm and fight his way into a pilot's chair which, despite modifications, was still overwhelmed by his massive form. The Wookie flipped several tiny switches with digits seemingly too big for the task. Those great paws drifted with surprising grace over the controls.

A deep throbbing started somewhere within the ship as the engines were activated. Luke and Ben began strapping themselves into the vacant seats in the main passageway.

Outside the docking-bay entrance a long, leathery snout protruded from dark folds of cloth, and somewhere in the depths to either side of that imposing proboscis, eyes stared intently. They turned, along with the rest of the head, as a squad of eight Imperial troops rushed up. Perhaps not surprisingly, they headed straight for the enigmatic figure who whispered something to the lead trooper and gestured to the docking bay.

The information must have been provocative. Activating their weapons and raising them to firing position, the troops charged en masse down the docking-bay entrance.

A glint of light on moving metal caught Solo's eyes as the unwelcome outlines of the first troops showed themselves. Solo thought it unlikely they would pause to engage in casual conversation. His suspicion was confirmed before he could open his mouth to protest their intrusion, as several dropped to their knees and opened fire on him. Solo ducked back inside, turning to yell forward.

"Chewie—deflector shields, quick! Get us out of here!"

A throaty roar of acknowledgment came back to him.

Drawing his own pistol, Solo managed to snap off a couple of bursts from the comparative safety of the hatchway. Seeing that their quarry was neither helpless nor comatose, the exposed troops dove for cover.

The low throbbing rose to a whine, then to a deafening howl as Solo's hand came down on the quick-release button. Immediately the overhead hatchcover slammed shut.

As the retreating troops raced out of the docking-bay entrance, the ground was trembling steadily. They ran smack into a second squad, which had just arrived in response to the rapidly spreading emergency call. One of the soldiers, gesticulating wildly, tried to explain to the newly arrived ranking officer what had happened back in the bay.

As soon as the panting trooper had finished, the officer whipped out a compact communicator and shouted into it, "Flight deck . . . they're trying to escape! Send everything you've got after this ship."

All across Mos Eisley, alarms began to sound, spreading out from docking bay ninety-four in concentric circles of concern.

Several soldiers scouring one alleyway reacted to the citywide alarm at the same time as they saw the small freighter lift gracefully into the clear blue sky above Mos Eisley. It shrank to a pinpoint before any of them thought to bring a weapon to bear.

Luke and Ben were already undoing their acceleration straps as Solo walked past them, moving toward the cockpit with the easy, loose-limbed stride of the experienced spacer. Once forward, he fell rather than sat in the pilot's seat and immediately began checking readouts and gauges. In the seat next to him Chewbacca was growling and grunting like a poorly tuned speeder engine. He turned from studying his own instruments long enough to jab a massive finger at the tracking screen.

Solo gave it a quick glance, then turned irritably to his own panel. "I know, I know . . . looks like two, maybe three destroyers. Somebody certainly dislikes our passengers. Sure picked ourselves a hot one this time. Try to hold them off somehow until I can finish the programming for the supralight jump. Angle the deflectors for maximum shielding."

With those instructions he ceased conversing with the huge Wookie as his hands flew over the computer input terminals. Solo did not even turn around when a small cylindrical shape appeared in the doorway behind him. Artoo Detoo beeped a few remarks, then scurried away.

Rear scanners showed the baleful lemon eye of Tatooine shrinking rapidly behind them. It wasn't rapid enough to eliminate the three points of light that indicated the presence of the pursuing Imperial warships.

Although Solo had ignored Artoo, he turned to acknowledge the entrance of his human passengers. "We've got two more coming in from different angles," he told them, scrutinizing the remorseless instrumentation. "They're going to try to box up before we can jump. Five ships . . . What did you two do to attract that kind of company?"

"Can't you outrun them?" Luke asked sarcastically, ignoring the pilot's question. "I thought you said this thing was fast."

"Watch your mouth, kid, or you'll find yourself floating home. There's too many of 'em, for one thing. But, we'll be safe enough once we've made the jump into hyperspace." He grinned knowingly. "Can't nobody track another ship accurately at supralight speeds. Plus, I know a few tricks that ought to lose any persistent stick-tights. I wish I'd known you boys were so popular."

"Why?" Luke said challengingly. "Would you have refused to take us?"

"Not necessarily," the Corellian replied, refusing to be baited. "But I sure's hell would've boosted your fare."

Luke had a retort poised on his lips. It was wiped out as he threw up his arms to ward off a brilliant red flash which gave black space outside the viewport the temporary aspect of the surface of a sun. Kenobi, Solo, and even Chewbacca did likewise, since the proximity of the explosion nearly overrode the phototropic shielding.

"Here's where the situation gets interesting," Solo muttered.

"How long before you can make the jump?" Kenobi inquired easily, apparently unconcerned that at any second they all might cease to exist.

"We're still within the gravitational influence of Tatooine," came the cool response. "It will be a few minutes yet before the navigation computer can compensate and effect an accurate jump. I could override its decision, but the hyperdrive would likely shred itself. That would give me a nice hold full of scrap metal in addition to you four."

"'A few minutes," Luke blurted, staring at the screens. "At the rate they're gaining . . ."

"Traveling through hyperspace isn't like dusting crops, boy. Ever tried calculating a hyperspace jump?" Luke had to shake his head. "It's no mean trick. Be nice if we rushed it and passed right through a star or some other friendly spatial phenom like a black hole. That would end our trip real quick."

Fresh explosions continued to flare close by despite Chewbacca's best efforts at evasion. On Solo's console a red warning light began to flash for attention.

"What's that?" Luke wondered nervously.

"We're losing a deflector shield," Solo informed him with the air of a man about to have a tooth pulled. "Better strap yourselves back in. We're almost ready to make the jump. It could get bad if we take a near-burst at the wrong moment."

Back in the main hold area Threepio was already locked tightly into his seat by metal arms stronger than any acceleration straps. Artoo swayed back and forth under the concussion produced by increasingly powerful energy bursts against the ship's deflectors.

"Was this trip really necessary?" the tall robot muttered in desperation. "I'd forgotten how much I hate space travel." He broke off as Luke and Ben appeared and began strapping themselves back into their chairs.

Oddly, Luke was thinking of a dog he had once owned when an immensely powerful something wrenched at the ship's hull with the strength of a fallen angel.

Admiral Motti entered the quiet conference room, his face streaked by the linear lights lining the walls. His gaze went to the spot where Governor Tarkin stood before the curved viewscreen, and he bowed slightly. Despite the evidence of the small green gem of a world entered in the screen, he formally announced, "We have entered the Alderaan system. We await your order."

The door signaled and Tarkin made a falsely gentle gesture to the admiral. "Wait a moment yet, Motti."

The door slid aside and Leia Organa entered, flanked by two armed guards, followed by Darth Vader.

"I am—," Tarkin began.

"I know who you are," she spat, "Governor Tarkin. I should have expected to find you holding Vader's leash. I thought I recognized your unique stench when I was first brought on board."

"Charming to the last," Tarkin declared in a fashion which suggested he was anything but charmed. "You don't know how hard I found it to sign the order for your termination." His expression changed to one of mock sorrow. "Of course, had you cooperated in our investigation, things might be otherwise. Lord Vader has informed me that your resistance to our traditional methods of inquiry—"

"Torture, you mean," she countered a trifle shakily.

"Let us not bandy semantics," Tarkin smiled.

"I'm surprised you had the courage to take the responsibility for issuing the order on yourself."

Tarkin sighed reluctantly. "I am a dedicated man, and the pleasures I reserve for myself are few. One of them is that before your execution I should like you to be my guest at a small ceremony. It will certify this battle station's operational status while at the same time ushering in a new era of Imperial technical supremacy. This station is the final link in the new-forged Imperial chain which will bind the million systems of the galactic Empire together once and for all. Your petty Alliance will no longer be of any concern to us. After today's demonstration no one will dare to oppose Imperial decree, not even the Senate."

Organa looked at him with contempt. "Force will not keep the Empire together. Force has never kept anything together for very long. The more you tighten your grip, the more systems will slip through your fingers. You're a foolish man, Governor. Foolish men often choke to death on their own delusions."

Tarkin smiled a death's-head smile, his face a parchment skull's. "It will be interesting to see what manner of passing Lord Vader has in mind for you. I am certain it will be worthy of you—and of him.

"But before you leave us, we must demonstrate the power of this station once and for all, in a conclusive fashion. In a way, you have determined the choice of subject for this demonstration. Since you have proven reluctant to supply us with the location of the rebel stronghold, I have deemed it appropriate to select as an alternate subject your home planet of Alderaan."

"No! You can't! Alderaan is a peaceful world, with no standing armies. You can't . . ."

Tarkin's eyes gleamed. 'You would prefer another target? A military target, perhaps? We're agreeable . . . name the system." He shrugged elaborately. "I grow tired of such games. For the last time, where is the main rebel base?"

A voice announced over a hidden speaker that they had approached within antigrav range of Alderaan—approximately six planetary diameters. That was enough to accomplish what all of Vader's infernal devices had failed to.

"Dantooine," she whispered, staring at the deck, all pretense at defiance gone now. "They're on Dantooine."

Tarkin let out a slow sigh of satisfaction, then turned to the black figure nearby. "There, you see, Lord Vader? She can be reasonable. One needs only frame the question properly to elicit the desired response." He directed his attention to the other officers. "After concluding our little test here we shall make haste to move on to Dantooine. You may proceed with the operation, gentlemen."

It took several seconds for Tarkin's words, so casually uttered, to penetrate. *"What!"* Organa finally gasped.

"Dantooine," Tarkin explained, examining his fingers, "is too far from the centers of Imperial population to serve as the subject of an effective demonstration. You will understand that for reports of our power to spread rapidly through the Empire we require an obstreperous world more centrally located. Have no fear, though. We will deal with your rebel friends on Dantooine as soon as possible.'

"But you said . . ." Organa started to protest.

"The only words which have meaning are the last ones spoken," Tarkin declared cuttingly. "We will proceed with the destruction of Alderaan as planned. Then you will enjoy watching with us as we obliterate the Dantooine center of this stupid and futile rebellion."

He gestured to the two soldiers flanking her. "Escort her to the principal observation level and," he smiled, "make certain she is provided with an unobstructed view."

☐ VIII

SOLO was busily checking readouts from gauges and dials in the hold area. Occasionally he would pass a small box across various sensors, study the result, and cluck with pleasure.

"You can stop worrying about your Imperial friends," he told Luke and Ben. "They'll never be able to track us now. Told you I'd lose them."

Kenobi might have nodded briefly in response, but he was engaged in explaining something to Luke.

"Don't everybody thank me at once," Solo grunted, slightly miffed. "Anyway, navigation computer calculates our arrival in Alderaan orbit at oh-two-hundred. I'm afraid after this little adventure I'll have to forge a new registration."

He returned to his checking, passing in front of a

small circular table. The top was covered with small squares lit from beneath, while computer monitors were set into each side. Tiny three-dimensional figures were projected above the tabletop from various squares.

Chewbacca sat hunched over one side of the table, his chin resting in massive hands. His great eyes glowing and facial whiskers wrinkled upward, he gave every sign of being well pleased with himself.

At least, he did until Artoo Detoo reached up with a stubby clawed limb across from him and tapped his own computer monitor. One of the figures walked abruptly across the board to a new square and stopped there.

An expression of puzzlement, then anger crossed the Wookie's face as he studied the new configuration. Glaring up and over the table, he vented a stream of abusive gibberish on the inoffensive machine. Artoo could only beep in reply, but Threepio soon interceded on behalf of his less eloquent companion and began arguing with the hulking anthropoid.

"He executed a fair move. Screaming about it won't help you."

Attracted by the commotion, Solo looked back over his shoulder, frowning slightly. "Let him have it. Your friend's way ahead anyhow. It's not wise to upset a Wookie."

"I can sympathize with that opinion, sir," Threepio countered, "but there is principle at stake here. There are certain standards any sentient creature must hold to. If one compromises them for any reason, including intimidation, then one is abrogating his right to be called intelligent."

"I hope you'll both remember that," Solo advised him, "when Chewbacca is pulling the arms off you and your little friend."

"Besides that, however," Threepio continued without missing a beat, "being greedy or taking advantage of someone in a weakened position is a clear sign of poor sportsmanship."

That elicited a beep of outrage from Artoo, and the two robots were soon engaged in violent electronic argument while Chewbacca continued jabbering at each in turn, occasionally waving at them though the translucent pieces waiting patiently on the board.

Oblivious to the altercation, Luke stood frozen in the middle of the hold. He held an activated lightsaber in position over his head. A low hum came from the ancient instrument while Luke lunged and parried under Ben Kenobi's instructive gaze. As Solo glanced from time to time at Luke's awkward movements, his lean features were sprinkled with smugness.

"No, Luke, your cuts should flow, not be so choppy," Kenobi instructed gently. "Remember, the force is omnipresent. It envelops you as it radiates from you. A Jedi warrior can actually feel the force as a physical thing."

"It is an energy field, then?" Luke inquired.

"It is an energy field and something more," Kenobi went on, almost mystically. "An aura that at once controls and obeys. It is a nothingness that can accomplish miracles." He looked thoughtful for a moment.

"No one, not even the Jedi scientists, were able to truly define the force. Possibly no one ever will. Sometimes there is as much magic as science in the explanations of the force. Yet what is a magician but a practicing theorist? Now, let's try again."

The old man was hefting a silvery globe about the size of a man's fist. It was covered with fine antennae, some as delicate as those of a moth. He flipped it toward Luke and watched as it halted a couple of meters away from the boy's face.

Luke readied himself as the ball circled him slowly, turning to face it as it assumed a new position. Abruptly it executed a lightning-swift lunge, only to freeze about a meter away. Luke failed to succumb to the feint, and the ball soon backed off.

Moving slowly to one side in an effort to get around

the ball's fore sensors, Luke drew the saber back pre-
paratory to striking. As he did so the ball darted in
behind *him*. A thin pencil of red light jumped from
one of the antennae to the back of Luke's thigh,
knocking him to the deck even as he was bringing his
saber around—too late.

Rubbing at his tingling, sleeping leg, Luke tried to
ignore the burst of accusing laughter from Solo.
"Hocus-pocus religions and archaic weapons are no
substitute for a good blaster at your side," the pilot
sneered.

"You don't believe in the force?" asked Luke,
struggling back to his feet. The numbing effect of the
beam wore off quickly.

"I've been from one end of this galaxy to the
other," the pilot boasted, "and I've seen a lot of
strange things. Too many to believe there couldn't be
something like this 'force.' Too many to think that
there could be some such controlling one's actions. *I*
determine my destiny—not some half-mystical energy
field." He gestured toward Kenobi. "I wouldn't follow
him so blindly, if I were you. He's a clever old man,
full of simple tricks and mischief. He might be using
you for his own ends."

Kenobi only smiled gently, then turned back to face
Luke. "I suggest you try it again, Luke," he said
soothingly. "You must try to divorce your actions
from conscious control. Try not to focus on anything
concrete, visually or mentally. You must let your mind
drift, drift; only then can you use the force. You have
to enter a state in which you act on what you sense,
not on what you think beforehand. You must cease
cogitation, relax, stop thinking . . . let yourself drift . . .
free . . . free . . ."

The old man's voice had dropped to a mesmeriz-
ing buzz. As he finished, the chrome bulb darted at
Luke. Dazed by Kenobi's hypnotic tone, Luke didn't
see it charge. It's doubtful he saw much of anything
with clarity. But as the ball neared, he whirled with
amazing speed, the saber arcing up and out in a pe-

culiar fashion. The red beam that the globe emitted was neatly deflected to one side. Its humming stopped and the ball bounced to the deck, all animation gone.

Blinking as if coming awake from a short nap, Luke stared in absolute astonishment at the inert remote.

"You see, you can do it," Kenobi told him. "One can teach only so much. Now you must learn to admit the force when you want it, so that you can learn to control it consciously."

Moving to one side, Kenobi took a large helmet from behind a locker and walked over to Luke. Placing the helmet over his head effectively eliminated the boy's vision.

"I can't see," Luke muttered, turning around and forcing Kenobi to step back out of range of the dangerously wavering saber. "How can I fight?"

"With the force," old Ben explained. "You didn't really 'see' the seeker when it went for your legs the last time, and yet you parried its beam. Try to let that sensation flow within you again."

"I *can't* do it," Luke moaned. "I'll get hit again."

"Not if you let yourself trust *you*," Kenobi insisted, none too convincingly for Luke. "This is the only way to be certain you're relying wholly on the force."

Noticing that the skeptical Corellian had turned to watch, Kenobi hesitated momentarily. It did Luke no good to have the self-assured pilot laugh every time a mistake was made. But coddling the boy would do him no good either, and there was no time for it anyway. Throw him in and hope he floats, Ben instructed himself firmly.

Bending over the chrome globe, he touched a control at its side. Then he tossed it straight up. It arched toward Luke. Braking in midfall, the ball plummeted stonelike toward the deck. Luke swung the saber at it. While it was a commendable try, it wasn't nearly fast enough. Once again the little antenna glowed. This time the crimson needle hit Luke square on the seat of his pants. Though it wasn't an incapacitating blow, it felt like one; and Luke let out a yelp of pain as he spun, trying to strike his invisible tormentor.

"Relax!" old Ben urged him. "Be free. You're trying to use your eyes and ears. Stop predicting and use the rest of your mind."

Suddenly the youth stopped, wavering slightly. The seeker was still behind him. Changing direction again, it made another dive and fired.

Simultaneously the lightsaber jerked around, as accurate as it was awkward in its motion, to deflect the bolt. This time the ball didn't fall motionless to the deck. Instead it backed up three meters and remained there, hovering.

Aware that the drone of the seeker remote no longer assaulted his ears, a cautious Luke peeked out from under the helmet. Sweat and exhaustion competed for space on his face.

"Did I—?"

"I told you you could," Kenobi informed him with pleasure. "Once you start to trust your inner self there'll be no stopping you. I told you there was much of your father in you."

"I'd call it luck," snorted Solo as he concluded his examination of the readouts.

"In my experience there is no such thing as luck, my young friend—only highly favorable adjustments of multiple factors to incline events in one's favor."

"Call it what you like," the Corellian sniffed indifferently, "but good against a mechanical remote is one thing. Good against a living menace is another."

As he was speaking a small telltale light on the far side of the hold had begun flashing. Chewbacca noticed it and called out to him.

Solo glanced at the board, then informed his passengers, "We're coming up on Alderaan. We'll be slowing down shortly and going back under lightspeed. Come on, Chewie."

Rising from the game table, the Wookie followed

his partner toward the cockpit. Luke watched them depart, but his mind wasn't on their imminent arrival at Alderaan. It was burning with something else, something that seemed to grow and mature at the back of his brain as he dwelt on it.

"You know," he murmured, "I did feel something. I could almost 'see' the outlines of the remote." He gestured at the hovering device behind him.

Kenobi's voice when he replied was solemn. "Luke, you've taken the first step into a larger universe."

Dozens of humming, buzzing instruments lent the freighter's cockpit the air of a busy hive. Solo and Chewbacca had their attention locked on the most vital of those instruments.

"Steady . . . stand by, Chewie." Solo adjusted several manual compensators. "Ready to go sublight . . . ready . . . cut us in, Chewie."

The Wookie turned something on the console before him. At the same time Solo pulled back on a comparatively large lever. Abruptly the long streaks of Doppler-distorted starlight slowed to hyphen shapes, then finally to familiar bolts of fire. A gauge on the console registered zero.

Gigantic chunks of glowing stone appeared out of the nothingness, barely shunted aside by the ship's deflectors. The strain caused the *Millennium Falcon* to begin shuddering violently.

"What the—?" a thoroughly startled Solo muttered. Next to him, Chewbacca offered no comment of his own as he flipped off several controls and activated others. Only the fact that the cautious Solo always emerged from supralight travel with his deflectors up —just in case any of many unfriendly folks might be waiting for him—had saved the freighter from instant destruction.

Luke fought to keep his balance as he made his way into the cockpit. "What's going on?"

"We're back in normal space," Solo informed him, "but we've come out in the middle of the worst asteriod storm I've ever seen. It's not on any of our charts." He peered hard at several indicators. "According to the glactic atlas, our position is correct. Only one thing is missing: Alderaan."

"Missing? But—that's crazy!"

"I won't argue with you," the Corellian replied grimly, "but look for yourself." He gestured out the port. "I've triple-checked the coordinates, and there's nothing wrong with the nav 'puter. We ought to be standing out one planetary diameter from the surface. The planet's glow should be filling the cockpit, but—there's nothing out there. Nothing but debris." He paused. "Judging from the level of wild energy outside and the amount of solid waste, I'd guess that Alderaan's been . . . blown away. Totally."

"Destroyed," Luke whispered, overwhelmed at the specter raised by such an unimaginable disaster. "But —how?"

"The Empire," a voice declared firmly. Ben Kenobi had come in behind Luke, and his attention was held by the emptiness ahead as well as the import behind it.

"No." Solo was shaking his head slowly. In his own way even he was stunned by the enormity of what the old man was suggesting. That a human agency had been responsible for the annihilation of an entire population, of a planet itself . . .

"No . . . the entire Imperial fleet couldn't have done this. It would take a thousand ships massing a lot more firepower than has ever existed."

"I wonder if we should get out of here," Luke was murmuring, trying to see around the rims of the port. "If by some chance it was the Empire . . ."

"I don't know what's happened here," an angry Solo cursed, "but I'll tell you one thing. The Empire isn't—"

Muffled alarms began humming loudly as a synchronous light flashed on the control console. Solo bent to the appropriate instrumentation.

"Another ship," he announced. "Can't judge the type yet."

"A survivor, maybe—someone who might know what happened," Luke ventured hopefully.

Ben Kenobi's next words shattered more than that hope. "That's an Imperial fighter."

Chewbacca suddenly gave an angry bark. A huge flower of destruction blossomed outside the port, battering the freighter violently. A tiny, double-winged ball raced past the cockpit port.

"It followed us!" Luke shouted.

"From Tatooine? It couldn't have," objected a disbelieving Solo. "Not in hyperspace."

Kenobi was studying the configuration the tracking screen displayed. "You're quite right, Han. It's the short-range Tie fighter."

"But where did it come from?" the Corellian wanted to know. "There are no Imperial bases near here. It couldn't have been a Tie job."

"You saw it pass."

"I know. It looked like a Tie fighter—but what about a base?"

"It's leaving in a big hurry," Luke noted, studying the tracker. "No matter where it's going, if it identifies us we're in big trouble."

"Not if I can help it," Solo declared. "Chewie, jam its transmission. Lay in a pursuit course."

"It would be best to let it go," Kenobi ventured thoughtfully. "It's already too far out of range."

"Not for long."

Several minutes followed, during which the cockpit was filled with a tense silence. All eyes were on the tracking screen and viewport.

At first the Imperial fighter tried a complex evasive course, to no avail. The surprisingly maneuverable freighter hung tight on its tail, continuing to make up the distance between them. Seeing that he couldn't shake his pursuers, the fighter pilot had obviously opened up his tiny engine all the way.

Ahead, one of the multitude of stars was becoming steadily brighter. Luke frowned. They were moving fast, but not nearly fast enough for any heavenly object to brighten so rapidly. Something here didn't make sense.

"Impossible for a fighter that small to be this deep in space on its own," Solo observed.

"It must have gotten lost, been part of a convoy or something," Luke hypothesized.

Solo's comment was gleeful. "Well, he won't be around long enough to tell anyone about us. We'll be on top of him in a minute or two."

The star ahead continued to brighten, its glow evidently coming from within. It assumed a circular outline.

"He's heading for that small moon," Luke murmured.

"The Empire must have an outpost there," Solo admitted. "Although, according to the atlas, Alderaan had no moons." He shrugged it off. "Galactic topography was never one of my best subjects. I'm only interested in worlds and moons with customers on them. But I think I can get him before he gets there; he's almost in range."

They drew steadily nearer. Gradually craters and mountains on the moon became visible. Yet there was something extremely odd about them. The craters were far too regular in outline, the mountains far too vertical, canyons and valleys impossibly straight and regularized. Nothing as capricious as volcanic action had formed those features.

"That's no moon," Kenobi breathed softly. "That's a space station."

"But it's too big to be a space station," Solo objected. "The size of it! It can't be artifical—it can't!"

"I have a very strange feeling about this," was Luke's comment.

Abruptly the usually calm Kenobi was shouting. "Turn the ship around! Let's get out of here!"

"Yes, I think you're right, old man. Full reverse, Chewie."

The Wookie started adjusting controls, and the freighter seemed to slow, arcing around in a broad curve. The tiny fighter leaped instantly toward the monstrous station until it was swallowed up by its overpowering bulk.

Chewbacca chattered something at Solo as the ship shook and strained against unseen forces.

"Lock in auxiliary power!" Solo ordered.

Gauges began to whine in protest, and by ones and twos every instrument on the control console sequentially went berserk. Try as he might, Solo couldn't keep the surface of the gargantuan station from looming steadily larger, larger—until it became the heavens.

Luke stared wildly at secondary installations as big as mountains, dish antennae larger than all of Mos Eisley. "Why are we still moving toward it?"

"Too late," Kenobi whispered softly. A glance at Solo confirmed his concern.

"We're caught in a tractor beam—strongest one I ever saw. It's dragging us in," the pilot muttered.

"You mean, there's nothing you can do?" Luke asked, feeling unbelievably helpless.

Solo studied the overloaded sensor readouts and shook his head. "Not against this kind of power. I'm on full power myself, kid, and it's not shifting out of course a fraction of a degree. It's no use. I'm going to have to shut down or we'll melt our engines. But they're not going to suck me up like so much dust without a fight!"

He started to vacate the pilot's chair, but was restrained by an aged yet powerful hand on his shoulder. An expression of concern was on the old man's face—and yet, a suggestion of something somewhat less funereal.

"If it's a fight you cannot win—well, my boy, there are always alternatives to fighting . . ."

The true size of the battle station became apparent as the freighter was pulled closer and closer. Running around the station's equator was an artificial cluster of metal mountains, docking ports stretching beckoning fingers nearly two kilometers above the surface.

Now only a miniscule speck against the gray bulk of the station, the *Millennium Falcon* was sucked toward one of those steel pseudopods and finally swallowed by it. A lake of metal closed off the entryway, and the freighter vanished as if it had never existed.

Vader stared at the motley array of stars displayed on the conference-room map while Tarkin and Admiral Motti conferred nearby. Interestingly, the first use of the most powerful destructive machine ever constructed had seemingly had no influence at all on that map, which in itself represented only a tiny fraction of this section of one modest-sized galaxy.

It would take a microbreakdown of a portion of this map to reveal a slight reduction in spatial mass, caused by the disapearance of Alderaan. Alderaan, with its many cities, farms, factories, and towns—and traitors, Vader reminded himself.

Despite his advances and intricate technological methods of annihilation, the actions of mankind remained unnoticeable to an uncaring, unimaginably vast universe. If Vader's grandest plans ever came to pass, all that would change.

He was well aware that despite all their intelligence and drive, the vastness and wonder were lost on the two men who continued to chatter monkeylike behind him. Tarkin and Motti were talented and ambitious, but they saw things only on the scale of human pettiness. It was a pity, Vader thought, that they did not possess the scope to match their abilities.

Still, neither man was a Dark Lord. As such, little more could be expected of them. These two were useful now, and dangerous, but someday they, like Alderaan, would have to be swept aside. For now he could not afford to ignore them. And while he would have preferred the company of equals, he had to admit reluctantly that at this point, he *had* no equals.

Nonetheless, he turned to them and insinuated himself into their conversation. "The defense systems on

Alderaan, despite the Senator's protestations to the contrary, were as strong as any in the Empire. I should conclude that our demonstration was as impressive as it was thorough."

Tarkin turned to him, nodding. "The Senate is being informed of our action at this very moment. Soon we will be able to announce the extermination of the Alliance itself, as soon as we have dealt with their main military base. Now that their main source of munitions, Alderaan, has been eliminated, the rest of those systems with secessionist inclinations will fall in line quickly enough, you'll see."

Tarkin turned as an Imperial officer entered the chamber. "Yes, what is it, Cass?"

The unlucky officer wore the expression of the mouse chosen to bell the cat. "Governor, the advance scouts have reached and circumnavigated Dantooine. They have found the remains of a rebel base . . . which they estimate has been deserted for some time. Years, possibly. They are proceeding with an extensive survey of the remainder of the system."

Tarkin turned apoplectic, his face darkening to a fine pomegranate fury. "She lied! She lied to us!"

No one could see, but it seemed that Vader must have smiled behind his mask. "Then we are even in the first exchange of 'truths.' I told you she would never betray the rebellion—unless she thought her confession could somehow destroy us in the process."

"Terminate her immediately!" The Governor was barely able to form words.

"Calm yourself, Tarkin," Vader advised him. "You would throw away our only link to the real rebel base so casually? She can still be of value to us."

"*Fagh!* You just said it yourself, Vader: we'll get nothing more out of her. I'll find that hidden fortress if I have to destroy every star system in this sector. I'll—"

A quiet yet demanding beep interrupted him.

"Yes, what is it?" he inquired irritably.

A voice reported over an unseen speaker. "Sirs,

we've captured a small freighter that was entering the remains of Alderaan. A standard check indicates that its markings apparently match that of the ship which blasted its way out of the quarantine at Mos Eisley, Tatooine system, and went hyper before the Imperial blockade craft there could close on it."

Tarkin looked puzzled. "Mos Eisley? Tatooine? What is this? What's this all about, Vader?"

"It means, Tarkin, that the last of our unresolved difficulties is about to be eliminated. Someone apparently received the missing data tapes, learned who transcribed them, and was trying to return them to her. We may be able to facilitate their meeting with the Senator."

Tarkin started to say something, hesitated, then nodded in understanding. "How convenient. I leave this matter in your hands, Vader."

The Dark Lord bowed slightly, a gesture which Tarkin acknowledged with a perfunctory salute. Then he spun and strode from the room, leaving Motti looking from man to man in confusion.

The freighter sat listlessly in the docking hangar of the huge bay. Thirty armed Imperial troopers stood before the lowered main ramp leading into the ship. They snapped to attention when Vader and a Commander approached. Vader halted at the base of the ramp, studying the vessel as an officer and several soldiers came forward.

"There was no reply to our repeated signals, sir, so we activated the ramp from outside. We've made no contact with anyone aboard either by communicator or in person," the officer reported.

"Send your men in," Vader ordered.

Turning, the officer relayed the command to a noncom, who barked orders. A number of the heavily armored soldiers made their way up the ramp and entered the outer hold. They advanced with appreciable caution.

Inside, two men covered a third as he advanced.

Moving in groups of three in this fashion, they rapidly spread through the ship. Corridors rang hollowly under metal-shod feet, and doors slid aside willingly as they were activated.

"Empty," the Sergeant in charge finally declared in surprise. "Check the cockpit."

Several troopers made their way forward and slid the portal aside, only to discover the pilot's chairs as vacant as the rest of the freighter. The controls were deactivated and all systems shut down. Only a single light on the console winked on and off fitfully. The Sergeant moved forward, recognized the source of the light, and activated the appropriate controls. A printout appeared on a nearby screen. He studied it intently, then turned to convey the information to his superior, who was waiting by the main hatch.

That worthy listened carefully before he turned and called down to the Commander and Vader. "There is no one aboard; the ship is completely deserted, sirs. According to the ship's log, her crew abandoned ship immediately after lift-off, then set her on automatics for Alderaan."

"Possibly a decoy," the Commander ventured aloud. "Then they should still be on Tatooine!"

"Possibly," Vader admitted reluctantly.

"Several of the escape pods have been jettisoned," the officer went on.

"Did you find any 'droids on board?" Vader called.

"No, sir—nothing. If there were any, they must have abandoned the ship along with the organic crew."

Vader hesitated before replying. When he did so, uncertainty was evident in his voice. "This doesn't feel right. Send a fully equipped scanning team on board. I want every centimeter of that ship checked out. See to it as soon as possible." With that, he whirled and stalked from the hangar, pursued by the infuriating feeling that he was overlooking something of vital importance.

The rest of the assembled soldiers were dismissed

by the officer. On board the freighter, a last lone figure left off examining the space beneath the cockpit consoles and ran to join his comrades. He was anxious to be off this ghost ship and back in the comfortable surroundings of the barracks. His heavy footsteps echoed through the once more empty freighter.

Below, the muffled sounds of the officer giving final orders faded, leaving the interior in complete quiet. The quivering of a portion of the floor was the only movement on board.

Abruptly the quivering became a sharp, upheaval. Two metal panels popped upward, followed by a pair of tousled heads. Han Solo and Luke looked around quickly, then managed to relax a little when it became clear that the ship was as empty as it sounded.

"Lucky you'd built these compartments," Luke commented.

Solo was not as cheerily confident. "Where did you think I kept smuggled goods—in the main hold? I admit I never expected to smuggle myself in them." He started violently at a sudden sound, but it was only another of the panels shifting aside.

"This is ridiculous. It isn't going to work. Even if I could take off and get past the closed hatch"—he jabbed a thumb upward—"we'd never get past that tractor beam."

Another panel opened, revealing the face of an elderly imp. "You leave that to me."

"I was afraid you'd say something like that," muttered Solo. "You're a damn fool, old man."

Kenobi grinned at him. "What does that say of the man who allows himself to be hired by a fool?"

Solo muttered something under his breath as they pulled themselves clear of the compartments, Chewbacca doing so with a good deal of grunting and twisting.

Two technicians had arrived at the base of the ramp. They reported to the two bored soldiers guarding it.

"The ship's all yours," one of the troopers told them. "If the scanners pick up anything, report it immediately."

The men nodded, then strained to lug their heavy equipment up the ramp. As soon as they disappeared inside, a loud crash was heard. Both guards whirled, then heard a voice call, "Hey, down there, could you give us a hand with this?"

One trooper looked at his companion, who shrugged. They both started up the ramp, muttering at the inefficiency of mere technicians. A second crashing sound reverberated, but now there was no one left to hear it.

But the absence of the two troopers *was* noticed, soon thereafter. A gantry officer passing the window of a small command office near the freighter entrance glanced out, frowning when he saw no sign of the guards. Concerned but not alarmed, he moved to a comlink and spoke into it as he continued to stare at the ship.

"THX-1138, why aren't you at your post? THX-1138, do you copy?"

The speaker gave back only static.

"THX-1138, why don't you reply?" The officer was beginning to panic when an armored figure descended the ramp and waved toward him. Pointing to the portion of his helmet covering his right ear, the figure tapped it to indicate the comlink inside wasn't working.

Shaking his head in disgust, the gantry officer gave his busy aide an annoyed look as he made for the door. "Take over here. We've got another bad transmitter. I'm going to see what I can do. He activated the door, took a step forward as it slid aside—and stumbled backward in a state of shock.

Filling the door completely was a towering hairy form. Chewbacca leaned inward and with a bone-splintering howl flattened the benumbed officer with one swipe of a pan-sized fist.

The aide was already on his feet and reaching for

his sidearm when a narrow energy beam passed completely through him, piercing his heart. Solo flipped up the faceplate of his trooper helmet, then slid it back into place as he followed the Wookie into the room. Kenobi and the 'droids squeezed in behind him, with Luke, also clad in the armor of a luckless Imperial soldier, bringing up the rear.

Luke was looking around nervously as he shut the door behind them. "Between his howling and your blasting everything in sight, it's a wonder the entire station doesn't know we're here."

"Bring 'em on," Solo demanded, unreasonably enthused by their success so far. "I prefer a straight fight to all this sneaking around."

"Maybe you're in a hurry to die," Luke snapped, "but I'm not. All this sneaking around has kept us alive."

The Corellian gave Luke a sour eye but said nothing.

They watched as Kenobi operated an incredibly complex computer console with the ease and confidence of one long accustomed to handling intricate machinery. A screen lit up promptly with a map of sections of the battle station. The old man leaned forward, scrutinizing the display carefully.

Meanwhile, Threepio and Artoo had been going over an equally complicated control panel nearby. Artoo suddenly froze and began whistling wildly at something he had found. Solo and Luke, their momentary disagreement over tactics forgotten, rushed over to where the robots were standing. Chewbacca busied himself hanging the gantry officer up by his toes.

"Plug him in," Kenobi suggested, looking over from his place before the larger readout. "He should be able to draw information from the entire station network. Let's see if he can find out where the tractor-beam power unit is located."

"Why not just disconnect the beam from here, sir?" Luke wanted to know.

It was Solo who replied derisively, "What, and have them lock it right back on us before we can get a ship's length outside the docking bay?"

Luke looked crestfallen. "Oh. I hadn't thought of that."

"We have to break the tractor at its power source in order to execute a clean escape, Luke," old Ben chided gently as Artoo punched a claw arm into the open computer socket he had discovered. Immediately a galaxy of lights came to life on the panel in front of him and the room was filled with the hum of machinery working at high speed.

Several minutes passed while the little 'droid sucked up information like a metal sponge. Then the hum slowed and he turned to beep something back at them.

"He's found it, sir!" Threepio announced excitedly.

"The tractor beam is coupled to the main reactors at seven locations. Most of the pertinent data is restricted, but he'll try to pull the critical information through to the monitor."

Kenobi turned his attention from the larger screen to a small readout near Artoo. Data began to race across it too fast for Luke to see, but apparently Kenobi somehow made something of the schematic blur. "I don't think there's any way you boys can help with this," he told them. "I must go alone."

"That suits me fine," said Solo readily. "I've already done more than I bargained for on this trip. But I think putting that tractor beam out of commission's going to take more than your magic, old man."

Luke wasn't put off so easily. "I want to go with you."

"Don't be impatient, young Luke. This requires skills you haven't yet mastered. Stay and watch over the 'droids and wait for my signal. They must be delivered to the rebel forces or many more worlds will meet the same fate as Alderaan. Trust in the force, Luke—and wait."

With a last look at the flow of information on the

monitor, Kenobi adjusted the lightsaber at his waist. Stepping to the door, he slid it aside, looked once left, once right, and, disappeared down a long, glowing hallway.

As soon as he was gone Chewbacca growled and Solo nodded agreement. "You said it, Chewie!" He turned to Luke. "Where'd you dig up that old fossil?"

"Ben Kenobi—*General* Kenobi—is a great man," Luke protested loftily.

"Great at getting us into trouble," Solo snorted. " 'General,' my afterburners! He's not going to get us out of here."

"You got any better ideas?" Luke shot back challengingly.

"Anything would be better than just waiting here for them to come and pick us up. If we—"

A hysterical whistling and hooting came from the computer console. Luke hurried over to Artoo Detoo. The little 'droid was all but hopping about on stubby legs.

"What now?" Luke asked Threepio.

The taller robot looked puzzled himself. "I'm afraid I don't understand either, sir. He says, 'I found her,' and keeps repeating, 'She's here, she's here!' "

"Who? Who has he found?"

Artoo turned a flat blinking face toward Luke and whistled frantically.

"Princess Leia," Threepio announced after listening carefully. "Senator Organa—they seem to be one and the same. I believe she may be the person in the message he was carrying."

That three-dimensional portrait of indescribable beauty coalesced in Luke's mind again. "The Princess? She's here?"

Attracted by the commotion, Solo wandered over. "Princess? What's going on?"

"Where? Where is she?" Luke demanded breathlessly, ignoring Solo completely.

Artoo whistled on while Threepio translated. "Level

five, detention block AA-23. According to the information, she is scheduled for slow termination."

"No! We've got to do something."

"What are you three blabbering about?" an exasperated Solo demanded.

"She's the one who programmed the message into Artoo Detoo," Luke explained hurriedly, "the one we were trying to deliver to Alderaan. We've got to help her."

"Now, just a minute," Solo cautioned him. "This is going awful fast for me. Don't get any funny ideas. When I said I didn't have any 'better ideas' I meant it. The old man said to wait here. I don't like it, but I'm not going off on some crazy maze through this place."

"But Ben didn't know she was here," Luke half pleaded, half argued. "I'm sure that if he knew he would have changed his plans." Anxiety turned to thoughtfulness. "Now, if we could just figure a way to get into that detention block . . ."

Solo shook his head and stepped back. "Huh-uh— I'm not going into any Imperial detention blocks."

"If we don't do something, they're going to execute her. A minute ago you said you didn't just want to sit here and wait to be captured. Now all you want to do is stay. Which is it, Han?"

The Corellian looked troubled—and confused. "Marching into a detention area's not what I had in mind. We're likely to end up there anyway—why rush it?"

"But they're going to execute her!"

"Better her than me."

"Where's your sense of chivalry, Han?"

Solo considered. "Near as I can recall, I traded it for a ten-carat chrysopaz and three bottles of good brandy about five years ago on Commenor."

"I've seen her," Luke persisted desperately. "She's beautiful."

"So's life."

"She's a rich and powerful Senator," Luke pressed,

hoping an appeal to Solo's baser instincts might be more effective. "If we could save her, the reward could be substantial."

"Uh . . . rich?" Then Solo looked disdainful. "Wait a minute . . . Reward, from whom? From the government on Alderaan?" He made a sweeping gesture toward the hangar and by implication the space where Alderaan had once orbited.

Luke thought furiously. "If she's being held here and is scheduled to be executed, that means she must be dangerous in some way to whoever destroyed Alderaan, to whoever had this station built. You can bet it had something to do with the Empire instituting a reign of full repression.

"I'll tell you who'll pay for her rescue, and for the information she holds. The Senate, the rebel Alliance, and every concern that did business with Alderaan. She could be the sole surviving heir of the off-world wealth of the entire system! The reward could be more wealth than you can imagine."

"I don't know . . . I can imagine quite a bit." He glanced at Chewbacca, who grunted a terse reply. Solo shrugged back at the big Wookie. "All right, we'll give it a try. But you'd better be right about that reward. What's your plan, kid?"

Luke was momentarily taken aback. All his energies up till now had been concentrated on persuading Solo and Chewbacca to aid in a rescue attempt. That accomplished, Luke became aware he had no idea how to proceed. He had grown used to old Ben and Solo giving directions. Now the next move was up to him.

His eyes were caught by several metal circlets dangling from the belt of Solo's armor. "Give me those binders and tell Chewbacca to come over here."

Solo handed Luke the thin but quite unbreakable cuffs and relayed the request to Chewbacca. The Wookie lumbered over and stood waiting next to Luke.

"Now, I'm going to put these on you," Luke began, starting to move behind the Wookie with the cuffs, "and—"

Chewbacca made a sound low in his throat, and Luke jumped in spite of himself. "Now," he began again, "Han is going to put these on you and . . ." He sheepishly handed the binders to Solo, uncomfortably aware of the enormous anthropoid's glowing eyes on him.

Solo sounded amused as he moved forward. "Don't worry, Chewie. I think I know what he has in mind."

The cuffs barely fit around the thick wrists. Despite his partner's seeming confidence in the plan, the Wookie wore a worried, frightened look as the restraints were activated.

"Luke, sir." Luke looked over at Threepio. "Pardon me for asking, but, ah—what should Artoo and I do if someone discovers us here in your absence?"

"Hope they don't have blasters," Solo replied.

Threepio's tone indicated he didn't find the answer humorous. "That isn't very reassuring."

Solo and Luke were too engrossed in their coming expedition to pay much attention to the worried robot. They adjusted their helmets. Then, with Chewbacca wearing a half-real downcast expression, they started off along the corridor where Ben Kenobi had disappeared.

☐ IX

AS they traveled farther and deeper into the bowels of the gigantic station, they found it increasingly difficult to maintain an air of casual indifference. Fortunately, those who might have sensed some nervousness on the part of the two armored troopers would regard it as only natural, considering their huge, dangerous Wookie captive. Chewbacca also made it impossible for the two young men to be as inconspicuous as they would have liked.

The farther they traveled, the heavier the traffic became. Other soldiers, bureaucrats, technicians, and mechanicals bustled around them. Intent on their own assignments, they ignored the trio completely, only a few of the humans sparing the Wookie a curious glance. Chewbacca's morose expression and the seeming confidence of his captors reassured the inquisitive.

Eventually they reached a wide bank of elevators. Luke breathed a sigh of relief. The computer-controlled transport ought to be capable of taking them just about anywhere on the station in response to a verbal command.

There was a nervous second when a minor official raced to get aboard. Solo gestured sharply, and the other, without voicing a protest, shifted to the next elevator tube in line.

Luke studied the operating panel, then tried to sound at once knowledgeable and important as he spoke into the pickup grid. Instead, he sounded nervous and scared, but the elevator was a pure-response mechanism, not programmed to differentiate the appropriateness of emotions conveyed vocally. So the door slid shut and they were on their way. After what felt like hours but was in reality only minutes, the door opened and they stepped out into the security area.

It had been Luke's hope they would discover something like the old-fashioned barred cells of the kind used on Tatooine in towns like Mos Eisley. Instead, they saw only narrow ramps bordering a bottomless ventilation shaft. These walkways, several levels of them, ran parallel to smooth curving walls which held faceless detention cells. Alert-looking guards and energy gates seemed to be everywhere they looked.

Uncomfortably aware that the longer they stood frozen in place, the sooner someone was bound to come over and ask unanswerable questions, Luke searched frantically for a course of action.

"This isn't going to work," Solo whispered, leaning toward him.

"Why didn't you say so before?" a frustrated, frightened Luke shot back.

"I think I did. I—"

"Shsshl!"

Solo shut up as Luke's worst fears were realized. A tall, grim-looking officer approached them. He frowned as he examined the silent Chewbacca.

"Where are you two going with this—thing?"

Chewbacca snarled at the remark, and Solo quieted him with a hasty jab in the ribs. A panicky Luke found himself replying almost instinctively. "Prisoner transfer from block TS-138."

The officer looked puzzled. "I wasn't notified. I'll have to clear it."

Turning, the man walked to a small console nearby and began entering his request. Luke and Han hurriedly surveyed the situation, their gaze traveling from alarms, energy gates, and remote photosensors to the three other guards stationed in the area.

Solo nodded to Luke as he unfastened Chewbacca's cuffs. Then he whispered something to the Wookie. An ear-splitting howl shook the corridor as Chewbacca threw up both hands, grabbing Solo's rifle from him.

"Look out!" a seemingly terrified Solo shouted. "It's loose. It'll rip us all apart!"

Both he and Luke had darted clear of the rampaging Wookie, pulled out their pistols, and were blasting away at him. Their reaction was excellent, their enthusiasm undeniable, and their aim execrable. Not a single shot came close to the dodging Wookie. Instead, they blasted automatic cameras, energy-rate controls, and the three dumbfounded guards.

At this point it occurred to the officer in charge that the abominable aim of the two soldiers was a bit too selectively efficient. He was preparing to jab the general alarm when a burst from Luke's pistol caught him in the midsection and he fell without a word to the gray deck.

Solo rushed to the open comlink speaker, which was screeching anxious questions about what was going on. Apparently there were audio as well as visual links between this detention station and elsewhere.

Ignoring the barrage of alternate threats and queries, he checked the readout set in the panel nearby. "We've got to find out which cell this Princess of yours is in. There must be a dozen levels and— Here it is. Cell 2187. Go on—Chewie and I'll hold them here."

Luke nodded once and was racing down the narrow walkway.

After gesturing for the Wookie to take up a position where he could cover the elevators, Solo took a deep breath and responded to the unceasing calls from the comlink.

"Everything's under control," he said into the pick-up, sounding reasonably official. "Situation normal."

"It didn't sound like that," a voice snapped back in a no-nonsense tone. "What happened?"

"Uh, well, one of the guards experienced a weapon malfunction," Solo stammered, his temporary official-ese lapsing into nervousness. "No problem now—we're all fine, thanks. How about you?"

"We're sending a squad up," the voice announced suddenly.

Han could almost smell the suspicion at the other end. What to say? He spoke more eloquently with the business end of a pistol.

"Negative—negative. We have an energy leak. Give us a few minutes to lock it down. Large leak—very dangerous."

"Weapon malfunction, energy leak . . . Who is this? What's your operating—?"

Pointing his pistol at the panels, Solo blew the instrumentation to silent scraps. "It was a dumb conversation anyway," he murmured. Turning, he shouted down the corridor, "Hurry it up, Luke! We're going to have company."

Luke heard, but he was absorbed in running from one cell to the next and studying the numbers glowing above each doorway. The cell 2187, it appeared, did not exist. But it did, and he found it just as he was about to give up and try the next level down.

For a long moment he examined the featureless convex metal wall. Turning his pistol to maximum and hoping it wouldn't melt in his hand before it broke through, he opened fire on the door. When the weapon became too hot to hold, he tossed it from hand to hand. As he did so the smoke had time to clear, and he saw with some surprise that the door had been blown away.

Peering through the smoke with an uncomprehending look on her face was the young woman whose portrait Artoo Detoo had projected in a garage on Tatooine several centuries ago, or so it seemed.

She was even more beautiful than her image, Luke decided, staring dazedly at her. "You're even—more beautiful—than I—"

Her look of confusion and uncertainty was replaced by first puzzlement and then impatience. "Aren't you a little short for a storm trooper?" she finally commented.

"What? Oh—the uniform." He removed the helmet, regaining a little composure at the same time. "I've come to rescue you. I'm Luke Skywalker."

"I beg your pardon?" she said politely.

"I said, I've come to rescue you. Ben Kenobi is with me. We've got your two 'droids—"

The uncertainty was instantly replaced by hope at the mention of the oldster's name. "Ben Kenobi!" She looked around Luke, ignoring him as she searched for the Jedi. "Where is he? Obi-wan!"

Governor Tarkin watched as Darth Vader paced rapidly back and forth in the otherwise empty conference room. Finally the Dark Lord paused, glancing around as though a great bell only he could hear had rung somewhere close by.

"He is here," Vader stated unemotionally.

Tarkin looked startled. "Obi-wan Kenobi! That's impossible. What makes you think so?"

"A stirring in the force, of a kind I've felt only in the presence of my old master. It is unmistakable."

"Surely—surely he must be dead by now."

Vader hesitated, his assurance suddenly gone. "Perhaps . . . It is gone now. It was only a brief sensation."

"The Jedi are extinct," declared Tarkin positively. "Their fire was quenched decades ago. You, my friend, are all that's left of their ways."

A comlink buzzed softly for attention. "Yes?" Tarkin acknowledged.

"We have an emergency alert in detention block AA-23."

"The Princess!" Tarkin yelped, jumping to his feet. Vader whirled, trying to stare through the walls.

"I knew it—Obi-wan *is* here. I knew I could not mistake a stirring in the force of such power."

"Put all sections on alert," Tarkin ordered through the comlink. Then he turned to stare at Vader. "If you're right, he must not be allowed to escape."

"Escape may not be Obi-wan Kenobi's intention," Vader replied, struggling to control his emotions. "He is the last of the Jedi—and the greatest. The danger he presents to us must not be underestimated—yet only I can deal with him." His head snapped around to stare fixedly at Tarkin. "Alone."

Luke and Leia had started back up the corridor when a series of blinding explosions ripped the walkway ahead of them. Several troopers had tried coming through the elevator, only to be crisped one after another by Chewbacca. Disdaining the elevators, they had blasted a gaping hole through a wall. The opening was too large for Solo and the Wookie to cover completely. In twos and threes, the Imperials were working their way into the detention block.

Retreating down the walkway, Han and Chewbacca encountered Luke and the Princess. "We can't go back that way!" Solo told them, his face flushed with excitement and worry.

"No, it looks like you've managed to cut off our only escape route," Leia agreed readily. "This is a detention area, you know. They don't build them with multiple exits."

Breathing heavily, Solo turned to look her up and down. "Begging your forgiveness, Your Highness," he said sarcastically, "but maybe you'd prefer it back in your cell?" She looked away, her face impassive.

"There's got to be another way out," Luke muttered, pulling a small transmitter unit from his belt and carefully adjusting the frequency: *"See Threepio . . . See Threepio!"*

A familiar voice responded with gratifying speed. "Yes, sir?"

"We've been cut off here. Are there *any* other ways out of the detention area—anything at all?"

Static crackled over the tiny grid as Solo and Chewbacca kept the Imperial troops bottled up at the other end of the walkway.

"What was that . . . ? I didn't copy."

Back in the gantry office Artoo Detoo beeped and whistled frantically as Threepio adjusted controls, fighting to clear the awkward transmission. "I said, all systems have been alerted to your presence, sir. The main entry seems to be the only way in or out of the cell block." He pressed instruments, and the view on the nearby readouts changed steadily. "All other information on your section is restricted."

Someone began banging on the locked door to the office—evenly at first and then, when no response was forthcoming from within, more insistently.

"Oh, no!" Threepio groaned.

The smoke in the cell corridor was now so intense that it was difficult for Solo and Chewbacca to pick their targets. That was fortunate inasmuch as they were now badly outnumbered and the smoke confused the Imperials' fire with equal thoroughness.

Every so often one of the soldiers would attempt to move closer, only to stand exposed as he penetrated the smoke. Under the accurate fire of the two smugglers, he would rapidly join the accumulating mass of motionless figures on the rampway flooring.

Energy bolts continued to ricochet wildly through the block as Luke moved close to Solo.

"There isn't any other way out." he yelled over the deafening roar of concentrated fire.

"Well, they're closing in on us. What do we do now?"

"This is some rescue," an irritated voice complained from behind them. Both men turned to see a thoroughly disgusted Princess eyeing them with regal disapproval. "When you came in here, didn't you have a plan for getting out?"

Solo nodded toward Luke. "He's the brains, sweetheart."

Luke managed an embarrassed grin and shrugged helplessly. He turned to help return fire, but before he could do so, the Princess had snatched the pistol from his hand.

"Hey!"

Luke stared as she moved along the wall, finally locating a small grate nearby. She pointed the pistol at it and fired.

Solo gazed at her in disbelief. "What do you think you're doing?"

"It looks like it's up to me to save our skins. Get into that garbage chute, flyboy!"

While the others looked on in amazement, she jumped feet first into the opening and disappeared. Chewbacca rumbled threateningly, but Solo slowly shook his head.

"No, Chewie, I don't want you to rip her apart. I'm not sure about her yet. Either I'm beginning to like her, or I'm going to kill her myself." The Wookie snorted something else, and Solo yelled back at him, "Go on in, you furry oaf! I don't care what you smell. This is no time to go dainty on me."

Shoving the reluctant Wookie toward the tiny opening, Solo helped jam the massive bulk through. As soon as he disappeared, the Corellian followed him in. Luke fired off a last series of blasts, more in the hope of creating a covering smoke than hitting anything, slid into the chute, and was gone.

Not wanting to incur further losses in such a confined space, the pursuing soldiers had momentarily halted to await the arrival of reinforcements and heavier weapons. Besides, they had their quarry trapped, and despite their dedication, none of them were anxious to die needlessly.

The chamber Luke tumbled into was dimly lit. Not that the light was needed to discern its contents. He smelled the decay long before he was dumped into it. Unadorned except for the concealed illuminants, the garbage room was at least a quarter full of slimy muck, much of which had already achieved a state of decomposition sufficient to wrinkle Luke's nose.

Solo was stumbling around the edge of the room, slipping and sinking up to his knees in the uncertain footing in an attempt to locate an exit. All he found was a small, thick hatchway which he grunted and heaved to pry open. The hatchcover refused to budge.

"The garbage chute was a wonderful idea," he told the Princess sardonically, wiping the sweat from his forehead. "What an incredible smell you've discovered. Unfortunately, we can't ride out of here on a drifting odor, and there doesn't seem to be any other exit. Unless I can get this hatch open."

Stepping back, he pulled his pistol and fired at the cover. The bolt promptly went howling around the room as everyone sought cover in the garbage. A last glance and the bolt detonated almost on top of them.

Looking less dignified by the moment, Leia was the first to emerge from the pungent cover. "Put that thing away," she told Solo grimly, "or you're going to get us all killed."

"Yes, Your Worship," Solo muttered in snide supplication. He made no move to reholster his weapon as he glanced back up toward the open chute above. "It won't take long for them to figure out what happened to us. We had things well under control—until you led us down here."

"Sure you did," she shot back, brushing refuse from her hair and shoulders. "Oh, well, it could be worse. . . ."

As if in reply, a piercing, horrible moaning filled the room. It seemed to come from somewhere beneath them. Chewbacca let out a terrified yowl of his own and tried to flatten himself against a wall. Luke drew his own pistol and peered hard at various clumps of debris, but saw nothing.

"What was that?" Solo asked.

"I'm not too sure." Luke suddenly jumped, looking down and behind him. "Something just moved past me, I think. Watch out—"

With shocking suddenness Luke disappeared straight down into the garbage.

"It's got Luke!" the Princess shouted. "It took him under!" Solo looked around frantically for something to shoot at.

As abruptly as he had vanished, Luke reappeared —and so did part of something else. A thick whitish tentacle was wrapped tight around his throat.

"Shoot it, kill it!" Luke screamed.

"Shoot it! I can't even see it," Solo protested.

Once again Luke was sucked under by whatever that gruesome appendage was attached to. Solo stared helplessly around the multicolored surface.

There was a distant rumble of heavy machinery, and two opposing walls of the chamber moved inward several centimeters. The rumble ceased and then it was quiet again. Luke appeared unexpectedly close to Solo, scrabbling his way clear of the suffocating mess and rubbing at the welt on his neck.

"What happened to it?" Leia wondered, eyeing the quiescent garbage warily.

Luke looked genuinely puzzled. "I don't know. It had me—and then I was free. It just let me go and disappeared. Maybe I didn't smell bad enough for it."

"I've got a very bad feeling about this," Solo murmured.

Again the distant rumble filled the room; again the walls began their inward march. Only this time neither sound nor movement showed any sign of stopping.

"Don't just stand there gaping at each other!" the Princess urged them. "Try to brace them with something."

Even with the thick poles and old metal beams Chewbacca could handle, they were unable to find anything capable of slowing the walls' advance. It seemed as if the stronger the object was that they placed against the walls, the easier it was snapped.

Luke pulled out his comlink, simultaneously trying to talk and will the walls to retreat. "Threepio . . . come in, Threepio!" A decent pause produced no response, causing Luke to look worriedly at his companions.

"I don't know why he doesn't answer." He tried again. "See Threepio, come in. Do you read?"

"See Threepio," the muted voice continued to call, "come in, See Threepio." It was Luke's voice and it issued softly in between buzzings from the small hand comlink resting on the deserted computer console. Save for the intermittent pleading, the gantry office was silent.

A tremendous explosion drowned out the muffled pleadings. It blew the office door clean across the room, sending metal fragments flying in all directions. Several of them struck the comlink, sending it flying to the floor and cutting off Luke's voice in mid-transmission.

In the wake of the minor cataclysm four armed and ready troopers entered through the blown portal. Initial study indicated the office was deserted—until a dim, frightened voice was heard coming from one of the tall supply cabinets near the back of the room.

"Help, help! Let us out!"

Several of the troopers bent to inspect the immobile bodies of the gantry officer and his aide while others opened the noisy cabinet. Two robots, one tall and humanoid, the other purely mechanical and three-legged, stepped out into the office. The taller one gave the impression of being half unbalanced with fear.

"They're madmen, I tell you, madmen!" He gestured urgently toward the doorway. "I think they said something about heading for the prison level. They just left. If you hurry, you might catch them. That way, that way!"

Two of the troopers inside joined those waiting in the hallway in hustling off down the corridor. That left two guards to watch over the office. They totally ignored the robots as they discussed what might have taken place.

"All the excitement has overloaded the circuitry in my companion here," Threepio explained carefully. "If you don't mind, I'd like to take him down to Maintenance."

"Hmmm?" One of the guards looked up indifferently and nodded to the robot. Threepio and Artoo hurried out the door without looking back. As they departed it occurred to the guard that the taller of the two 'droids was of a type he had never seen before. He shrugged. That was not surprising on a station of this size.

"That was too close," Threepio muttered as they scurried down an empty corridor. "Now we'll have to find another information-control console and plug you back in, or everything is lost."

The garbage chamber grew remorselessly smaller, the smoothly fitting metal walls moving toward one another with stolid precision. Larger pieces of refuse performed a concerto of snapping and popping that was rising toward a final shuddering crescendo.

Chewbacca whined pitifully as he fought with all his incredible strength and weight to hold back one of the walls, looking like a hirsute Tantalus approaching his final summit.

"One thing's for sure," Solo noted unhappily. "We're all going to be much thinner. This could prove popular for slimming. The only trouble is its permanence."

Luke paused for breath, shaking the innocent comlink angrily. "What could have happened to Threepio?"

"Try the hatch again," advised Leia. "It's our only hope."

Solo shielded his eyes and did so. The ineffectual blast echoed mockingly through the narrowing chamber.

The service bay was unoccupied, everyone apparently having been drawn away by the commotion elsewhere. After a cautious survey of the room Threepio beckoned for Artoo to follow. Together they commenced a hurried search of the many service panels. Artoo let out a beep, and Threepio rushed to him. He waited impatiently as the smaller unit plugged the receptive arm carefully into the open socket.

A superfast flurry of electronics spewed in undisciplined fashion from the grid of the little 'droid. Threepio made cautioning motions.

"Wait a minute, slow down!" The sounds dropped to a crawl. "That's better. They're where? They what? Oh, no! They'll only come out of there as a liquid!"

Less than a meter of life was left to the trapped occupants of the garbage room. Leia and Solo had been forced to turn sideways, had ended up facing each other. For the first time the haughtiness was gone from the Princess's face. Reaching out, she took Solo's hand, clutching it convulsively as she felt the first touch of the closing walls.

Luke had fallen and was lying on his side, fighting to keep his head above the rising ooze. He nearly choked on a mouthful of compressed sludge when his comlink began buzzing for attention.

"Threepio!"

"Are you there, sir?" the 'droid replied. "We've had some minor problems. You would not believe—"

"Shut up, Threepio!" Luke screamed into the unit. "And shut down all the refuse units on the detention level or immediately below it. Do you copy? Shut down the refuse—"

Moments later Threepio grabbed at his head in pain as a terrific screeching and yelling sounded over the comlink.

"No, shut them *all* down!" he implored Artoo. "Hurry! Oh, listen to them—they're dying, Artoo! I curse this metal body of mine. I was not fast enough. It was my fault. My poor master—all of them . . . no, no, *no!*"

The screaming and yelling, however, continued far beyond what seemed like a reasonable interval. In fact, they were shouts of relief. The chamber walls had reversed direction automatically with Artoo's shutdown and were moving apart again.

"Artoo, Threepio," Luke hollered into the comlink, "it's all right, we're all right! Do you read me? We're okay—you did just fine."

Brushing distastefully at the clinging slime, he made his way as rapidly as possible toward the hatch-cover. Bending, he scraped accumulated detritus away, noting the number thus revealed.

"Open the pressure-maintenance hatch on unit 366-117891."

"Yes, sir," came Threepio's acknowledgment.

They may have been the happiest words Luke had ever heard.

☐ X

LINED with power cables and circuitry conduits that rose from the depths and vanished into the heavens, the service trench appeared to be hundreds of kilometers deep. The narrow catwalk running around one side looked like a starched thread glued on a glowing ocean. It was barely wide enough for one man to traverse.

One man edged his way along that treacherous walkway now, his gaze intent on something ahead of him instead of the awesome metal abyss below. The clacking sounds of enormous switching devices resounded like captive leviathans in the vast open space, tireless and never sleeping.

Two thick cables joined beneath an overlay panel. It was locked, but after careful inspection of sides, top and bottom, Ben Kenobi pressed the panel cover in a particular fashion causing it to spring aside. A blinking computer terminal was revealed beneath.

With equal care he performed several adjustments to the terminal. His actions were rewarded when several indicator lights on the board changed from red to blue.

Without warning, a secondary door close behind him opened. Hurriedly reclosing the panel cover, the old man slipped deeper into the shadows. A detachment of troopers had appeared in the portal, and the officer in charge moved to within a couple of meters of the motionless, hidden figure.

"Secure this area until the alert has been cancelled."

As they began to disperse, Kenobi became one with the dark.

Chewbacca grunted and wheezed, and barely succeeded in forcing his thick torso through the hatch-

154

way opening with Luke's and Solo's help. That accomplished, Luke turned to take stock of their surroundings.

The hallway they had emerged into showed dust on the floor. It gave the impression of not having been used since the station had been built. Probably it was only a repair access corridor. He had no idea where they were.

Something hit the wall behind them with a massive *thunk,* and Luke yelled for everyone to watch out as a long, gelatinous limb worked its way through the hatch and flailed hopefully about in the open corridor. Solo aimed his pistol at it as Leia tried to slip past the half-paralyzed Chewbacca.

"Somebody get this big hairy walking carpet out of my way." Suddenly she noticed what Solo was preparing to do. "No, wait! It'll be heard!"

Solo ignored her and fired at the hatchway. The burst of energy was rewarded with a distant roar as an avalanche of weakened wall and beaming all but buried the creature in the chamber beyond.

Magnified by the narrow corridor, the sounds continued to roll and echo for long minutes afterward. Luke shook his head in disgust, realizing that someone like Solo who spoke with the mouth of a gun might not always act sensibly. Until now he had sort of looked up to the Corellian. But the senseless gesture of firing at the hatchway brought them, for the first time in Luke's mind, to the same level.

The Princess's actions were more surprising than Solo's, however. "Listen," she began, staring up at him, "I don't know where you came from, but I'm grateful." Almost as an afterthought she glanced back at Luke, adding, "To the both of you." Her attention turned back to Solo. "But from now on you do as I tell you."

Solo gaped at her. This time the smug smile wouldn't come. "Look, Your Holiness," he was finally able to stammer, "let's get something straight. I take orders only from one person—me."

"It's a wonder you're still alive," she shot back smoothly. A quick look down the corridor and she had started determinedly off in the other direction.

Solo looked at Luke, started to say something, then hesitated and simply shook his head slowly. "No reward is worth this. I don't know if there's enough credit in the universe to pay for putting up with *her* ... Hey, slow down!"

Leia had started around a bend in the corridor, and they ran swiftly to catch up with her.

The half dozen troops milling around the entrance to the power trench were more interested in discussing the peculiar disturbance in the detention block than in paying attention to their present boring duty. So engrossed were they in speculation as to the cause of the trouble that they failed to notice the fey wraith behind them. It moved from shadow to shadow like a night-stalking ferret, freezing when one of the troopers seemed to turn slightly in its direction, moving on again as if walking on air.

Several minutes later one of the troopers frowned inside his armor, turning to where he thought he had sensed a movement near the opening to the main passageway. There was nothing but an undefinable something which the ghost-like Kenobi had left behind. Acutely uncomfortable yet understandably unwilling to confess to hallucinations, the trooper turned back to the more prosaic conversation of his fellows.

Someone finally discovered the two unconscious guards tied in the service lockers on board the captured freighter. Both men remained comatose despite all efforts to revive them.

Under the direction of several bickering officers, troopers carried their two armorless comrades down the ramp and toward the nearest hospital bay. On the way they passed two forms hidden by a small opened service panel. Threepio and Artoo went unnoticed, despite their proximity to the hangar.

As soon as the troops had passed, Artoo finished removing a socket cover and hurriedly shoved his sensor arm into the opening. Lights commenced a wild flashing on his face and smoke started issuing from several seams in the small 'droid before a frantic Threepio could pull the arm free.

Immediately the smoke vanished, the undisciplined blinking faded to normalcy. Artoo emitted a few wilted beeps, successfully giving the impression of a human who had expected a glass of mild wine and instead unwittingly downed several gulps of something 180 proof.

"Well, next time watch where you stick your sensors," Threepio chastised his companion. "You could have fried your insides." He eyed the socket. "That's a power outlet, stupid, not an information terminal."

Artoo whistled a mournful apology. Together they hunted for the proper outlet.

Luke, Solo, Chewbacca, and the Princess reached the end of an empty hallway. It dead-ended before a large window which overlooked a hangar, giving them a sweeping, tantalizing view of the freighter just below.

Pulling out his comlink and looking around them with increasing nervousness, Luke spoke into the pickup. "See Threepio . . . do you copy?"

There was a threatening pause, then, "I read you, sir. We had to abandon the region around the office."

"Are you both safe?"

"For the moment, though I'm not sanguine about my old age. We're in the main hangar, across from the ship."

Luke looked toward the bay window in surprise. "I can't see you across the bay—we must be right above you. Stand by. We'll join you as soon as we can." He clicked off, smiling suddenly at Threepio's reference to his "old age." Sometimes the tall 'droid was more human than people.

"Wonder if the old man was able to knock out the

tractor," Solo was muttering as he surveyed the scene below. A dozen or so troopers were moving in and out of the freighter.

"Getting back to the ship's going to be like flying through the five Fire Rings of Fornax."

Leia Organa turned long enough to glance in surprise from the ship to Solo. "You came here in that wreck? You're braver than I thought."

At once praised and insulted, Solo wasn't sure how to react. He settled for giving her a dirty look as they started back down the hallway, Chewbacca bringing up the rear.

Rounding a corner, the three humans came to an abrupt halt. So did the twenty Imperial troopers marching toward them. Reacting naturally—which is to say, without thinking—Solo drew his pistol and charged the platoon, yelling and howling in several languages at the top of his lungs.

Startled by the totally unexpected assault and wrongly assuming their attacker knew what he was doing, the troopers started to back away. Several wild shots from the Corellian's pistol initiated complete panic. Ranks and composure shattered, the troopers broke and fled down the passage.

Drunk with his own prowess, Solo continued the chase, turning to shout back at Luke, "Get to the ship. I'll take care of these!"

"Are you out of your mind?" Luke yelled at him. "Where do you think you're going?"

But Solo had already rounded a far bend in the corridor and didn't hear. Not that it would have made any difference.

Upset at his partner's disappearance, Chewbacca let out a thunderous if unsettled howl and rushed down the hallway after him. That left Luke and Leia standing alone in the empty corridor.

"Maybe I was too hard on your friend," she confessed reluctantly. "He certainly is courageous."

"He certainly is an idiot!" a furious Luke countered tightly. "I don't know what good it'll do us if he gets himself killed." Muted alarms suddenly sounded from the bay below and behind them.

"That's done it," Luke growled disgustedly. "Let's go." Together they started off in search of a way down to a hangar-deck level.

Solo continued his rout of all opposition, running at top speed down the long hallway, yelling and brandishing his pistol. Occasionally he got off a shot whose effect was more valuable psychologically than tactically.

Half the troops had already scattered down various subpassages and corridors. The ten troopers he continued to harry still raced headlong away from him, returning his fire only indifferently. Then they came up against a dead end, which forced them to turn and confront their opponents.

Seeing that the ten had halted, Solo likewise slowed. Gradually he came to a complete stop. Corellian and Imperials regarded one another silently. Several of the troopers were staring, not at Han but past him.

It suddenly occurred to Solo that he was very much alone, and the same thought was beginning to seep into the minds of the guards he was confronting. Embarrassment gave way rapidly to anger. Rifles and pistols started to come up. Solo took a step backward, fired one shot, then turned and ran like hell.

Chewbacca heard the whistle and crump of energy weapons firing as he lumbered lightly down the corridor. There was something odd about them, though: they sounded as if they were coming closer instead of moving away.

He was debating what to do when Solo came tearing around a corner and nearly ran him down. Seeing ten troopers in pursuit, the Wookie decided to reserve his questions for a less confused moment. He turned and followed Solo back up the hallway.

Luke grabbed the Princess and pulled her back into a recess. She was about to retort angrily at his brusqueness when the sound of marching feet caused her to shrink back into the darkness with him.

A squad of soldiers hurried past, responding to the alarms that continued to ring steadily. Luke looked out at the retreating backs and tried to catch his breath. "Our only hope of reaching the ship is from the other side of the hangar. They already know some-one's here." He started back down the corridor, mo-tioning for her to follow.

Two guards appeared at the far end of the passage-way, paused, and pointed directly at them. Turning, Luke and Leia began running back the way they had come. A larger squad of troopers rounded the far bend and came racing toward them.

Blocked ahead and behind, they hunted frantically for another way out. Then Leia spotted the cramped subhallway and gestured to it.

Luke fired at the nearest of their pursuers and joined her in running down the narrow passage. It looked like a minor service corridor. Behind them, pursuit sounded deafeningly loud in the confining space. But at least it minimized the amount of fire the troops could concentrate on them.

A thick hatchway appeared ahead. The lighting beyond turned dimmer, raising Luke's hopes. If they could lock the hatch even for a few moments and lose themselves somewhere beyond, they might have a chance of shaking their immediate tormentors.

But the hatch stayed open, showing no inclination to close automatically. Luke was about to let out a shout of triumph when the ground suddenly vanished ahead of him. His toes hanging over nothingness, he flailed to regain his balance, succeeding just in time to nearly go over the edge of the retracted catwalk anyway as the Princess plowed into him from behind.

The catwalk had been reduced to a stub protruding into empty air. A cool draft caressed Luke's face as he studied walls that soared to unseen heights overhead and plunged to fathomless depths below. The service shaft was employed in circulating and recycling the atmosphere of the station.

At the moment Luke was too frightened and concerned to be angry with the Princess for nearly sending them over the edge. Besides, other dangers competed for his attention. A burst of energy exploded above their heads, sending metal slivers flying.

"I think we made a wrong turn," he murmured, firing back at the advancing troops and illuminating the narrow corridor behind them with destruction.

An open hatchway showed on the other side of the chasm. It might as well have been a light-year away. Hunting along the rim of the doorway, Leia located a switch and hit it quickly. The hatch door behind them slid shut with a resounding boom. At least that cut off fire from the rapidly nearing soldiers. It also left the two fugitives balanced precariously on a small section of catwalk barely a meter square. If the remaining section were to unexpectedly withdraw into the wall, they would see more of the battle station's interior than either wished.

Gesturing for the Princess to move aside as much as possible, Luke shielded his eyes and aimed the pistol at the hatch controls. A brief burst of energy melted them flush with the wall, insuring that no one could open it easily from the other side. Then he turned his attention to the vast cavity blocking their path to the opposite portal. It beckoned invitingly—a small yellow rectangle of freedom.

Only the soft rush of air from below sounded until Luke commenetd, "This is a shield-rated door, but it won't hold them back very long."

"We've got to get across there somehow," Leia agreed, once more examining the metal bordering the sealed doorway. "Find the controls for extending the bridge."

Some desperate searching produced nothing, while an ominous pounding and hissing sounded from behind the frozen door. A small spot of white appeared in the center of the metal, then began to spread and smoke.

"They're coming through!" Luke groaned.

The Princess turned carefully to stare across the gap. "This must be a single-unit bridge, with the controls only on the other side."

Reaching up to the point at the panel holding the unreachable controls, Luke's hand caught on something at his waist. A frustrated glance downward revealed the cause—and engendered a bit of practical insanity.

The cable coiled tightly in small loops was thin and fragile seeming, but it was general military-issue line and would have supported Chewbacca's weight easily. It certainly ought to hold Leia and himself. Pulling the cable free of the waist catch, he gauged its length, matching it against the width of the abyss. This should span the distance with plenty to spare.

"What now?" the Princess inquired curiously.

Luke didn't reply. Instead, he removed a small but heavy power unit from the utility belt of his armor and tied one end of the cable around it. Making sure the wrapping was secure, he stepped as close to the edge of their uncertain perch as he dared.

Whirling the weighted end of the cord in increasing circles, he let it arc across the gorge. It struck an outcropping of cylindrical conduits on the other side and fell downward. With forced patience he pulled the loose line back in, then recoiled it for another try.

Once again the weighted end orbited in ever greater circles, and again he flung it across the gap. He could feel the rising heat behind him as he let it go, heat from the melting metal doorway.

This time the heavy end looped around an outcropping of pipes above, wrapped itself several times around, and slipped, battery end down, into a crack between them. Leaning backward, he tugged and pulled on the cable, pulling on it at the same time as he tried

to rest all his weight on it. The cable showed no sign
of parting.

Wrapping the other end of the line several times
around his waist and right arm, he reached out and
pulled the Princess close to him with the other. The
hatch door behind them was now a molten white,
and liquid metal was running steadily from its borders.

Something warm and pleasant touched Luke's lips,
alerting every nerve in his body. He looked down in
shock at the Princess, his mouth still tingling from
the kiss.

"Just for luck," she murmured with a slight, almost
embarrassed smile as she put her arms around him.
"We're going to need it."

Gripping the thin cable as tightly as possible with
his left hand, Luke put his right over it, took a
deep breath, and jumped out into air. If he had mis-
calculated the degree of arc in their swing, they
would miss the open hatch and slam into the metal
wall to either side or below it. If that happened he
doubted he could maintain his grip on the rope.

The heart-halting transit was accomplished in less
time than that thought. In a moment Luke was on the
other side, scrambling on his knees to make sure they
didn't fall back into the pit. Leia released her hold on
him with admirable timing. She rolled forward and
into the open hatchway, climbing gracefully to her
feet as Luke fought to untangle himself from the cable.

A distant whine became a loud hiss, then a groan as
the hatch door on the other side gave way. It collapsed inward and tumbled into the depths. If it
touched bottom, Luke didn't hear it.

A few bolts struck the wall nearby. Luke turned
his own weapon on the unsuccessful troopers and
returned the fire even as Leia was pulling him into
the passageway behind.

Once clear of the door he hit the activating switch.
It shut tightly behind them. They would have several
minutes, at least, without having to worry about being
shot in the back. On the other hand, Luke didn't have

the slightest idea where they were, and he found himself wondering what had happened to Han and Chewbacca.

Solo and his Wookie partner had succeeded in shaking a portion of their pusuers. But it seemed that whenever they slipped free of several soldiers, more appeared to take their place. No question about it: the word was out on them.

Ahead, a series of shield doors was beginning to close.

"Hurry, Chewie!" Solo urged.

Chewbacca grunted once, breathing like an overused engine. Despite his immense strength, the Wookie was not built for long-distance sprinting. Only his enormous stride had enabled him to keep pace with the lithe Corellian. Chewbacca left a couple of hairs in one of the doors, but both slipped inside just before the five layers slammed shut.

"That ought to hold them for a while," Solo crowed with delight. The Wookie growled something at him, but his partner fairly fluoresced with confidence.

"Of course I can find the ship from here—Corellians can't get lost." There came another growl, slightly accusing this time. Solo shrugged. "Tocneppil doesn't count; he wasn't a Corellian. Besides, I was drunk."

Ben Kenobi ducked into the shadows of a narrow passageway, seeming to become part of the metal itself as a large cluster of troopers hurried past him. Pausing to make certain they had all passed, he checked the corridor ahead before starting down it. But he failed to see the dark silhouette which eclipsed the light far behind him.

Kenobi had avoided one patrol after another, slowly working his way back toward the docking bay holding the freighter. Just another two turns and he should be at the hangar. What he would do then would be determined by how inconspicuous his charges had been.

That young Luke, the adventurous Corellian and his partner, and the two robots had been involved in something other than quiet napping he already suspected from the amount of activity he had observed while making his way back from the power trench. Surely all those troops hadn't been out hunting just for him!

But something else was troubling them, judging from the references he had overheard concerning a certain important prisoner, now escaped. That discovery had puzzled him, until he considered the restless natures of both Luke and Han Solo. Undoubtedly they were involved in some fashion.

Ben sensed something directly ahead and slowed cautiously. It had a most familiar feel to it, a half-remembered mental odor he could not quite place.

Then the figure stepped out in front of him, blocking his entry to the hangar not five meters away. The outline and size of the figure completed the momentary puzzle. It was the maturity of the mind he had sensed that had temporarily confused him. His hand moved naturally to the hilt of his deactivated saber.

"I have been waiting a long time, Obi-wan Kenobi," Darth Vader intoned solemnly. "We meet again at last. The circle has been completed." Kenobi sensed satisfaction beneath the hideous mask. "The presence I sensed earlier could only have been you."

Kenobi regarded the great form blocking his retreat and nodded slowly. He gave the impression of being more curious than impressed. "You still have much to learn."

"You were once my teacher," Vader admitted, "and I learned much from you. But the time of learning has long passed, and I am the master now."

The logic that had constituted the missing link in his brilliant pupil remained as absent as before. There would be no reasoning here, Kenobi knew. Igniting his saber, he assumed the pose of warrior-ready, a movement accomplished with the ease and elegance of a dancer.

Rather roughly, Vader imitated the movement. Several minutes followed without motion as the two men remained staring at each other, as if waiting for some proper, as yet unspoken signal.

Kenobi blinked once, shook his head, and tried to clear his eyes, which had begun to water slightly. Sweat beaded up on his forehead, and his eyelids fluttered again.

"Your powers are weak," Vader noted emotionlessly. "Old man, you should never have come back. It will make your end less peaceful than you might have wished."

"You sense only a part of the force, Darth," Kenobi murmured with the assurance of one to whom death is merely another sensation, like sleeping or making love or touching a candle. "As always, you perceive its reality as little as a utensil perceives the taste of food."

Executing a move of incredible swiftness for one so old, Kenobi lunged at the massive shape. Vader blocked the stab with equal speed, riposting with a counterslash that Kenobi barely parried. Another parry and Kenobi countered again, using this opportunity to move around the towering Dark Lord.

They continued to trade blows, with the old man now backing toward the hangar. Once, his saber and Vader's locked, the interaction of the two energy fields producing a violent sparking and flashing. A low buzzing sound rose from the straining power units as each saber sought to override the other.

Threepio peeked around the entrance to the docking bay, worriedly counting the number of troopers milling around the deserted freighter.

"Where could they be? Oh, oh."

He ducked back out of sight just as one of the guards glanced in his direction. A second, more cautious appraisal was more rewarding. It revealed Han

Solo and Chewbacca hugging the wall of another tunnel on the far side of the bay.

Solo also was nonplussed at the number of guards. He muttered, "Didn't we just leave this party?"

Chewbacca grunted, and both turned, only to relax and lower their weapons at the sight of Luke and the Princess.

"What kept you?" Solo quipped mirthlessly.

"We ran into," Leia explained, panting heavily, "some old friends."

Luke was staring at the freighter. "Is the ship all right?"

"Seems okay," was Solo's analysis. "It doesn't look like they've removed anything or disturbed her engines. The problem's going to be getting to it."

Leia suddenly pointed to one of the opposite tunnels. "Look!"

Illuminated by the flare from contacting energy fields, Ben Kenobi and Darth Vader were backing toward the bay. The fight attracted the attention of others beside the Senator. Every one of the guards moved in for a better view of the Olympian conflict.

"Now's our chance," Solo observed, starting forward.

All seven of the troopers guarding the ship broke and rushed toward the combatants, going to the Dark Lord's aid. Threepio barely ducked aside as they ran past him. Turning back into the alcove, he yelled to his companion.

"Unplug yourself, Artoo. We're leaving." As soon as the Artoo unit slipped his sensor arm free of the socket, the two 'droids began to slowly edge out into the open bay.

Kenobi heard the approaching commotion and spared a glance back into the hangar. The squad of troopers bearing down on him was enough to show that he was trapped.

Vader took immediate advantage of the momentary distraction to bring his saber over and down. Kenobi somehow managed to deflect the sweeping blow, at once parrying and turning a complete circle.

"You still have your skill, but your power fades. Prepare to meet the force, Obi-wan."

Kenobi gauged the shrinking distance between the oncoming troops and himself, then turned a pitying gaze on Vader. "This is a fight you cannot win, Darth. Your power has matured since I taught you, but I too have grown much since our parting. If my blade finds its mark, you will cease to exist. But if you cut me down, I will only become more powerful. Heed my words."

"Your philosophies no longer confuse me, old man," Vader growled contemptuously. "I am the master now."

Once again he lunged forward, feinting, and then slashing in a deadly downward arc with the saber. It struck home, cutting the old man cleanly in half. There was a brief flash as Kenobi's cloak fluttered to the deck in two neat sections.

But Ben Kenobi was not in it. Wary of some tricks, Vader poked at the empty cloak sections with the saber. There was no sign of the old man. He had vanished as though he had never existed.

The guards slowed their approach and joined Vader in examining the place where Kenobi had stood seconds before. Several of them muttered, and even the awesome presence of the Sith Lord couldn't keep a few of them from feeling a little afraid.

Once the guards had turned and dashed for the far tunnel, Solo and the others started for the starship —until Luke saw Kenobi cut in two. Instantly he shifted direction and was moving toward the guards.

"Ben!" he screamed, firing wildly toward the troops. Solo cursed, but turned to fire in support of Luke.

One of the energy bolts struck the safety release on the tunnel blast door. The emergency hold broken, the heavy door fairly exploded downward. Both the guards and Vader leaped clear—the guards into the bay and Vader backward, to the opposite side of the door.

Solo had turned and started for the entrance to the ship, but he paused as he saw Luke running toward the guards.

"It's too late!" Leia yelled at him. "It's over."

"No!" Luke half shouted, half sobbed.

A familiar, yet different voice rang in his ears—Ben's voice. "Luke . . . listen!" was all it said.

Bewildered, Luke turned to hunt for the source of that admonition. He only saw Leia beckoning to him as she followed Artoo and Threepio up the ramp.

"Come on! There's no time."

Hesitating, his mind still on that imagined voice (or was it imagined?), a confused Luke took aim and felled several soldiers before he, too, whirled and retreated into the freighter.

☐ XI

DAZED, Luke staggered toward the front of the ship. He barely noticed the sound of energy bolts, too weak to penetrate the ship's deflectors, exploding harmlessly outside. His own safety was currently of little concern to him. With misty eyes he stared as Chewbacca and Solo adjusted controls.

"I hope that old man managed to knock out that tractor beam," the Corellian was saying, "or this is going to be a very short ride."

Ignoring him, Luke returned to the hold area and slumped into a seat, his head falling into his hands. Leia Organa regarded him quietly for a while, then removed her cloak. Moving to him, she placed it gently around his shoulders.

"There wasn't anything you could have done," she whispered comfortingly. "It was all over in an instant."

"I can't believe he's gone," came Luke's reply, his voice a ghost of a whisper. "I can't."

Solo shifted a lever, staring nervously ahead. But the massive bay door was constructed to respond to the approach of any vessel. The safety feature now served to facilitate their escape as the freighter slipped quickly past the still-opening door and out into free space.

"Nothing," Solo sighed, studying several readouts with profound satisfaction. "Not so much as an erg of come-hither. He did it, all right."

Chewbacca rumbled something, and the pilot's attention shifted to another series of gauges. "Right, Chewie. I forget, for a moment, that there are other ways of persuading us to return." His teeth flashed in a grin of determination. "But the only way they'll get us back in that traveling tomb is in pieces. Take over."

Whirling, he ran out of the cockpit. "Come with me, kid," he shouted at Luke as he entered the hold. "We're not out of this yet."

Luke didn't respond, didn't move, and Leia turned an angry face to Solo. "Leave him alone. Can't you see what the old man meant to him?"

An explosion jarred the ship, nearly tumbling Solo to the deck.

"So what? The old man gave himself to give us a chance to get away. You want to waste that, Luke? You want Kenobi to have wasted himself?"

Luke's head came up and he stared with vacant eyes at the Corellian. No, not quite vacant . . . There was something too old and unpleasant shining blindly in the back of them. Without a word, he threw off the cloak and joined Solo.

Giving him a reassuring smile, Solo gestured down a narrow accessway. Luke looked in the indicted direction, smiled grimly, and rushed down it as Solo started down the opposing passage.

Luke found himself in a large rotating bubble protruding from the side of the ship. A long, wicked-

looking tube whose purpose was instantly apparent
projected from the apex of the transparent hemis-
phere. Luke settled himself into the seat and commenced a rapid study of the controls. Activator here,
firing grip here . . . He had fired such weapons a
thousand times before—in his dreams.

Forward, Chewbacca and Leia were searching the
speckled pit outside for the attacking fighters represented by firepricks on several screens. Chewbacca
suddenly growled throatily and pulled back on several
controls as Leia let out a yelp.

"Here they come."

The starfield wheeled around Luke as an Imperial
Tie fighter raced toward him and then swung overhead to vanish into the distance. Within the tiny cockpit its pilot frowned as the supposedly battered
freighter darted out of range. Adjusting his own con-
rols, he swung up and over in a high arc intended to
take him on a fresh intercept course with the escaping ship.

Solo fired at another fighter, and its pilot nearly
slammed his engine through its mountings as he
fought to avoid the powerful energy bolts. As he did
so, his hurried maneuver brought him under and
around to the other side of the freighter. Even as he
was lowering the glare reflector over his eyes, Luke
opened up on the racing fighter.

Chewbacca was alternating his attention between
the instruments and the tracking screens, while Leia
strained to separate distant stars from nearby assassins.

Two fighters dove simultaneously on the twisting,
spiraling freighter, trying to line their weapons on
the unexpectedly flexible craft. Solo fired at the de-
scending globes, and Luke followed with his own
weapon a second later. Both fired on the starship and
then shot past.

"They're coming in too fast," Luke yelled into his
comlink.

Another enemy bolt struck the freighter forward

and was barely shunted aside by its deflectors. The cockpit shuddered violently, and gauges whined in protest at the quantity of energy they were being asked to monitor and compensate for.

Chewbacca muttered something to Leia, and she murmured a soft reply as if she almost understood.

Another fighter unloosed a barrage on the freighter, only this time the bolt pierced an overloaded screen and actually struck the side of the ship. Though partially deflected, it still carried enough power to blow out a large control panel in the main passageway, sending a rain of sparks and smoke in all directions. Artoo Detoo started stolidly toward the miniature inferno as the ship lurched crazily, throwing the less stable Threepio into a cabinet full of component chips.

A warning light began to wink for attention in the cockpit. Chewbacca muttered to Leia, who stared at him worriedly and wished for the gift of Wookie-gab.

Then a fighter floated down on the damaged freighter, right into Luke's sights. His mouth moving silently, Luke fired at it. The incredibly agile little vessel darted out of his range, but as it passed beneath them Solo picked it up instantly, and commenced a steady following fire. Without warning the fighter erupted in an incredible flash of multicolored light, throwing a billion bits of superheated metal to every section of the cosmos.

Solo whirled and gave Luke a victory wave, which the younger man gleefully returned. Then they turned back to their weapons as yet another fighter stormed over the freighter's hull, firing at its transmitter dish.

In the middle of the main passageway, angry flames raged around a stubby cylindrical shape. A fine white powdery spray issued from Artoo Detoo's head. Wherever it touched, the fire retreated sharply.

Luke tried to relax, to become a part of the weapon. Almost without being aware of it, he was firing at a retreating Imperial. When he blinked, it was to see the flaming fragments of the enemy craft forming a perfect ball of light outside the turret. It was his turn to spin and flash the Corellian a grin of triumph.

In the cockpit, Leia paid close attention to scattered readouts as well as searching the sky for additional ships. She directed her voice toward an open mike.

"There are still two more of them out there. Looks like we've lost the lateral monitors and the starboard deflector shield."

"Don't worry," Solo told her, with as much hope as confidence, "she'll hold together." He gave the walls a pleading stare. "You hear me, ship? Hold together! Chewie, try to keep them on our port side. If we—"

He was forced to break off as a Tie fighter seemed to materialize out of nowhere, energy bolts reaching out from it toward him. Its companion craft came up on the freighter's other side and Luke found himself firing steadily at it, ignoring the immensely powerful energy it threw at him. At the last possible instant before it passed out of range, he swung the weapon's nozzle minutely, his finger tightening convulsively on the fire control. The Imperial fighter turned into a rapidly expanding cloud of phosphorescing dust. The other fighter apparently considered the shrunken odds, turned, and retreated at top speed.

"We've made it!" Leia shouted, turning to give the startled Wookie an unexpected hug. He growled at her—very softly.

Darth Vader strode into the control room where Governor Tarkin stood staring at a huge, brilliantly lit screen. It displayed a sea of stars, but it was not the spectacular view which absorbed the Governor's thoughts at the moment. He barely glanced around as Vader entered.

"Are they away?" the Dark Lord demanded.

"They've just completed the jump to hyperspace. No doubt they are at this very moment congratulating themselves on their daring and success." Now Tarkin turned to face Vader, a hint of warning in his tone.

"I'm taking an awful chance, on your insistence, Vader. This had better work. Are you certain the homing beacon is secure aboard their ship?"

Vader exuded confidence beneath the reflective black mask. "There is nothing to fear. This will be a day long remembered. It already has been witness to the final extinction of the Jedi. Soon it will see the end of the Alliance and the rebellion."

Solo switched places with Chewbacca, the Wookie grateful for the opportunity to relinquish the controls. As the Corellian moved aft to check the extent of the damage, a determined-looking Leia passed him in the corridor.

"What do you think, sweetheart?" Solo inquired, well pleased with himself. "Not a bad bit of rescuing. You know, sometimes I amaze even myself."

"That doesn't sound too hard," she admitted readily. "The important thing is not my safety, but the fact that the information in the R-2 'droid is still intact."

"What's that 'droid carrying that's so important, anyway?"

Leia considered the blazing starfield forward. "Complete technical schematics of the battle station. I only hope that when the data is analyzed, a weakness can be found. Until then, until the station itself is destroyed, we must go on. This war isn't over yet."

"It is for me," objected the pilot. "I'm not on this mission for your revolution. Economics interest me, not politics. There's business to be done under any government. And I'm not doing it for you, Princess. I expect to be well paid for risking my ship and my hide."

"You needn't worry about your reward," she assured him sadly, turning to leave. "If money is what you love . . . that's what you will receive."

On leaving the cockpit she saw Luke coming forward, and she spoke softly to him in passing. "Your friend is indeed a mercenary. I wonder if he really cares about anything—or anybody."

Luke stared after her until she disappeared into the main hold area, then whispered, *"I do . . . I care."* Then he moved into the cockpit and sat in the seat Chewbacca had just vacated.

"What do you think of her, Han?"

Solo didn't hesitate. "I try not to."

Luke probably hadn't intended his response to be audible, but Solo overheard his murmur of "Good" none the less.

"Still," Solo ventured thoughtfully, "she's got a lot of spirit to go with her sass. I don't know, do you think it's possible for a Princess and a guy like me . . . ?"

"No," Luke cut him off sharply. He turned and looked away.

Solo smiled at the younger man's jealousy, uncertain in his own mind whether he had added the comment to bait his naive friend—or because it was the truth.

Yavin was not a habitable world. The huge gas giant was patterned with pastel high-altitude cloud formations. Here and there the softly lambent atmosphere was molded by cyclonic storms composed of six-hundred-kilometer-per-hour winds which boiled rolling gases up from the Yavinesque troposphere. It was a world of lingering beauty and quick death for any who might try to penetrate to its comparatively small core of frozen liquids.

Several of the giant planet's numerous moons, however, were planet-sized themselves, and of these, three could support humanoid life. Particularly inviting was the satellite designated by the system's discoverers as number four. It shone like an emerald in Yavin's necklace of moons, rich with plant and animal life. But it was not listed among those worlds supporting human settlement. Yavin was located too far from the settled regions of the galaxy.

Perhaps the latter reason, or both, or a combination of causes still unknown had been responsible for whatever race had once risen from satellite four's jungles, only to disappear quietly long before the first human explorer set foot on the tiny world. Little was known of them save that they left a number of impressive monuments, and that they were one of the many races which had aspired to the stars only to have their desperate reach fall short.

Now all that remained were the mounds and foliage-clad clumps formed by jungle-covered buildings. But though they had sunk back into the dust, their artifacts and their world continued to serve an important purpose.

Strange cries and barely perceptible moans sounded from every tree and copse; hoots and growls and strange mutterings issued from creatures content to remain concealed in the dense undergrowth. Whenever dawn broke over moon the fourth, heralding one of its long days, an especially feral chorus of shrieks and weirdly modulated screams would resound through the thick mist.

Even stranger sounds surged continually from one particular place. Here lay the most impressive of those edifices which a vanished race had raised toward the heavens. It was a temple, a roughly pyramidal structure so colossal that it seemed impossible it could have been built without the aid of modern gravitonic construction techniques. Yet all evidence pointed only to simple machines, hand technology—and, perhaps, devices alien and long lost.

While the science of this moon's inhabitants had led them to a dead end as far as offworld travel was concerned, they had produced several discoveries which in certain ways surpassed similar Imperial accomplishments—one of which involved a still unexplained method of cutting and transporting gargantuan blocks of stone from the crust of the moon.

From these monstrous blocks of solid rock, the massive temple had been constructed. The jungle had scaled even its soaring crest, clothing it in rich green and brown. Only near its base, in the temple front, did the jungle slide away completely, to reveal a long, dark entrance cut by its builders and enlarged to suit the needs of the structure's present occupants.

A tiny machine, its smooth metal sides and silvery hue incongruous amidst the all-pervasive green, appeared in the forest. It hummed like a fat, swollen beetle as it conveyed its cluster of passengers toward the open temple base. Crossing a considerable clearing, it was soon swallowed up by the dark maw in the front of the massive structure, leaving the jungle once more in the paws and claws of invisible squallers and screechers.

The original builders would never have recognized the interior of their temple. Seamed metal had replaced rock, and poured paneling did service for chamber division in place of wood. Nor would they have been able to see the buried layers excavated into the rock below, layers which contained hangar upon hangar linked by powerful elevators.

A landspeeder came to a gradual stop within the temple, whose first level was the uppermost of those ship-filled hangars. Its engine died obediently as the vehicle settled to the ground. A noisy cluster of humans waiting nearby ceased their conversation and rushed toward the craft.

Fortunately Leia Organa quickly emerged from the speeder, or the man who reached it first might have pulled her bodily from it, so great was his delight at the sight of her. He settled for giving her a smothering hug as his companion called their own greetings.

"You're safe! We'd feared you'd been killed." Abruptly he composed himself, stepped away from her, and executed a formal bow. "When we heard about Alderaan, we were afraid that you were . . . lost along with the rest of the population."

"All that is past history, Commander Willard," she said. "We have a future to live for. Alderaan and its people are gone." Her voice turned bitter cold, frightening in so delicate-looking a person. "We must see that such does not happen again.

"We don't have time for our sorrows, Commander," she continued briskly. "The battle station has surely tracked us here."

Solo started to protest, but she shut him up with logic and a stern look.

"That's the only explanation for the ease of our escape. They sent only four Tie fighters after us. They could as easily have launched a hundred."

Solo had no reply for that, but continued to fume silently. Then Leia gestured at Artoo Detoo.

"You must use the information locked in this R-2 'droid to form a plan of attack. It's our only hope. The station itself is more powerful than anyone suspected." Her voice dropped. "If the data does not yield a weakness, there will be no stopping them."

Luke was then treated to a sight unique in his experience, unique in most men's. Several rebel technicians walked up to Artoo Detoo, positioned themselves around him, and gently hoisted him in their arms. This was the first, and probably the last time he would ever see a robot being carried respectfully by men.

Theoretically, no weapon could penetrate the exceptionally dense stone of the ancient temple, but Luke had seen the shattered remains of Alderaan and knew that for those in the incredible battle station the entire moon would present simply another abstract problem in mass-energy conversion.

Little Artoo Detoo rested comfortably in a place of honor, his body radiating computer and data-bank hookups like a metal hairdo. On an array of screens and readouts nearby the technical information stored on the submicroscopic record tape within the robot's brain was being played out. Hours of it—diagrams, charts, statistics.

First the rush of material was slowed and digested by more sophisticated computer minds. Then the most critical information was turned over to human analysts for detailed evaluation.

All the while See Threepio stood close to Artoo, marveling at how so much complex data could be stored in the mind of so simple a 'droid.

The central briefing room was located deep within the bowels of the temple. The long, low-ceiling auditorium was dominated by a raised dais and huge electronic display screen at its far end. Pilots, navigators, and a sprinkling of Artoo units filled the seats. Impatient, and feeling very out of place, Han Solo and Chewbacca stood as far away from the stage, with its assemblage of officers and Senators, as possible. Solo scanned the crowd, searching for Luke. Despite some common sense entreaties, the crazy kid had gone and joined the regular pilots. He didn't see Luke, but he recognized the Princess as she talked somberly with some bemedaled oldster.

When a tall, dignified gentleman with too many deaths on his soul moved to stand by the far side of the screen, Solo turned his attention to him, as did everyone else in the room. As soon as an expectant silence had gripped the crowd, General Jan Dodonna adjusted the tiny mike on his chest and indicated the small group seated close to him.

"You all know these people," he intoned with quiet power. "They are the Senators and Generals whose worlds have given us support, whether open or covert. They have come to be with us in what may well prove to be the decisive moment." He let his gaze touch many in the crowd, and none who were so favored remained unmoved.

"The Imperial battle station you now all have heard of is approaching from the far side of Yavin and its sun. That gives us a little extra time, but it must be stopped—once and for all—before it can reach this moon, before it can bring its weaponry to bear on us as it did on Alderaan." A murmur ran through the crowd at the mention of that world, so callously obliterated.

"The station," Dodonna went on, "is heavily shielded and mounts   more firepower than half the Imperial fleet. But its defenses were designed to fend off large-scale, capital ship assaults. A small, one- or two-man fighter should be able to slip through its defensive screens."

A slim, supple man who resembled an older version of Han Solo rose. Dodonna acknowledged his presence. "What is it, Red Leader?"

The man gestured toward the display screen, which showed a computer portrait of the battle station. "Pardon me for asking, sir, but what good are our *snub* fighters going to be against *that?*"

Dodonna considered. "Well, the Empire doesn't think a one-man fighter is any threat to anything except another small ship, like a Tie fighter, or they would have provided tighter screens. Apparently they're convinced that their defensive weaponry can fend off any light attacks.

"But an analysis of the plans provided by Princess Leia has revealed what we think is a weakness in the station's design. A big ship couldn't get near it, but an X- or Y-wing fighter might.

"It's a small thermal exhaust port. Its size belies its importance, as it appears to be an unshielded shaft that runs directly into the main reactor system powering the station. Since this serves as an emergency outlet for waste heat in the event of reactor overproduction, its usefulness would be eliminated by particle shielding. A direct hit would initiate a chain reaction that will destroy the station."

Mutterings of disbelief ran through the room. The more experienced the pilot, the greater his expressed disbelief.

"I didn't say your approach would be easy," Dodonna admonished them. He gestured at the screen. "You must maneuver straight in down this shaft, level off in the trench, and skim the surface to—this point. The target is only two meters across. It will take a precise hit at exactly ninety degrees to reach the reactor systematization. And only a direct hit will start the complete reaction.

"I said the port wasn't particle-shielded. However, it is completely ray-shielded. That means no energy beams. You'll have to use proton torpedoes."

A few of the pilots laughed humorlessly. One of them was a teenaged fighter jockey seated next to Luke who bore the unlikely name of Wedge Antilles. Artoo Detoo was there also, seated next to another Artoo unit who emitted a long whistle of hopelessness.

"A two-meter target at maximum speed—with a torpedo, yet," Antilles snorted. "That's impossible even for the computer."

"But it's not impossible," protested Luke. "I used to bulls-eye womp-rats in my T-16 back home. They're not much bigger than two meters."

"Is that so?" the rakishly uniformed youth noted derisively. "Tell me, when you were going after your particular varmint, were there a thousand other, what did you call it, 'womp-rats' armed with power rifles firing up at you?" He shook his head sadly.

"With all that firepower on the station directed at us, this will take a little more than barnyard marksmanship, believe me."

As if to confirm Antilles' pessimism, Dodonna indicated a string of lights on the ever-changing schematic. "Take special note of these emplacements. There's a heavy concentration of firepower on the latitudinal axes, was well as several dense circumpolar clusters.

"Also, their field generators will probably create a lot of distortion, especially in and around the trench. I figure that maneuverability in that sector will be less than point three." This produced more murmurs and a few groans from the assembly.

"Remember," the General went on, "you must achieve a direct hit. Yellow squadron will cover for

Red on the first run. Green will cover Blue on the second. Any questions?"

A muted buzz filled the room. One man stood, lean and handsome—too much so, it seemed, to be ready to throw away his life for something as abstract as freedom.

"What if both runs fail, What happens after that?"

Dodonna smiled tightly. "There won't be any 'after that.' " The man nodded slowly, understandingly, and sat down. "Anyone else?" Silence now, pregnant with expectation.

"Then man your ships, and may the force be with you."

Like oil draining from a shallow pot, the seated ranks of men, women, and machines rose and flowed toward the exits.

Elevators hummed busily, lifting more and more deadly shapes from buried depths to the staging area in the primary temple hangar as Luke, Threepio, and Artoo Detoo walked toward the hangar entrance.

Neither the bustling flight crews, nor the pilots performing final checkouts, nor the massive sparks thrown off as power couplings were disconnected captured Luke's attention at the moment. Instead, it was held by the activity of two far more familiar figures.

Solo and Chewbacca were loading a pile of small strongboxes onto an armored landspeeder. They were completely absorbed with this activity, ignoring the preparations going all around them.

Solo glanced up briefly as Luke and the robots approached, then returned to his loading. Luke simply watched sadly, conflicting emotions careening confusedly off one another inside him. Solo was cocky, reckless, intolerant, and smug. He was also brave to a fault, instructive, and unfailingly cheery. The combination made for a confusing friend—but a friend nonetheless.

"You got your reward," Luke finally observed, indicating the boxes. Solo nodded once. "And you're leaving, then?"

"That's right, kid. I've got some old debts to pay off, and even if I didn't, I don't think I'd be fool enough to stick around here." He eyed Luke appraisingly. "You're pretty good in a scrap, kid. Why don't you come with us? I could use you."

The mercenary gleam in Solo's eyes only made Luke mad. "Why don't you look around you and see something besides yourself for a change? You know what's going to happen here, what they're up against. They could use a good pilot. But you're turning your back on them."

Solo didn't appear upset at Luke's tirade. "What good's a reward if you're not around to spend it? Attacking that battle station isn't my idea of courage— more like suicide."

"Yeah . . . Take care of yourself, Han," Luke said quietly, turning to leave. "But I guess that's what you're best at, isn't it?" He started back into the hangar depths, flanked by the two 'droids.

Solo stared after him, hesitated, then called, "Hey, Luke . . . may the force be with you." Luke looked back to see Solo wink at him. He waved—sort of. Then he was swallowed up by moving mechanics and machinery.

Solo returned to his work, lifted a box—and stopped, to see Chewbacca gazing fixedly at him.

"What are you staring at, gruesome? I know what I'm doing. Get back to work!"

Slowly, still eyeing his partner, the Wookie returned to the task of loading the heavy crates.

Sorrowful thoughts of Solo vanished when Luke saw the petite, slim figure standing by his ship—the ship he had been granted.

"Are you sure this is what you want?" Princess Leia asked him. "It could be a deadly reward."

Luke's eyes were filled with the sleek, venomous metal shape. "More than anything."

"Then what's wrong?"

Luke looked back at her and shrugged. "It's Han. I thought he'd change his mind. I thought he'd join us."

"A man must follow his own path," she told him, sounding now like a Senator. "No one can choose it for him. Han Solo's priorities differ from ours. I wish it were otherwise, but I can't find it in my heart to condemn him." She stood on tiptoes, gave him a quick, almost embarrassed kiss, and turned to go. "May the force be with you."

"I only wish," Luke murmured to himself as he started back to his ship, "Ben were here."

So intent was he on thoughts of Kenobi, the Princess, and Han that he didn't notice the larger figure which tightly locked on to his arm. He turned, his initial anger gone instantly in astonishment as he recognized the figure.

"Luke!" the slightly older man exclaimed. "I don't believe it! How'd you get here? Are you going out with us?"

"Biggs!" Luke embraced his friend warmly. "Of course I'll be up there with you." His smile faded slightly. "I haven't got a choice, anymore." Then he brightened again. "Listen, have I got some stories to tell you . . ."

The steady whooping and laughing the two made was in marked contrast to the solemnity with which the other men and women in the hangar went about their business. The commotion attracted the attention of an older, war-worn man known to the younger pilots only as Blue Leader.

His face wrinkled with curiosity as he approached the two younger men. It was a face scorched by the same fire that flickered in his eyes, a blaze kindled not by revolutionary fervor but by years of living through and witnessing far too much injustice. Behind that fatherly visage a raging demon fought to escape. Soon, very soon, he would be free to let it loose.

Now he was interested in these two young men,

who in a few hours were likely to be particles of frozen meat floating about Yavin. One of them he recognized.

"Aren't you Luke Skywalker? Have you been checked out on the Incom T-65?"

"Sir," Biggs put in before his friend could reply, "Luke's the best bush pilot in the outer-rim territories."

The older man patted Luke reassuringly on the back as they studied his waiting ship. "Something to be proud of. I've got over a thousand hours in an Incom skyhopper myself." He paused a moment before going on.

"I met your father once when I was just a boy, Luke. He was a great pilot. You'll do all right out there. If you've got half your father's skill, you'll do a damn sight better than all right."

"Thank you, sir. I'll try."

"There's not much difference control-wise between an X-wing T-65," Blue Leader went on, "and a skyhopper." His smile turned ferocious. "Except the payload's of a somewhat different nature."

He left them and hurried toward his own ship. Luke had a hundred questions to ask him, and no time for even one.

"I've got to get aboard my own boat, Luke. Listen, you'll tell me your stories when we come back. All right?"

"All right. I told you I'd make it here someday, Biggs."

"You did." His friend was moving toward a cluster of waiting fighters, adjusting his flight suit. "It's going to be like old times, Luke. We're a couple of shooting stars that can't be stopped!"

Luke laughed. They used to reassure themselves with that cry when they piloted starships of sandhills and dead logs behind the flaking, pitted buildings of Anchorhead . . . years and years ago.

Once more Luke turned toward his ship, admiring its deadly lines. Despite Blue Leader's assurances, he had to admit that it didn't look much like an Incom skyhopper. Artoo Detoo was being snuggled into the R-2 socket behind the fighter cockpit. A forlorn metal figure stood below, watching the operation and shuffling nervously about.

"Hold on tight," See Threepio was cautioning the smaller robot. "You've got to come back. If you don't come back, who am I going to have to yell at?" For Threepio, that query amounted to an overwhelming outburst of emotion.

Artoo beeped confidently down at his friend, however, as Luke mounted the cockpit entry. Farther down the hangar he saw Blue Leader already set in his acceleration chair and signaling to his ground crew. Another roar was added to the monstrous din filling the hangar area as ship after ship activated its engines. In that enclosed rectangle of temple the steady thunder was overpowering.

Slipping into the cockpit seat, Luke studied the various controls as ground attendants began wiring him via cords and umbilicals into the ship. His confidence increased steadily. The instrumentation was necessarily simplified and, as Blue Leader had indicated, much like his old skyhopper.

Something patted his helmet, and he glanced left to see the crew chief leaning close. He had to shout to be heard above the deafening howl of multiple engines. "That R-2 unit of yours seems a little beat-up. Do you want a new one?"

Luke glanced briefly back at the secured 'droid before replying. Artoo Detoo looked like a permanent piece of the fighter.

"Not on your life. That 'droid and I have been through a lot together. All secure, Artoo?" The 'droid replied with a reassuring beep.

As the ground chief jumped clear, Luke commenced the final checkout of all instruments. It slowly occurred to him what he and the others were about to attempt. Not that his personal feelings could override his decision to join them. He was no longer an individual, functioning solely to satisfy his personal needs. Something now bound him to every other man and woman in this hangar.

All around him, scattered scenes of good-bye were taking place—some serious, some kidding, all with the true emotion of the moment masked by efficiency. Luke turned away from where one pilot left a mechanic, possibly a sister or wife, or just a friend, with a sharp, passionate kiss.

He wondered how many of them had their own little debts to settle with the Empire. Something crackled in his helmet. In response, he touched a small lever. The ship began to roll forward, slowly but with increasing speed, toward the gaping mouth of the temple.

☐ XII

LEIA Organa sat silently before the huge display screen on which Yavin and its moons were displayed. A large red dot moved steadily toward the fourth of those satellites. Dodonna and several other field commanders of the Alliance stood behind her, their eyes also intent on the screen. Tiny green flecks began to appear around the fourth moon, to coalesce into small clouds like hovering emerald gnats.

Dodonna put a hand on her shoulder. It was comforting. "The red represents the progress of the Imperial battle station as it moves deeper into Yavin's system."

"Our ships are all away," a Commander behind him declared.

A single man stood alone in the cylindrical hold, secured to the top of a rapier-thin tower. Staring through fixed-mount electrobinoculars, he was the sole visible representative of the vast technology buried in the green purgatory below.

Muted cries, moans, and primeval gurglings drifted up to him from the highest treetops. Some were frightening, some less so, but none were as indicative of power held in check as the four silvery starships which burst into view above the observer. Keeping a tight formation, they exploded through humid air to vanish in seconds into the morning cloud cover far above. Sound-shadows rattled the trees moments later, in a forlorn attempt to catch up to the engines which had produced them.

Slowly assuming attack formations combining X- and Y-wing ships, the various fighters began to move outward from the moon, out past the oceanic atmosphere of giant Yavin, out to meet the technologic executioner.

The man who had observed the byplay between Biggs and Luke now lowered his glare visor and adjusted his half-automatic, half-manual gunsights as he checked the ships to either side of him.

"Blue boys," he addressed his intership pickup, "this is Blue Leader. Adjust your selectors and check in. Approaching target at one point three . . ."

Ahead, the bright sphere of what looked like one of Yavin's moons but wasn't began to glow with increasing brightness. It shone with an eerie metallic glow utterly unlike that of any natural satellite. As he watched the giant battle station make its way around the rim of Yavin, Blue Leader's thoughts traveled back over the years. Over the uncountable injustices, the innocents taken away for interrogation and never heard from again—the whole multitude of evils incurred by an increasingly corrupt and indifferent Imperial government. All those terrors and agonies were concentrated, magnified, represented by the single bloated feat of engineering they were approaching now.

"This is it, boys," he said to the mike. "Blue Two, you're too far out. Close it up, Wedge."

The young pilot Luke had encountered in the temple briefing room glanced to starboard, then back to his instruments. He executed a slight adjustment, frowning. "Sorry, boss. My ranger seems to be a few points off. I'll have to go on manual."

"Check, Blue Two. Watch yourself. All ships, stand by to lock S-foils in attack mode."

One after another, from Luke and Biggs, Wedge and the other members of Blue assault squadron, the replies came back. "Standing by . . ."

"Execute," Blue Leader commanded, when John D. and Piggy had indicated they were in readiness.

The double wings on the X-wing fighters split apart, like narrow seeds. Each fighter now displayed four wings, its wing-mounted armament and quadruple engines now deployed for maximum firepower and maneuverability.

Ahead, the Imperial station continued to grow. Surface features became visible as each pilot recognized docking bays, broadcast antennae, and other man-made mountains and canyons.

As he neared that threatening black sphere for the second time, Luke's breathing grew faster. Automatic life-support machinery detected the respiratory shift and compensated properly.

Something began to buffet his ship, almost as if he were back in his skyhopper again, wrestling with the unpredictable winds of Tatooine. He experienced a bad moment of uncertainty until the calming voice of Blue Leader sounded in his ears.

"Wer'e passing through their outer shields. Hold tight. Lock down freeze-floating controls and switch your own deflectors on, double front."

The shaking and buffeting continued, worsened. Not knowing how to compensate, Luke did exactly what he should have: remained in control and followed orders. Then the turbulence was gone and the deathly cold peacefulness of space had returned.

"That's it, we're through," Blue Leader told them quietly. "Keep all channels silent until we're on top of them. It doesn't look like they're expecting much resistance."

Though half the great station remained in shadow, they were now near enough for Luke to be able to discern individual lights on its surface. A ship that could show phases matching a moon . . . once again he marveled at the misplaced ingenuity and effort which had gone into its construction. Thousands of lights scattered across its curving expanse gave it the appearance of a floating city.

Some of Luke's comrades, since this was their first sight of the station, were even more impressed. "Look at the size of that thing!" Wedge Antilles gasped over his open pickup.

"Cut the chatter, Blue Two," Blue Leader ordered. "Accelerate to attack velocity."

Grim determination showed in Luke's expression as he flipped several switches above his head and began adjusting his computer target readout. Artoo Detoo reexamined the nearing station and thought untranslatable electronic thoughts.

Blue Leader compared the station with the location of their proposed target area. "Red Leader," he called toward the pickup, "this is Blue Leader. We're in position; you can go right in. The exhaust shaft is farther to the north. We'll keep 'em busy down here."

Red Leader was the physical opposite of Luke's squadron commander. He resembled the popular notion of a credit accountant—short, slim, shy of face. His skills and dedication, however, easily matched those of his counterpart and old friend.

"Wer'e starting for the target shaft now, Dutch. Stand by to take over if anything happens."

"Check, Red Leader," came the other's reply. "We're going to cross their equatorial axis and try to draw their main fire. May the force be with you."

From the approaching swarm, two squads of fighters broke clear. The X-wing ships dove directly for the bulge of the station, far below, while the Y-ships curved down and northward over its surface.

Within the station, alarm sirens began a mournful, clangorous wail as slow-to-react personnel realized that the impregnable fortress was actually under organized attack. Admiral Motti and his tacticians had expected the rebels' resistance to be centered around a massive defense of the moon itself. They were completely unprepared for an offensive response consisting of dozens of tiny snub ships.

Imperial efficiency was in the process of compensating for this strategic oversight. Soldiers scrambled to man enormous defensive-weapons emplacements. Servodrivers thrummed as powerful motors aligned the huge devices for firing. Soon a web of annihilation began to develop the station as energy weapons, electrical bolts, and explosive solids ripped out at the oncoming rebel craft.

"This is Blue Five," Luke announced to his mike as he nose dived his ship in a radical attempt to confuse any electronic predictors below. The gray surface of the battle station streaked past his ports. "I'm going in."

"I'm right behind you, Blue Five," a voice recognizable as Biggs's sounded in his ears.

The target in Luke's sights was as stable as that of the Imperial defenders was evasive. Bolts flew from the tiny vessel's weapons. One started a huge fire on the dim surface below, which would burn until the crew of the station could shut off the flow of air to the damaged section.

Luke's glee turned to terror as he realized he couldn't swerve his craft in time to avoid passing through the fireball of unknown composition. "Pull out, Luke, pull out!" Biggs was screaming at him.

But despite commands to shift course, the automatic pressors wouldn't allow the necessary centrifugal force. His fighter plunged into the expanding ball of superheated gases.

Then he was through and clear, on the other side. A rapid check of his controls enabled him to relax. Passage through the intense heat had been insufficient to damage anything vital—though all four wings bore streaks of black, carbonized testimony to the nearness of his escape.

Hell-flowers bloomed outside his ship as he swung it up and around in a sharp curve. "You all right, Luke?" came Biggs's concerned query.

"I got a little toasted, but I'm okay."

A different, stern voice sounded. "Blue Five," warned the squadron leader, "you'd better give yourself more lead time or you're going to destroy yourself as well as the Imperial construction."

"Yes, sir. I've got the hang of it now. Like you said, it's not *exactly* like flying a skyhopper."

Energy bolts and sun-bright beams continued to create a chromatic maze in the space above the station as the rebel fighters crisscrossed back and forth over its surface, firing at whatever looked like a decent target. Two of the tiny craft concentrated on a power terminal. It blew up, throwing lightning-sized electric arcs from the station's innards.

Inside, troopers, mechanicals, and equipment were blown in all directions by subsidiary explosions as the effects of the blast traveled back down various conduits and cables. Where the explosion had hulled the station, escaping atmosphere sucked helpless soldiers and 'droids out into a bottomless black tomb.

Moving from position to position, a figure of dark calm amid the chaos, was Darth Vader. A harried Commander rushed up to him and reported breathlessly.

"Lord Vader, we count at least thirty of them, of two types. They are so small and quick the fixed guns cannot follow them accurately. They continuously evade the predictors."

"Get all Tie crews to their fighters. We'll have to go out after them and destroy them ship by ship."

Within numerous hangars red lights began flashing and an insistent alarm started to ring. Ground crews worked frantically to ready ships as flight-suited Imperial pilots grabbed for helmets and packs.

"Luke," requested Blue Leader as he skimmed

smoothly through a rain of fire, "let me know when you're off the block."

"I'm on my way now."

"Watch yourself," the voice urged over the cockpit speaker. "There's a lot of fire coming from the starboard side of that deflection tower."

"I'm on it, don't worry," Luke responded confidently. Putting his fighter into a twisting dive, he sliced once more across metal horizons. Antennae and small protruding emplacements burst into transitory flame as bolts from his wing tips struck with deadly accuracy.

He grinned as he pulled up and away from the surface as intense lines of energy passed through space recently vacated. Darned if it *wasn't* like hunting womp-rats back home in the crumbling canyons of Tatooine's wastes.

Biggs followed Luke on a similar run, even as Imperial pilots prepared to lift clear of the station. Within the many docking bays technical crews rushed hurriedly to unlock power cables and conclude desperate final checks.

More care was taken in preparing a particular craft nearest one of the bay ports, the one into which Darth Vader barely succeeded in squeezing his huge frame. Once set in the seat he slid a second set of eye shields across his face.

The atmosphere of the war room back in the temple was one of nervous expectancy. Occasional blinks and buzzes from the main battle screen sounded louder than the soft sussuration of hopeful people trying to reassure one another. Near a far corner of the mass of flickering lights a technician leaned a little closer to his own readouts before speaking into the pickup suspended near his mouth.

"Squad leaders—attention; squad leaders—attention! We've picked up a new set of signals from the other side of the station. Enemy fighters coming your way."

Luke received the report at the same time as everyone else. He began hunting the sky for the predicted

Imperial craft, his gaze dropping to his instrumentation. "My scope's negative. I don't see anything."

"Maintain visual scanning," Blue Leader directed. "With all this energy flying, they'll be on top of you before your scope can pick them up. Remember, they can jam every instrument on your ship except your eyes."

Luke turned again, and this time saw an Imperial already pursuing an X-wing—an X-wing with a number Luke quickly recognized.

"Biggs!" he shouted. "You've picked one up. On your tail . . . watch it!"

"I can't see it," came his friend's panicked response. "Where is he? I can't see it."

Luke watched helplessly as Biggs's ship shot away from the station surface and out into clear space, closely followed by the Imperial. The enemy vessel fired steadily at him, each successive bolt seeming to pass a little closer to Biggs's hull.

"He's on me tight," the voice sounded in Luke's cockpit. "I can't shake him."

Twisting, spinning, Biggs looped back toward the battle station, but the pilot trailing him was persistent and showed no sign of relinquishing pursuit.

"Hang on, Biggs," Luke called, wrenching his ship around so steeply that straining gyros whined. "I'm coming in."

So absorbed in his pursuit of Biggs was the Imperial pilot that he didn't seee Luke, who rotated his own ship, flipped out of the concealing gray below and dropped in behind him.

Electronic crosshairs lined up according to the computer-readout instructions, and Luke fired repeatedly. There was a small explosion in space—tiny compared with the enormous energies being put out by the emplacements on the surface of the battle station. But the explosion was of particular significance to three people: Luke, Biggs, and, most particularly, to the pilot of the Tie fighter, who was vaporized with his ship.

"Got him!" Luke murmured.

"I've got one! I've got one!" came a less restrained cry of triumph over the open intercom. Luke identified the voice as belonging to a young pilot known as John D. Yes, that was Blue Six chasing another Imperial fighter across the metal landscape. Bolts jumped from the X-wing in steady succession until the Tie fighter blew in half, sending leaflike glittering metal fragments flying in all directions.

"Good shooting, Blue Six," the squadron leader commented. Then he added quickly, "Watch out, you've got one on your tail."

Within the fighter's cockpit the gleeful smile on the young man's face vanished instantly as he looked around, unable to spot his pursuer. Something flared brightly nearby, so close that his starboard port burst. Then something hit even closer and the interior of the now open cockpit became a mass of flames.

"I'm hit, I'm hit!"

That was all he had time to scream before oblivion took him from behind. Far above and to one side Blue Leader saw John D.'s ship expand in a fiery ball. His lips may have whitened slightly. Otherwise he might as well never have seen the X-wing explode, for all the reaction he displayed. He had more important things to do.

On the fourth moon of Yavin a spacious screen chose that moment to flicker and die, much as John D. had. Worried technicians began rushing in all directions. One turned a drawn face to Leia, the expectant Commanders, and one tall, bronzed robot.

"The high-band receiver has failed. It will take some time to fix . . ."

"Do the best you can," Leia snapped. "Switch to audio only."

Someone overheard, and in seconds the room was filled with the sounds of distant battle, interspersed with the voices of those involved.

"Tighten it up, Blue Two, tighten it up," Blue Leader was saying. "Watch those towers."

"Heavy fire, Boss," came the voice of Wedge Antilles, "twenty-three degrees."

"I see it. Pull in, pull in. We're picking up some interference."

"I can't believe it," Biggs was stammering. "I've never seen such firepower!"

"Pull in, Blue Five. Pull in." A pause, then, "Luke, do you read me? Luke?"

"I'm all right, Chief," came Luke's reply. "I've got a target. I'm going to check it out."

"There's too much action down there, Luke," Biggs told him. "Get out. Do you read me, Luke? Pull out."

"Break off, Luke," ordered the deeper tones of Blue Leader. "We've hit too much interference here. Luke, I repeat, break off! I can't see him. Blue Two, can you see Blue Five?"

"Negative," Wedge replied quickly. "There's a fire zone here you wouldn't believe. My scanner's jammed. Blue Five, where are you? Luke, are you all right?"

"He's gone," Biggs started to report solemnly. Then his voice rose. "No, wait . . . there he is! Looks like a little fin damage, but the kid's fine."

Relief swept the war room, and it was most noticeable in the face of the slightest, most beautiful Senator present.

On the battle station, troopers worn half to death or deafened by the concussion of the big guns were replaced by fresh crews. None of them had time to wonder how the battle was going, and at the moment none of them much cared, a malady shared by common soldiers since the dawn of history.

Luke skimmed daringly low over the station's surface, his attention riveted on a distant metal projection.

"Stick close, Blue Five," the squadron commander directed him. "Where are you going?"

"I've picked up what looks like a lateral stabilizer," Luke replied. "I'm going to try for it."

"Watch yourself, Blue Five. Heavy fire in your area."

Luke ignored the warning as he headed the fighter straight toward the oddly shaped protuberance. His determination was rewarded when, after saturating it with fire, he saw it erupt in a spectacular ball of superhot gas.

"Got it!" he exclaimed. "Continuing south for another one."

Within the rebel temple-fortress, Leia listened intently. She seemed simultaneously angry and frightened. Finally she turned to Threepio and muttered, "Why is Luke taking so many chances?" The tall 'droid didn't reply.

"Watch your back, Luke," Biggs's voice sounded over the speakers, "watch your back! Fighters above you, coming in."

Leia strained to see what she could only hear. She wasn't alone. "Help him, Artoo," Threepio was whispering to himself, "and keep holding on."

Luke continued his dive even as he looked back and spotted the object of Biggs's concern close on his tail. Reluctantly he pulled up and away from the station surface, abandoning his target. His tormentor was good, however, and continued closing on him.

"I can't shake him," he reported.

Something cut across the sky toward both ships. "I'm on him, Luke," shouted Wedge Antilles. "Hold on."

Luke didn't have to for very long. Wedge's gunnery was precise, and the Tie fighter vanished brightly shortly thereafter.

"Thanks, Wedge," Luke murmured, breathing a little more easily.

"Good shooting, Wedge." That was Biggs again. "Blue Four, I'm going in. Cover me, Porkins."

"I'm right with you, Blue Three," came the other pilot's assurance.

Biggs leveled them off, let go with full weaponry. No one ever decided exactly what it was he hit, but the small tower that blew up under his energy bolts was obviously more important than it looked.

A series of sequential explosions hopscotched across a large section of the battle station's surface, leaping from one terminal to the next. Biggs had already shot past the area of disturbance, but his companion, following slightly behind, received a full dose of whatever energy was running wild down there.

"I've got a problem," Porkins announced. "My converter's running wild." That was an understatement. Every instrument on his control panels had abruptly gone berserk.

"Eject—eject, Blue Four," advised Biggs. "Blue Four, do you read?"

"I'm okay," Porkins replied. "I can hold her. Give me a little room to run, Biggs."

"You're too low," his companion yelled. "Pull up, pull up!"

With his instrumentation not providing proper information, and at the altitude he was traveling, Porkins's ship was simple for one of the big, clumsy gun emplacements to track. It did as its designers had intended it should. Porkins's demise was as glorious as it was abrupt.

It was comparatively quiet near the pole of the battle station. So intense and vicious had been Blue and Green squadron's assault on the equator that Imperial resistence had concentrated there. Red Leader surveyed the false peace with mournful satisfaction, knowing it wouldn't last for long.

"Blue Leader, this is Red Leader," he announced into his mike. "We're starting our attack run. The exhaust port is located and marked. No flak, no enemy fighters up here—yet. Looks like we'll get at least one smooth run at it."

"I copy, Red Leader," the voice of his counterpart responded. "We'll try to keep them busy down here."

Three Y-wing fighters dropped out of the stars, diving toward the battle-station surface. At the last possible minute they swerved to dip into a deep artificial canyon, one of many streaking the northern pole of the Death Star. Metal ramparts raced past on three sides of them.

Red Leader hunted around, noticed the temporary absence of Imperial fighters. He adjusted a control and addressed his squadron.

"This is it, boys. Remember, when you think you're close, go in closer before you drop that rock. Switch all power to front deflector screens—never mind what they throw at you from the side. We can't worry about that now."

Imperial crews lining the trench rudely awoke to the fact that their heretofore ignored section of the station was coming under attack. They reacted speedily, and soon energy bolts were racing at the attacking ships in a steadily increasing volume. Occasionally one would explode near one of the onrushing Y-wings, jostling it without real damage.

"A little aggressive, aren't they," Red Two reported over his mike.

Red Leader reacted quietly. "How many guns do you think, Red Five?"

Red Five, known casually to most of the rebel pilots as Pops, somehow managed to make an estimate of the trench's defenses while simultaneously piloting his fighter through the growing hail of fire. His helmet was battered almost to the point of uselessness from the effects of more battles than anyone had a right to survive.

"I'd say about twenty emplacements," he finally decided, "some in the surface and some on the towers."

Red Leader acknowledged the information with a grunt as he pulled his computer-targeting visor down in front of his face. Explosions continued to rock the fighter. "Switch to targeting computers," he declared.

"Red Two," came one reply, "computer locked in and I'm getting a signal." The young pilot's rising excitement marked his reply.

But the senior pilot among all the rebels, Red Five, was expectantly cool and confident—though it didn't sound like it from what he murmured half to himself: "No doubt about it, this is going to be some trick."

Unexpectedly, all defensive fire from the surrounding emplacements ceased. An eerie quiet clung to the trench as the surface continued to blur past the skimming Y-wings.

"What's this?" Red Two blurted, looking around worriedly. "They stopped. Why?"

"I don't like it," growled Red Leader. But there was nothing to confuse their approach now, no energy bolts to avoid.

It was Pops who was first to properly evaluate this seeming aberration on the enemy's part. "Stabilize your rear deflectors now. Watch for enemy fighters."

"You pinned it, Pops," Red Leader admitted, studying a readout. "Here they come. Three marks at two-ten."

A mechanical voice continued to recite the shrinking distance to their target, but it wasn't shrinking fast enough. "We're sitting ducks down here," he observed nervously.

"We'll just have to ride it out," the old man told them all. "We can't defend ourselves and go for the target at the same time." He fought down old reflexes as his own screen revealed three Tie fighters in precision formation diving almost vertically down toward them.

"Three-eight-one-oh-four," Darth Vader announced as he calmly adjusted his controls. The stars whipped past behind him. "I'll take them myself. Cover me."

Red Two was the first to die, the young pilot never knowing what hit him, never seeing his executioner. Despite his experience, Red Leader was on the verge of panic when he saw his wingman dissolve in flame.

"We're trapped down here. No way to maneuver— trench walls are too close. We've got to loosen it up somehow. Got—"

"Stay on target," admonished an older voice. "Stay on target."

Red Leader took Pops's words like tonic, but it was all he could do to ignore the closing Tie fighters as the two remaining Y-wings continued to streak toward the target.

Above them, Vader permitted himself a moment of undisciplined pleasure as he readjusted his targeting 'puter. The rebel craft continued to travel a straight, unevasive course. Again Vader touched finger to fire control.

Something screeched in Red Leader's helmet, and fire started to consume his instrumentation. "It's no good," he yelled into his pickup, "I'm hit. I'm hit . . . !"

A second Y-wing exploded in a ball of vaporized metal, scattering a few solid shards of debris across the trench. This second loss proved too much even for Red Five to take. He manipulated controls, and his ship commenced rising in a slow curve out of the trench. Behind him, the lead Imperial fighter moved to follow.

"Red Five to Blue Leader," he reported. "Aborting run under heavy fire. Tie fighters dropped on us out of nowhere. I can't—wait—"

Astern, a silent, remorseless enemy was touching a deadly button once more. The first bolts struck just as Pops had risen high enough to commence evasive action. But he had pulled clear a few seconds too late.

One energy beam seared his port engine, igniting gas within. The engine blew apart, taking controls and stabiliziing elements with it. Unable to compensate, the out-of-control Y-wing began a long, graceful plunge toward the station surface.

"Are you all right, Red Five?" a troubled voice called over the intership system.

"Lost Tiree . . . lost Dutch," Pops explained slowly, tiredly. "They drop in behind you, and you can't maneuver in the trench. Sorry . . . it's your baby now. So long, Dave. . . ."

It was the last message of many from a veteran.

Blue Leader forced a crispness he didn't feel into his voice as he tried to shunt aside the death of his old friend. "Blue boys, this is Blue Leader. Rendezvous at mark six point one. All wings report in."

"Blue Leader, this is Blue Ten. I copy."

"Blue Two here," Wedge acknowledged. "Coming toward you, Blue Leader."

Luke was also waiting his turn to report when something beeped on his control board. A glance backward confirmed the electronic warning as he spotted an Imperial fighter slipping in behind him.

"This is Blue Five," he declared, his ship wobbling as he tried to lose the Tie fighter. "I have a problem here. Be right with you."

He sent his ship into a steep dive toward the metal surface, then cut sharply up to avoid a burst of defensive fire from emplacements below. Neither maneuver shook his pursuit.

"I see you, Luke," came a reassuring call from Biggs. "Stay with it."

Luke looked above, below, and to the sides, but there was no sign of his friend. Meanwhile, energy bolts from his trailing assailant were passing uncomfortably close.

"Blast it, Biggs, where are you?"

Something appeared, not to the sides or behind, but almost directly in front of him. It was bright and moving incredibly fast, and then it was firing just above him. Taken completely by surprise, the Imperial fighter came apart just as its pilot realized what had happened.

Luke turned for the rendezvous mark as Biggs shot past overhead. "Good move, Biggs. Fooled me, too."

"I'm just getting started," his friend announced as he twisted his ship violently to avoid the fire from below. He hove into view over Luke's shoulder and executed a victory roll. "Just point me at the target."

Back alongside Yavin's indifferent bulk, Dodonna finished an intense discussion with several of his principal advisors, then moved to the long-range transmitter.

"Blue Leader, this is Base One. Double-check your own attack prior to commencement. Have your wingmen hold back and cover for you. Keep half your group out of range to make the next run."

"Copy, Base One," the response came. "Blue Ten, Blue Twelve, join with me."

Two ships leveled off to flank the squadron commander. Blue Leader checked them out. Satisfied that they were positioned properly for the attack run, he set the group to follow in case they should fail.

"Blue Five, this is Blue Leader. Luke, take Blue Two and Three with you. Hold up here out of their fire and wait for my signal to start your own run."

"Copy, Blue Leader," Luke acknowledged, trying to slow his heart slightly. "May the force be with you. Biggs, Wedge, let's close it up." Together, the three fighters assumed a tight formation high above the firefight still raging between other rebel craft of Green and Yellow squadrons and the imperial gunners below.

The horizon flip-flopped ahead of Blue Leader as he commenced his approach to the station surface. "Blue Ten, Blue Twelve, stay back until we spot those fighters, then cover me."

All three X-wings reached the surface, leveled off, then arced into the trench. His wingmen dropped farther and farther behind until Blue Leader was seemingly alone in the vast gray chasm.

No defensive fire greeted him as he raced toward the distant target. He found himself looking around nervously, checking and rechecking the same instruments.

"This doesn't look right," he found himself muttering.

Blue Ten sounded equally concerned. "You should be able to pick up the target by now."

"I know. The disruption down here is unbelievable. I think my instruments are off. Is this the right trench?"

Suddenly, intense streaks of light began to shoot close by as the trench defenses opened up. Near misses shook the attackers. At the far end of the trench a huge tower dominated the metal ridge, vomiting enormous amounts of energy at the nearing ships.

"It's not going to be easy with that tower up there," Blue Leader declared grimly. "Stand by to close up a little when I tell you."

Abruptly the energy bolts ceased and all was silent and dark in the trench once again. "This is it," Blue Leader announced, trying to locate the attack from above that had to be coming. "Keep your eyes open for those fighters."

"All short- and long-range scopes are blank," Blue Ten reported tensely. "Too much interference here. Blue Five, can you see them from where you are?"

Luke's attention was riveted to the surface of the station. "No sign of— Wait!" Three rapidly moving points of light caught his eye. "There they are. Coming in point three five."

Blue Ten turned and looked in the indicated direction. Sun bounced off stabilizing fins as the Tie fighters looped downward. "I see them."

"It's the right trench, all right," Blue Leader exclaimed as his tracking scope suddenly began a steady beeping. He adjusted his targeting instrumentation, pulling the visor down over his eyes. "I'm almost in range. Targets ready . . . coming up. Just hold them off me for a few seconds—keep 'em busy."

But Darth Vader was already setting his own fire control as he dropped like a stone toward the trench. "Close up the formation. I'll take them myself."

Blue Twelve went first, both engines blown. A slight deviation in flight path and his ship slammed into the trench wall. Blue Ten slowed and accelerated, bobbed drunkenly, but could do little within the confines of those metal walls.

"I can't hold them long. You'd better fire while you can, Blue Leader—we're closing on you."

The squadron commander was wholly absorbed in lining up two circles within his targeting visor. "We're almost home. Steady, steady . . ."

Blue Ten glanced around frantically. "They're right behind me!"

Blue Leader was amazed at how calm he was. The targeting device was partly responsible, enabling him to concentrate on tiny, abstract images to the exclusion of all else, helping him to shut out the rest of the inimical universe.

"Almost there, almost there . . ." he whispered. Then the two circles matched, turned red, and a steady buzzing sounded in his helmet. "Torpedoes away, torpedoes away."

Immediately after, Blue Ten let his own missiles loose. Both fighters pulled up sharply, just clearing the end of the trench as several explosions billowed in their wake.

"It's a hit! We've done it!" Blue Ten shouted hysterically.

Blue Leader's reply was thick with disappointment. "No, we haven't. They didn't go in. They just exploded on the surface outside the shaft."

Disappointment killed them, too, as they neglected to watch behind them. Three pursuing Imperial fighters continued up out of the fading light from the torpedo explosions. Blue Ten fell to Vader's precision fire, then the Dark Lord changed course slightly to fall in behind the squadron commander.

"I'll take the last one," he announced coldly. "You two go back."

Luke was trying to pick the assault team out of the glowing gases below when Blue Leader's voice sounded over the communicator.

"Blue Five, this is Blue Leader. Move into position, Luke. Start your attack run—stay low and wait until you're right on top of it. It's not going to be easy."

"Are you all right?"

"They're on top of me—but I'll shake them."

"Blue Five to Blue pack," Luke ordered, "let's go!" The three ships peeled off and plunged toward the trench sector.

Meanwhile Vader finally succeeded in hitting his quarry, a glancing bolt that nonetheless started small, intense explosions in one engine. Its R-2 unit scrambled back toward the damaged wing and struggled to repair the crippled power plant.

"R-2, shut off the main feed to number-one starboard engine," Blue Leader directed quietly, staring resignedly at instruments which were running impossibilities. "Hang on tight, this could get rough."

Luke saw that Blue Leader was in trouble. "We're right above you, Blue Leader," he declared. "Turn to point oh five, and we'll cover for you."

"I've lost my upper starboard engine," came the reply.

"We'll come down for you."

"Negative, negative. Stay there and get set up for your attack run."

"You're sure you're all right?"

"I think so . . . Stand by for a minute."

Actually, it was somewhat less than a minute before Blue Leader's gyrating X-wing plowed into the surface of the station.

Luke watched the huge explosion dissipate below him, knowing without question its cause, sensing fully for the first time the helplessness of his situaton. "We just lost Blue Leader," he murmured absently, not particularly caring if his mike picked up the somber announcement.

On Yavin Four, Leia Organa rose from her chair and nervously began pacing the room. Normally perfect nails were now jagged and uneven from nervous chewing. It was the only indication of physical unease. The anxiety visible in her expression was far more revealing of her feelings, an anxiety and worry that filled the war room on the announcement of Blue Leader's death.

"Can they go on?" she finally asked Dodonna.

The general replied with gentle resolve. "They must."

"But we've lost so *many*. Without Blue or Red Leader, how will they regroup?"

Dodonna was about to reply, but held his words as more critical ones sounded over the speakers.

"Close it up, Wedge," Luke was saying, thousands of kilometers away. "Biggs, where are you?"

"Coming in right behind you."

Wedge replied soon after. "Okay, Boss, we're in position."

Dodonna's gaze went to Leia. He looked concerned.

The three X-wings moved close together high above the battle station's surface. Luke studied his instruments and fought irritably with one control that appeared to be malfunctioning.

Someone's voice sounded in his ears. It was a young-old voice, a familiar voice: calm, content, confident, and reassuring—a voice he had listened to intently on the desert of Tatooine and in the guts of the station below, once upon a time.

"Trust your feelings, Luke," was all the Kenobi-like voice said.

Luke tapped his helmet, unsure whether he had heard anything or not. This was no time for introspection. The steely horizon of the station tilted behind him.

"Wedge, Biggs, we're going in," he told his wingmen. "We'll go in full speed. Never mind finding the trench and then accelerating. Maybe that will keep those fighters far enough behind us."

"We'll stay far enough back to cover you," Biggs declared. "At that speed will you be able to pull out in time?"

"Are you kidding?" Luke sneered playfully as they began their dive toward the surface. "It'll be just like Beggars Canyon back home."

"I'm right with you, *boss*," noted Wedge, emphasizing the title for the first time. "Let's go . . ."

At high speed the three slim fighters charged the glowing surface, pulling out *after* the last moment. Luke skimmed so close over the station hull that the tip of one wing grazed a protruding antenna, sending metal splinters flying. Instantly they were enveloped in a meshwork of energy bolts and explosive projectiles. It intensified as they dropped down into the trench.

"We seem to have upset them," Biggs chortled, treating the deadly display of energy as though it were all a show being put on for their amusement.

"This is fine," Luke commented, surprised at the clear view ahead. "I can see everything."

Wedge wasn't quite as confident as he studied his own readouts. "My scope shows the tower, but I can't make out the exhaust port. It must be awfully small. Are you sure the computer can target it?"

"It better," Biggs muttered.

Luke didn't offer an evaluation—he was too busy holding a course through the turbulence produced by exploding bolts. Then, as if on command, the defensive fire ceased. He glanced around and up for sign of the expected Tie fighters, but saw nothing.

His hand went to drop the targeting visor into position, and for just a moment he hesitated. Then he swung it down in front of his eyes. "Watch yourselves," he ordered his companions.

"What about the tower?" Wedge asked worriedly.

"You worry about those fighters," Luke snapped. "I'll worry about the tower."

They rushed on, closing on the target every second. Wedge stared upward, and his gaze suddenly froze. "Here they come—oh point three."

Vader was setting his controls when one of his wingmen broke attack silence. "They're making their approach too fast—they'll never get out in time."

"Stay with them," Vader commanded.

"They're going too fast to get a fix," his other pilot announced with certainty.

Vader studied several readouts and found that his sensors confirmed the other estimates. "They'll still have to slow down before they reach that tower."

Luke contemplated the view in his targeting visor. "Almost home." Seconds passed and the twin circlets achieved congruence. His finger convulsed on the firing control. "Torpedoes away! Pull up, pull up."

Two powerful explosions rocked the trench, striking harmlessly far to one side of the minute opening. Three Tie fighters shot out of the rapidly dissipating fireball, closing on the retreating rebels. "Take them," Vader ordered softly.

Luke detected the pursuit at the same time as his companions. "Wedge, Biggs, split up—it's the only way we'll shake them."

The three ships dropped toward the station, then abruptly raced off in three different directions. All three Tie fighters turned and followed Luke.

Vader fired on the crazily dodging ship, missed, and frowned to himself. "The force is strong with this one. Strange. I'll take him myself."

Luke darted between defensive towers and wove a tight path around projecting docking bays, all to no avail. A single remaining Tie fighter stayed close behind. An energy bolt nicked one wing, close by an engine. It started to spark irregularly, threateningly. Luke fought to compensate and retain full control.

Still trying to shake his persistent assailant, he dropped back into a trench again. "I'm hit," he announced, "but not bad. Artoo, see what you can do with it."

The tiny 'droid unlocked himself and moved to work on the damaged engine as energy bolts flashed by dangerously close. "Hang on back there," Luke counseled the Artoo unit as he worked a path around projecting towers, the fighter spinning and twisting tightly through the topography of the station.

Fire remained intense as Luke randomly changed

direction and speed. A series of indicators on the control panel slowly changed color; three vital gauges relaxed and returned to where they belonged.

"I think you've got it, Artoo," Luke told him gratefully. "I think—there, that's it. Just try to lock it down so it can't work loose again."

Artoo beeped in reply while Luke studied the whirling panorama behind and above them. "I think we've lost those fighters, too. Blue group, this is Blue Five. Are you clear?" He manipulated several controls and the X-wing shot out of the trench, still followed by emplacement fire.

"I'm up here waiting, Boss," Wedge announced from his position high above the station. "I can't see you."

"I'm on my way. Blue Three, are you clear? Biggs?"

"I've had some trouble," his friend explained, "but I think I lost him."

Something showed again, damnably, on Biggs's screen. A glance behind showed the Tie fighter that had been chasing him for the past several minutes dropping in once more behind him. He swung down toward the station again.

"Nope, not yet," Biggs told the others. "Hold on, Luke. I'll be right there."

A thin, mechanical voice sounded over the speakers. "Hang on, Artoo, hang on!" Back at the temple headquarters, Threepio turned away from the curious human faces which had turned to stare at him.

As Luke soared high above the station another X-wing swung in close to him. He recognized Wedge's ship and began hunting around anxiously for his friend.

"We're goin' in, Biggs—join up. Biggs, are you all right? Biggs!" There was no sign of the other fighter. "Wedge, do you see him anywhere?"

Within the transparent canopy of the fighter bobbing close by, a helmeted head shook slowly. "Nothing," Wedge told him over the communicator. "Wait a little longer. He'll show."

Luke looked around, worried, studied several instruments, then came to a decision. "We can't wait; we've got to go now. I don't think he made it."

"Hey, you guys," a cheerful voice demanded to know, "what are you waiting for?"

Luke turned sharply to his right, in time to see another ship racing past and slowing slightly ahead of him. "Don't ever give up on old Biggs," the intercom directed as the figure in the X-wing ahead looked back at them.

Within the central control room of the battle station, a harried officer rushed up to a figure studying the great battle screen and waved a handful of printouts at him.

"Sir, we've completed an analysis of their attack plan. There is a danger. Should we break off the engagement or make plans to evacuate? Your ship is standing by."

Governor Tarkin turned an incredulous gaze on the officer, who shrank back. "Evacuate!" he roared. "At our moment of triumph? We are about to destroy the last remnants of the Alliance, and you call for evacuation? You overestimate their chances badly . . . Now, get out!"

Overwhelmed by the Governor's fury, the subdued officer turned and retreated from the room.

"We're going in," Luke declared as he commenced his dive toward the surface. Wedge and Biggs followed just aft.

"Let's go—Luke," a voice he had heard before sounded inside his head. Again he tapped his helmet and looked around. It sounded as if the speaker were standing just behind him. But there was nothing, only silent metal and nonverbal instrumentation. Puzzled, Luke turned back to his controls.

Once more, energy bolts reached out for them, passing harmlessly on both sides as the surface of the battle station charged up into his face. But the defensive fire wasn't the cause of the renewed trembling Luke suddenly experienced. Several critical gauges were beginning their swing back into the danger zone again.

He leaned toward the pickup. "Artoo, those stabilizing elements must have broken loose again. See if you can't lock it back down—I've got to have full control."

Ignoring the bumpy ride, the energy beams and explosions lighting space around him, the little robot moved to repair the damage.

Additional, tireless explosions continued to buffet the three fighters as they dropped into the trench. Biggs and Wedge dropped behind to cover for Luke as he reached to pull down the targeting visor.

For the second time a peculiar hesitation swept through him. His hand was slower yet as he finally pulled the device down in front of his eyes, almost as if the nerves were in conflict with one another. As expected, the energy beams stopped as if on signal and he was barreling down the trench unchallenged.

"Here we go again," Wedge declared as he spotted three Imperial fighters dropping down on them.

Biggs and Wedge began crossing behind Luke, trying to draw the coming fire away from him and confuse their pursuers. One Tie fighter ignored the maneuvers, continuing to gain inexorably on the rebel ships.

Luke stared into the targeting device—then reached up slowly to move it aside. For a long minute he pondered the deactivated instrument, staring at it as if hypnotized. Then he slid it sharply back in front of his face and studied the tiny screen as it displayed the shifting relationship of the X-wing to the nearing exhaust port.

"Hurry, Luke," Biggs called out as he wrenched his ship in time to narrowly avoid a powerful beam. "They're coming in faster this time. We can't hold them much longer."

With inhuman precision, Darth Vader depressed the fire control of his fighter again. A loud, desperate

shout sounded over the speakers, blending into a
final agonized scream of flesh and metal as Biggs's
fighter burst into a billion glowing splinters that
rained down on the bottom of the trench.

Wedge heard the explosion over his speakers and
hunted frantically behind him for the trailing enemy
ships. "We lost Biggs," he yelled toward his own
pickup.

Luke didn't reply immediately His eyes were watering, and he angrily wiped them clear. They were
blurring his view of the targeting readout.

"We're a couple of shooting stars, Biggs," he whispered huskily, "and we'll never be stopped." His ship
rocked slightly from a near miss and he directed his
words to his remaining wingman, biting down hard
on the end of each sentence.

"Close it up, Wedge. You can't do any more good
back there. Artoo, try to give me a little more power
on our rear reflectors."

The Artoo unit hurried to comply as Wedge pulled
up alongside Luke's ship. The trailing Tie fighters also
increased their speed.

"I'm on the leader," Vader informed his soldiers.
"Take the other one."

Luke flew just in front of Wedge, slightly to port
side. Energy bolts from the pursuing Imperials began to streak close about them. Both men crossed
each other's path repeatedly, striving to present as
confusing a target as possible.

Wedge was fighting with his controls when several
small flashes and sparks lit his control board. One
small panel exploded, leaving molten slag behind.
Somehow he managed to retain control of the ship.

"I've got a bad malfunction, Luke. I can't stay with
you."

"Okay, Wedge, get clear."

Wedge mumbled a heartfelt "Sorry" and peeled
up out of the trench.

Vader, concentrating his attention on the one ship
remaining before him, fired.

Luke didn't see the near-lethal explosion which burst close behind him. Nor did he have time to examine the smoking shell of twisted metal which now rode alongside one engine. The arms went limp on the little 'droid.

All three Tie fighters continued to chase the remaining X-wing down the trench. It was only a matter of moments before one of them caught the bobbing fighter with a crippling burst. Except now there were only two Imperials pursuing. The third had become an expanding cylinder of decomposing debris, bits and pieces of which slammed into the walls of the canyon.

Vader's remaining wingman looked around in panic for the source of the attack. The same distortion fields that confused rebel instrumentation now did likewise to the two Tie fighters.

Only when the freighter fully eclipsed the sun forward did the new threat become visible. It was a Corellian transport, far larger than any fighter, and it was diving directly at the trench. But it didn't move precisely like a freighter, somehow.

Whoever was piloting that vehicle must have been unconscious or out of his mind, the wingman decided. Wildly he adjusted controls in an attempt to avoid the anticipated collision. The freighter swept by just overhead, but in missing it the wingman slid too far to one side.

A small explosion followed as two huge fins of the paralleling Tie fighters intersected. Screaming uselessly into his pickup, the wingman fluttered toward the near trench wall. He never touched it, his ship erupting in flame before contact.

To the other side, Darth Vader's fighter began spinning helplessly. Unimpressed by the Dark Lord's desperate glower, various controls and instruments gave back readings which were brutally truthful. Completely out of control, the tiny ship continued spin-

ning in the opposite direction from the destroyed
wingman—out into the endless reaches of deep space.

Whoever was at the controls of the supple freighter
was neither unconscious nor insane—well, perhaps
slightly touched, but fully in command nonetheless.
It soared high above the trench, turning to run pro-
tectively above Luke.

"You're all clear now, kid," a familiar voice informed
him. "Now blow this thing so we can all go home."

This pep talk was followed by a reinforcing grunt
which could only have been produced by a particularly large Wookie.

Luke looked up through the canopy and smiled.
But his smile faded as he turned back to the targeting
visor. There was a tickling inside his head.

"Luke . . . trust me," the tickle requested, forming
words for the third time. He stared into the targeter.
The emergency exhaust port was sliding toward the
firing circle again, as it had once before—when he'd
missed. He hesitated, but only briefly this time, then
shoved the targeting screen aside. Closing his eyes,
he appeared to mumble to himself, as if in internal
conversation with something unseen. With the confidence of a blind man in familiar surroundings, Luke
moved a thumb over several controls; then touched
one. Soon after, a concerned voice filled the cockpit
from the open speakers.

"Base One to Blue Five, your targeting device is
switched off. What's wrong?"

"Nothing," Luke murmured, barely audible. "Nothing."

He blinked and cleared his eyes. Had he been
asleep? Looking around, he saw that he was out of
the trench and shooting back into open space. A
glance outside showed the familiar shape of Han Solo's
ship shadowing him. Another, at the control board,
indicated that he had released his remaining torpedoes, although he couldn't remember touching the
firing stud. Still, he must have.

The cockpit speakers were alive with excitment. "You did it! You did it!" Wedge was shouting over and over. "I think they went right in."

"Good shot kid." Solo complimented him, having to raise his voice to be heard over Chewbacca's unrestrained howling.

Distant, muted rumblings shook Luke's ship, an omen of incipient success. He must have fired the torpedoes, mustn't he? Gradually he regained his composure.

"Glad . . . you were here to see it. Now let's get some distance between us and that thing before it goes. I hope Wedge was right."

Several X-wings, Y-wings, and one battered-looking freighter accelerated away from the battle station, racing toward the distant curve of Yavin.

Behind them small flashes of fading light marked the receding station. Without warning, something appeared in the sky in place of it which was brighter than the glowing gas giant, brighter than its far-off sun. For a few seconds the eternal night became day. No one dared look directly at it. Not even multiple shields set on high could dim that awesome flare.

Space filled temporarily with trillions of microscopic metal fragments, propelled past the retreating ships by the liberated energy of a small artificial sun. The collapsed residue of the battle station would continue to consume itself for several days, forming for that brief span of time the most impressive tombstone in this corner of the cosmos.

☐ XIII

A cheering, gleeful throng of technicians, mechanics, and other inhabitants of the Alliance headquarters swarmed around each fighter as it touched down and taxied into the temple hangar. Several of the other surviving pilots had already vacated their ships and were waiting to greet Luke.

On the opposite side of the fighter, the crowd was far smaller and more restrained. It consisted of a couple of technicians and one tall, humanoid 'droid who watched worriedly as the humans mounted the scorched fighter and lifted a badly burned metal hulk from its back.

"Oh, my! Artoo?" Threepio pleaded, bending close to the carbonized robot. "Can you hear me? Say something." His unwinking gaze turned to one of the techs. "You can repair him, can't you?"

"We'll do our best." The man studied the vaporized metal, the dangling components. "He's taken a terrible beating."

"You must repair him! Sir, if any of my circuits or modules will help, I'll gladly donate them . . ."

They moved slowly away, oblivious to the noise and excitement around them. Between robots and the humans who repaired them there existed a very special relationship. Each partook a little of the other and sometimes the dividing line between man and machine was more blurred than many would admit.

The center of the carnival atmosphere was formed by three figures who battled to see who could compli-

ment the others the most. When it came to congrat-
ulatory back-slapping, however, Chewbacca won by
default. There was laughter as the Wookie looked
embarrassed at having nearly flattened Luke in his
eagerness to greet him.

"I knew you'd come back," Luke was shouting, "I
just knew it! I would've been nothing but dust if you
hadn't sailed in like that, Han!"

Solo had lost none of his smug self-assurance. "Well,
I couldn't very well let a flying farm boy go up against
that station all by himself. Besides, I was beginning to
realize what could happen, and I felt terrible about
it, Luke—leaving you to maybe take all the credit
and get all the reward."

As they laughed, a lithe figure, robes flowing,
rushed up to Luke in a very unsenatorial fashion. "You
did it, Luke, you did it!" Leia was shouting.

She fell into his arms and hugged him as he spun
her around. Then she moved to Solo and repeated
the embrace. Expectantly, the Corellian was not quite
as embarrassed.

Suddenly awed by the adulation of the crowd, Luke
turned away. He gave the tired fighter a look of ap-
proval, then found his gaze traveling upward, up
to the ceiling high overhead. For a second he thought
he heard something faintly like a gratified sigh, a re-
laxing of muscles a crazy old man had once performed in moments of pleasure. Of course, it was
probably the intruding hot wind of a steaming jungle
world, but Luke smiled anyway at what he thought
he saw up there.

There were many rooms in the vast expanse of the
temple which had been converted for modern service
by the technicians of the Alliance. Even in their desperate need, however, there was something too clean
and classically beautiful about the ruins of the ancient
throne room for the architects to modify. They had
left it as it was, save for scouring it clear of creeping jungle growth and debris.

For the first time in thousands of years that spacious chamber was full. Hundreds of rebel troops and technicians stood assembled on the old stone floor, gathered together for one last time before dispersing to new posts and distant homes. For the first time ever the massed ranks of pressed uniforms and polished semi-armor stood arrayed together in a fitting show of Alliance might.

The banners of the many worlds which had lent support to the rebellion fluttered in the gentle breeze formed inside. At the far end of a long open aisle stood a vision gowned in formal white, barred with chalcedony waves—Leia Organa's signet of office.

Several figures appeared at the far end of the aisle. One, massive and hirsute, showed signs of running for cover, but was urged on down the open row by his companion. It took several minutes for Luke, Han, Chewie, and Threepio to cover the distance to the other end.

They stopped before Leia, and Luke recognized General Dodonna among the other dignitaries seated nearby. There was a pause and a gleaming, familiar Artoo unit joined the group, moving to stand next to a thoroughly awestruck Threepio.

Chewbacca shuffled nervously, giving every indication of wishing he were someplace else. Solo silenced him as Leia rose and came forward. At the same time banners tilted in unison and all those gathered in the great hall turned to face the dais.

She placed something heavy and golden around Solo's neck, then Chewbacca's—having to strain to do so—and finally around Luke's. Then she made a signal to the crowd, and the rigid discipline dissolved as every man, woman, and mechanical present was permitted to give full vent to their feelings.

As he stood awash in the cheers and shouts, Luke found that his mind was neither on his possible future with the Alliance nor on the chance of traveling adventurously with Han Solo and Chewbacca. Instead, unlikely as Solo had claimed it might be, he found his full attention occupied by the radiant Leia Organa.

She noticed his unabashed stare, but this time she only smiled.